Titles by Mary Kennedy

Talk Radio Mysteries

DEAD AIR
REEL MURDER
STAY TUNED FOR MURDER

Dream Club Mysteries

NIGHTMARES CAN BE MURDER
DREAM A LITTLE SCREAM

Praise for

Nightmares Can Be Murder

"A dream come true for cozy readers everywhere."

—Lorna Barrett, *New York Times* bestselling author of the Booktown Mysteries

"A wry and clever debut. Huge fun."

—Carolyn Hart, national bestselling author of the Death on Demand Mysteries

"A fun series that goes where no sleuth has gone before. Once you pick this book up, you won't look at dreams in the same way. Or mysteries."

—Carolyn Haines, award-winning author of the Sarah Booth Delaney Mysteries

"Kennedy, who previously penned the Talk Radio Mystery series, introduces a fresh premise to the cozy genre. Balancing a murder plot with humorous characters and a genteel Southern setting, this is a terrific start to a new series."

—*Library Journal*

"Readers may start analyzing their own dreams after reading Kennedy's latest tale . . . Kennedy pens a lively mystery, made unique by the Dream Club getting together to see if they can solve a murder before one of their own members is targeted."

—*RT Book Reviews*

"Entertaining . . . well written . . . The author of the Talk Radio Mystery series continues to craft mysteries with sharp humor and witty dialogue. She succeeds in educating readers who will spend their days analyzing what the subconscious has been telling them at night."

—Kings River Life Magazine

continued . . .

"This is a clever premise, and I found the club members' dreams and the group interpretations thought provoking . . . The mystery was well designed . . . populated with characters who are sure to delight." —MyShelf.com

Dream a Little Scream

Mary Kennedy

BERKLEY PRIME CRIME, NEW YORK

An imprint of Penguin Random House LLC
375 Hudson Street, New York, New York 10014

DREAM A LITTLE SCREAM

A Berkley Prime Crime Book / published by arrangement with the author

ISBN: 978-0-425-26806-3

PUBLISHING HISTORY
Berkley Prime Crime mass-market edition / August 2015

PRINTED IN THE UNITED STATES OF AMERICA

10 9 8 7 6 5 4 3 2 1

Cover illustration by Bill Brunning.
Cover design by Lesley Worrell.
Interior text design by Kelly Lipovich.

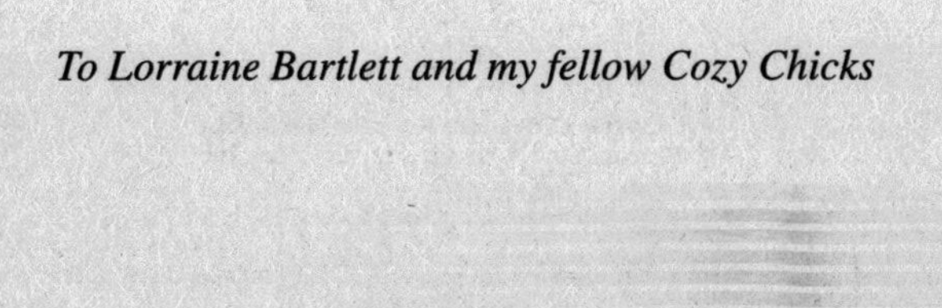

To Lorraine Bartlett and my fellow Cozy Chicks

Acknowledgments

A big thank-you to my editor, Michelle Vega, for her endless patience and expert editorial guidance. The wonderful staff at Berkley Prime Crime deserves a special shout-out for their marketing expertise and drop-dead-gorgeous covers.

I owe a debt of gratitude to my creative and energetic agent, Holly Root, who makes all things possible.

A special thanks to my husband, Alan, plot genius and computer guru, who smooths over technical (and creative) glitches for me.

Thank you to my pal, Bill Parrilli, who is my go-to guy for eccentric Florida characters, motorcycles, and the secret of making a perfectly dry martini.

And of course, thank you to my readers for enjoying my books and sending me words of encouragement.

1

"Do you suppose she'll pose for pictures with us? Or give me a few quotes for my book club newsletter?" Lucinda Macavy flashed a shy smile at Sybil Powers, her eyes bright with excitement. "It's not every day a celebrity chef like Sonia Scott comes to town," she added breathlessly. "It would be such an honor to meet her."

Lucinda, a thin woman wearing an expensive but unflattering clay-colored shift, leaned forward to inspect the goodies Ali had arranged on the coffee table. With a quick, birdlike movement, she added a napoleon, a lemon bar, and a blueberry scone to her bone china plate and then sat back, waiting for the group to respond.

It was a hot summer evening in Savannah and Ali had jacked up the AC before the members of the Dream Club arrived for their weekly meeting. Sybil looked flushed in one of her tropical caftans and was gulping down vast quantities of sweet tea served in mason jars. Persia Walker appeared thoughtful, fingering her chunky handmade necklace from Nepal.

My sister Ali, as always, looked cool, blond, and slender in white skinny jeans and and a pale yellow beaded top. As the proprietor of Oldies But Goodies, a Savannah candy shop, she dresses casually but always looks put together. The Dream Club meets weekly in her apartment above the shop, and she serves sweet tea, coffee, and a delicious array of pastries. She calls the Dream Club members her "beta tasters," and she adds the most popular items to the café menu downstairs.

When I arrived in Savannah a few months ago, the vintage candy shop, just a couple of blocks off the Historic District, was struggling. We've made a few changes since then, invested in some marketing, added a café menu, and things are looking up. We've gone from operating in the red to the black, and Ali likes to tease me that my MBA finally came in handy. I like to tell her that my advice as a high-powered business consultant has rubbed off on her.

We make a good team. Yin and yang. Ali is headstrong and impulsive, with a wild creative bent, and I'm more conservative, always looking out for the bottom line. My quick visit down south to help my sister took an unexpected turn: I fell in love with Savannah and decided to make it my home.

"Oh, for heaven's sake, Lucinda. She won't be bothered giving you quotes for a little newsletter," Dorien said sharply. "She's a celebrity and I bet all she cares about are articles in major newspapers," she went on, "so you'd just be wasting your time. You know the food critic Neal Garson will want to do a big piece on Sonia. She thanked him on the acknowledgment page of her new book. I've heard the two of them are like this." She held up her index finger intertwined with her middle finger and gave a knowing look like an actress in a soap opera.

"I think they dated back in high school," Minerva Harper said thoughtfully. Minerva and her sister Rose are octogenarians who seem to know everyone who has ever lived in, died in, or visited Savannah in the past seventy-five years.

"See what I mean," Dorien said triumphantly. "If anyone chats with Sonia about her cooking empire it will be Neal Garson, not you."

"I suppose you're right," Lucinda said diffidently. "Still . . . I'd certainly like to have a few moments with her."

"Buy her latest cookbook, and you'll get ten seconds with her and an autograph." Dorien snorted.

Ali raised her eyebrows and exchanged a look with me. I lifted my shoulders in a little shrug. We both know Dorien can be abrasive and has a way of dampening everyone's enthusiasm with her cutting remarks. The club members tolerate her rudeness and chalk it up to the fact that the woman has no idea she's being offensive. Plus she's fallen on hard times since her catering company took a nosedive. Dorien is a competent cook, but a few months ago she delivered a catered dinner to a dance instructor who later was found poisoned. Even though Dorien had no part in his death, it certainly had put a damper on her business.

"Maybe we should start the meeting," I said, glancing at my watch. We were due to head over to the television taping at eight sharp. Sonia Scott, a nationally known chef, was going to do a live broadcast at a local television studio, and our reporter friend, Sara, had managed to snare tickets for everyone.

"Good idea," Sybil said, fanning herself with a folded-up copy of *Southern Living*. Usually the thick stucco walls of the building keep the apartment cool, but this had been a brutally hot day, and now, even with the AC maxed out, the apartment seemed uncomfortably warm.

"We have a new member with us tonight," Ali announced. "Etta Mae Beasley." She nodded to a slight woman with hawkish features and piercing dark eyes. "Please tell us a little about yourself."

Etta Mae licked her lips nervously and rested her hands on her knees. I noticed her hands looked rough and chapped as if the woman had spent a great deal of time farming or gardening.

"I moved here from Brunswick, Georgia," she said slowly. "I've always been interested in dreams, so I'm really happy to be part of this group." She hesitated for a moment. "I know everyone seems excited over the arrival of Sonia Scott, but I have a sort of"—she paused delicately—"history with her, so I'm afraid I don't share your enthusiasm."

There was an awkward silence and Ali said quickly, "I'm so sorry to hear that, Etta Mae." She glanced at me, probably hoping I'd chime in. "I hope you'll join us at the taping anyway."

"Oh, I'll be there," Etta Mae said in a stronger voice. "I wouldn't miss it for the world." Her gaze traveled to a thick book with a glossy cover lying on an end table. "Is that what I think it is? Sonia's latest cookbook?" Her eyes widened in surprise as Dorien reached over and handed it to her. "How did you get it, if you don't mind my asking? The Southern Lights bookstore told me it wouldn't be available until tomorrow."

"One of my customers picked up a copy at Hilton Head yesterday," Ali said quickly. "The release day is tomorrow, but she saw them unpacking a box of Sonia's books at a local bookstore and managed to buy one. You can borrow it, if you like."

"I'd like that very much," Etta Mae said, her face hardening. "I bet this book is full of surprises." *Surprises?* It seemed like an odd thing to say. Another uncomfortable pause while Etta Mae shoved the book into a large quilted tote bag and didn't say another word. I had no idea what Etta Mae's "history" was with Sonia Scott, but it was obvious she wasn't a fan.

"Who's up first tonight?" Ali sat down and Scout gave a little meow and jumped into her lap. Barney and Scout are Ali's beloved cats, and no one is a stranger to them. Ali's question was just a formality; everyone knew the members take turns.

"I believe it's my turn," Rose Harper said in her quivery voice. She and her sister Minerva were dressed in nearly identical floral dresses, and their wispy white hair framed their faces like halos.

"Go ahead, Rose," Ali said encouragingly, just as we heard footsteps on the stairs leading up from the shop. Ali tensed and rushed to the landing but then laughed and touched her hand to her chest. "It's okay. We have another new member, Edward Giles." She greeted a thin man in his sixties with an angular face as he reached the top of the stairs. "Welcome, Edward. Please have a seat anywhere you like."

He glanced apologetically around the room and sat down on a leather hammock near the coffee table. "Sorry to be late; I was held up at the university."

"Edward is a professor in the botany department," Ali said warmly. "He knows all about herbalism and is an expert on nineteenth-century Savannah."

"But I'm here tonight to learn about dreams," he said, flushing a little. I wondered if he felt silly admitting his interest in dreams, or if he felt overwhelmed by the all-female Dream Club.

Ali quickly introduced the members by first names. "We're

running a bit late, Edward, so if you don't mind, we'll let Rose tell us about her dream."

Rose stared at the new guest. "Edward Giles," she said musingly. "Your mother was a Sudderth, I believe."

The professor's eyebrows flew up. "Why yes, her name was Hilda Sudderth. But how in the world—"

"My sister knows everything about genealogy," Minerva said complacently. "We're probably related."

"We are." Rose nodded her head vigorously. "Your maternal great-grandmother was married briefly to Thomas Newton of Charleston, who later had five children by Emily Cavendish." She stopped and thought for a moment. "We're third cousins, twice removed, I believe. I'll look it up tonight to be sure."

"That's astonishing," Edward said, leaning forward. "We could use you at the university library in our reference department. We have a lot of people who need help researching their ancestry."

"Oh, I'm retired," Rose said, "I just research the family history of my friends and relatives for fun. That's one of my passions in life," she added, "along with this club, of course."

"Rose . . ." Ali said, urging her on.

"Oh yes, my dream," Rose said. "I think this is an easy one. It's the House Dream." She looked around the circle and paused dramatically. "Some of you are probably familiar with it. It's supposed to be a classic."

"I've had that dream several times," Persia Walker said. She turned to Etta Mae and explained, "It's a very symbolic dream. You're walking through a beautiful house and it represents all your dreams and aspirations. Each room is more lovely than the next." Etta Mae nodded but didn't reply.

"I've hopped into that dream a few times," Sybil offered. "It's fascinating."

"You hopped in?" Edward looked perplexed. "How is that possible?"

"Sybil is a dream-hopper," Ali explained. "She has a very special talent. She can drop into other people's dreams and follow them just as if she were watching a movie. It's a unique ability; the rest of us don't have it."

Minerva gently nudged her sister. "Tell them about your dream, Rose," she said, pointedly glancing at her watch.

"I was in a beautiful house somewhere down south. I know it was in the South because I saw Spanish moss hanging from the trees in the backyard. I was standing in the kitchen looking out at a lovely garden. Everything was perfect, pristine. The kitchen was stark white and modern, like something out of *Architectural Digest*. Very high-end: white cabinets, white subway tiles along the backsplash, a big farmhouse sink, white marble countertops."

"Would anyone use marble on kitchen countertops?" Dorien asked. "Marble stains so easily, you know. Soapstone or granite are much more practical."

"Anything is possible in a dream," Rose said mildly. "There were copper pots hanging from the ceiling. They were gleaming; it was hard to believe they'd ever been used. The countertops were bare except for some lovely glass canisters. I think they must have been antiques. They were made of cut glass with silver lids. All of them were filled with spices and seeds and herbs. I opened one and it contained vanilla beans. The one next to it had cinnamon sticks, and a third one was stocked with tiny seeds I didn't recognize. They may have been sesame seeds, but they were larger, like nuts."

"How did you feel when you were wandering through the kitchen?" I asked. Rose always has very detailed dreams, and I wanted to hurry her along. I'm new to dream interpretation, but I know the emotional content of a dream is the key to analyzing it. Since Ali started the Dream Club a few months ago, the members have become surprisingly astute in uncovering the symbolic elements in a dream.

"First I felt very happy and carefree. Then I felt a sense of dread come over me, a premonition that something awful was about to take place," Rose said, her voice faltering. "I looked outside and the sky had turned gray, threatening. The beautiful kitchen, the lovely décor"—she shook her head as if to focus her thoughts—"everything was suddenly shrouded in shadows. I sensed that something sinister was about to happen. I felt an evil presence in the kitchen."

"Probably a demon," Persia said calmly. Etta Mae's eyes widened and she gave a jaw-dropping stare. I suppose Ali and I should have warned her that dream content isn't always puppies and sunsets. Sometimes a nefarious spirit or two appears and a thread of hidden danger inserts itself into the dream. The dreamer's mood can switch from euphoria to terror in a split second.

"It was just a feeling," Rose went on, "and I'm having trouble describing it." She paused and let out her breath slowly. "There was a book on the kitchen counter, a very old book with a brown leather cover. I remember it so clearly."

"Did it remind you of something?" Sybil asked, her bangle bracelets clanging as she reached for an éclair.

"Maybe." Rose squinted her eyes shut, as if she was trying to recall the image of the book. "I knew it was precious to many people and probably very valuable. I had the feeling it belonged to a family, a sort of keepsake that was handed down from generation to generation."

"That's amazing," Etta Mae said softly. She was leaning forward, listening raptly. "Did it have a title?"

Rose opened her eyes. "I can't recall," she said apologetically.

"What makes you think it was a family heirloom?" I asked.

"Just an impression I had," Rose said, blinking. "The pages were yellowed and some of them were sticking out, as if new pages had been inserted."

The room was silent, and I guessed no one had a clue how to interpret Rose's dream.

"Anything else?" Ali asked gently. I knew she was eager to leave for the television taping.

"The book," Rose said, her voice suddenly stronger. "When I finished walking through the house, I went back to the kitchen and picked it up to leaf through it. There was nothing there. Just blank pages. Every single one."

2

"What did you make of Rose's dream?" I asked Ali a couple of hours later. We were settled on folding chairs at the taping of Sonia's cooking show and the studio was buzzing with activity.

"No idea," she replied. "That was a tough one. Usually the House Dream ends with the dreamer coming to some resolution about a problem that's troubling them in real life. Rose's dream just seemed to trail off and she was left with a mysterious book and a sense of foreboding." She craned her neck to see past the Harper sisters, who were sitting right in front of us. "Has Sonia made her appearance yet?"

"There she is! Right in front of the guy following her with a microphone. I think he wants to do a sound check." I watched as he finally caught up with Sonia and pinned a tiny mic to the lapel of her pink linen blazer. She pretended to shout into the mic for comic effect and some crew members laughed and put their hands over their ears. Sonia has a reputation for clowning around with the crew, but she's all business when it comes to cooking.

Lucinda nudged me and said, "Excuse me for a minute. I just spotted someone I haven't seen in years." Moments later, she returned with her arm around a thin brunette, who gave us a shy smile. "Leslie, these are my dear friends Taylor and Ali Blake. They're new to Savannah and own the cutest little candy shop in the Historic District." As Leslie shook hands with us, Lucinda added, "Leslie was one of my students at the Academy."

"I hope you enjoy Savannah," Leslie said quietly to us. "It's a beautiful city."

"Leslie's husband works for Sonia's company; isn't that exciting?" Lucinda said in a bubbly voice. "And she has two beautiful little children. Do you suppose we could we meet your husband, dear?"

Leslie hesitated. "He's usually busy with last-minute details, but I can try to catch his eye." She gestured to a tall, dark-haired man who was standing at the front of the room, chatting with one of the technicians. When he spotted Leslie, he frowned but made his way down the aisle toward us. By the time he reached us, he'd rearranged his features into a more pleasant expression.

"I know you're busy, honey," Leslie said, "but this is Lucinda Macavy from the Academy and two of her friends."

"Taylor and Ali Blake," I offered.

"Nice to meet all of you," he said briefly. "Jeremy Watts." He seemed tense and preoccupied, eager to get back to the business at hand. "A good crowd," he added vaguely.

"Yes, everyone's excited over Sonia's visit," I told him. He nodded, barely listening, and quickly excused himself when a cameraman called out to him.

There was an awkward pause, and Leslie stared after her

husband, looking embarrassed at his brusque behavior. Ali and I exchanged a look. Jeremy Watts certainly wasn't Mr. Congeniality.

"I can't wait to have a good long chat with you," Lucinda said quickly, patting Leslie on the hand. "Do you want to follow me home or shall I give you directions?"

"Just write down your address and I'll use my GPS," Leslie said. "Jeremy and I came in separate cars. I need to get home to the children tonight and he's leaving right after the taping to do some advance work in Atlanta." Leslie smiled her thanks when Lucinda scribbled a note and passed it to her. "I'm so glad we ran into each other," she said with a broad smile. She returned to her seat near the front of the studio, and we settled back to enjoy the show. Sonia darted around the set, arranging flowers and crockery as the crew fumbled with the equipment, her raucous laugh bouncing off the walls. She seemed completely at ease and I remembered reading that the show was unscripted. The food was prepared ahead of time, and the recipes would flash on the screen as Sonia read the ingredients. She had a keen sense of theatrics and that, along with her sometimes bawdy sense of humor, was guaranteed to keep the viewers watching. Even people who didn't like to cook enjoyed Sonia's show.

Sara Rutledge walked in a side door and I waved her over. "I saved you a seat right next to me." I picked up the newspaper I'd placed on the folding chair next to mine. "It looks like a full house tonight."

"Thanks," she said, settling down next to me.

"It's the least I could do," I said with a grin. "After all, you're the one who got us the tickets." Sara is a freelance journalist who recently moved to Savannah. We've been friends since college, and I was thrilled to have her living so close to us. "Are you interviewing Sonia for the paper, or did Neal grab that one?"

"I got it," she said triumphantly. "Neal's taking his annual two-week vacation in Maine, so the timing couldn't be better. For me, I mean," she added with a giggle. "I did a quick sit-down with Sonia at Riverfront today and got some good quotes. I'll put it together with my background material and I think I'll get above the fold in the Sunday edition."

"That's impressive." I reached out my hand for a fist bump. "How did you manage to interview her without interruptions? Didn't the tourists at the Riverfront pester her for autographs?"

Sara shook her head. "No one even spotted her. She was wearing a baseball cap and sunglasses and we sat at an outdoor café. She picked an umbrella table hidden behind a palm tree, which was a smart move. I think the waiter recognized her, but he never said a word." Sara laughed. "I tipped him well, so he's happy."

"That was smart," Ali said as she waited for the taping to begin.

The back door to the studio was open to the parking lot and a few minutes later, I spotted a man and woman step out under the awning, deep in conversation. I assumed they were part of Sonia's entourage because the woman, a fortyish blonde, was holding a notebook with the Sonia Scott logo on it. There was something intimate about their body language, and I wondered if they were a couple. When the man lit a cigarette and offered it to her, I realized it was Jeremy Watts, Leslie's husband. The woman smiled and shook her head, touching his lapel, letting her gaze linger on his face just a second too long. Interesting.

The taping started then, and the next ninety minutes flew by. Sonia was at her best, talking directly to the camera, telling anecdotes about the recipes she was preparing. The menu called for grilled chicken with mango and oranges slices, scalloped cheese potatoes, and peach cobbler. These were all staples from her previous cookbooks, and she put them together effortlessly, all the while keeping up a playful banter.

The filming stopped for a few breaks and Sonia's bubbly persona vanished as she moved out of the bright lights, talking on her cell. I had hoped she might interact with the studio audience, but she seemed distant and preoccupied.

Sara raised her eyebrows. "She seems to switch off when the cameras do," she said shrewdly. "Interesting." Sara pulled out a pen and jotted a note in the steno pad she carried everywhere.

"You're not putting that in the article, are you?" I supposed it would be a juicy tidbit, but that kind of observation certainly wouldn't portray Sonia in a good light. Nobody likes a celebrity who ignores her fans.

"No, I'm just saving it, in case I write an in-depth piece about her down the road. The article I'm doing for the Sunday paper is a puff piece, all positive. But who knows? Someday I might do an unauthorized biography and this sort of detail might be important." I know Sara plans on moving to New York or Los Angeles and hopes to snare a job as an investigative reporter with a major paper. At the moment, she's happy to get freelance work writing arts and entertainment pieces in Savannah, but it barely pays the bills.

We were filing out after the taping when a harried-looking young woman carrying a clipboard approached Sara. It was the attractive blonde I had seen chatting outside the studio with Jeremy Watts. "Excuse me, are you Sara Rutledge from the newspaper?" When Sara nodded, she raced on, "It seems we're going to be in Savannah for another half day. Sonia's flight to Richmond tonight was canceled." She realized we were blocking traffic and motioned us over to the sidelines. "Sorry, I'm so frazzled, I forgot to introduce myself. I'm Olivia Hudson, Sonia's personal assistant."

"Nice to meet you. We chatted on the phone," Sara told her.

"Yes, I remember," Olivia raced on, barely acknowledging the comment. "This is all very last-minute, but we'd like to get as much mileage out of the tour as possible. Is there a place Sonia could meet with some fans tomorrow morning for a quick photo op? Maybe a bookstore, or a cooking school? I know I can get a few photographers to show up and I've got some of her earlier titles we can use as giveaways. Nothing formal—it's just a way for her to be seen chatting with the fans, you know. "

"What about a candy store?" Sara interjected. She grabbed my arm. "Here's someone you need to talk to. Taylor Blake. She and her sister Ali own a vintage candy store here in Savannah. It's also a café. They're both big fans of Sonia and recommend her cookbooks to all their customers."

"A candy store?" Olivia looked doubtful. "I suppose it's a possibility." She looked me up and down. "I don't think Sonia has ever done an appearance in a candy store—"

"It has lots of charm and it's right off the Historic District," Sara interrupted. "It would be perfect, and it's a big hit with the locals. I know they can guarantee you a good turnout, even on a weekday morning." I bit back a smile at Sara's eagerness. *If ever I could afford to hire a PR person, it would be Sara*, I thought. Meanwhile, Ali had joined us, a puzzled look clouding her face.

Sara quickly explained the situation and Ali's face lit up. "You know what would be fun?" Ali said. "We could offer a free sampling of classic Southern desserts for her visit. And, of course, we'd include some of her recipes. It would add a little interest to the event, and I think the fans would love it."

And it would be great publicity for Oldies But Goodies, I thought to myself. Only our regular customers seemed to know that we'd added a café to the vintage candy store. An appearance by Sonia Scott would definitely help to get the word out.

"Nothing with peanuts," Olivia said crisply. "She's really allergic to nuts and seeds."

"No peanuts, no nuts, no seeds," Ali agreed. Ali was beaming, practically vibrating with happiness.

"It's a deal, then," Olivia said, pocketing Ali's business card. "We'll be there at nine sharp. Just a quick stop en route to the airport. See you then!" she added before scurrying away. We watched as she raced back to Sonia, who had pulled off her mic and looked irritated, hands on hips.

"Chop, chop," I heard Sonia say in a snappish voice to one of her assistants. "Let's get back to the hotel. I'm exhausted." She pointed to the collection of dirty dishes and pans on the countertop. "Olivia, make sure these are cleaned and then pack everything up; you know which ones are mine. The cheap stuff belongs to the studio. And don't forget my copper frying pan like you did the last time." There was a sharp edge in her voice and Olivia immediately sprang into action like a well-trained greyhound. "Wake me at seven sharp with croissants and coffee. Skim milk, no sugar." She turned a beady-eyed stare at Olivia. "Got it?"

"I've got it," Olivia said in a tired voice.

"That limo had better be waiting at the curb, or heads are gonna roll," Sonia said, sweeping out of the studio.

"Wow, Sonia's a bit of a surprise in person, isn't she?" Ali asked as Lucinda walked up next to us.

"They call her 'a force of nature,'" I said, reading from a publicity handout.

Sara laughed. "Really? I'd say 'diva' would be more like it. I wonder what it's like to work for her."

"Well, it seems that one of my former students, Leslie, is married to an executive with Sonia's company," Lucinda said. "We chatted with them just before you arrived, Sara. Her husband, Jeremy, is such a fine-looking young man. I'd say they're a very happy couple, wouldn't you, Taylor?"

"Oh, I'm sure they are," I said with as much enthusiasm as I could muster. My mind was still reeling at the image of Olivia Hudson having a tête-à-tête outside the studio with the very married Jeremy Watts. Had I imagined the obvious attraction between them? Leslie had been in the studio audience when Olivia and Jeremy were having their private moment. Didn't she see what was so obvious to me? Or did she just turn a blind eye because of the children?

"I'm sure I'll hear some interesting tidbits from Leslie tonight," Lucinda said contentedly. "I bet she'll have a lot to tell me."

"I'm sure she will," I muttered under my breath. Having tea with Leslie might prove to be more than Lucinda had bargained for.

"What have we gotten ourselves into?" Ali asked me in a fade-away voice the next morning. She was clearly exhausted. We'd darted back to the shop last night, tidied up the kitchen, and polished the glass display cases until they sparkled. I washed and waxed the floor while Ali defrosted some goodies she'd stored away for our Dream Club meetings. Lemon squares and tiny cherry cheesecake tarts appeared as if by magic. Ali arranged the pastries on a long pine table that we pulled into the center aisle of the shop. Ali was very fussy about "presentation" and the pine table was covered with a blue chintz tablecloth.

Minverva and Rose Harper had offered to bring a few vases of pale pink roses and bright blue hydrangeas to add a festive air. Visitors could help themselves to the free treats and enjoy a glass of homemade lemonade or sweet tea while waiting for a quick meet and greet with Sonia.

"How much lemonade do we really need?" I said, squeezing my twenty-third lemon. I was tired and hot and my hair was hanging limply in my eyes.

"Do a few more," Ali said in her most encouraging voice. "I want to fill at least five of those cut-glass pitchers. And we'll have gallons of sweet tea, as well. Do you think we should serve lattes . . ." she began, and then broke off when she caught my expression. "Okay, we'll just go with the lemonade and the sweet tea," she said quickly. "It's too hot for lattes anyway."

"Howdy, y'all!" Sonia Scott swept into the shop at 9 a.m. sharp, followed by her personal assistant, Olivia Hudson, and the rest of her entourage. She turned up the volume on her smile when she spotted the table laden with homemade goodies. "Hope these are all Sonia Scott recipes," she said, wagging her finger at us playfully.

"Of course they are," Ali said gamely. "We wouldn't serve anything else." Ali gave me a broad wink and I hoped Sonia wouldn't inspect the dishes too closely.

"Well, let's get this show on the road, ladies. Time's a-wastin', and we need to be at the airport by noon."

"Actually, by eleven thirty," Olivia muttered under her breath.

"Whatever," Sonia said, waving her hand like she was

swatting at a fly. "Now, where do you want me to sit? This looks good," she said, plunking herself down on a padded armchair that Ali had arranged in front of a small table we used as a desk. Olivia immediately arranged three piles of books in front of Sonia, along with a Sharpie, and motioned for the people in the front row to come forward and have their books signed.

"Come on up here, honey, don't be shy," Sonia urged an awed-looking Lucinda Macavy. Lucinda's face was flushed with excitement; she was clearly dazzled at the idea of meeting the iconic chef. The Dream Club members—including Etta Mae Beasley and Edward Giles—had arrived early and snared seats in the very first row. "I thought I'd sign all these books and then when I run out, I can sign bookmarks and pose for pictures until we have to leave." She paused, her eyes sweeping over the audience. The place was packed. "Sound like a plan?" she asked with a grin.

Smiles all around and some scattered applause as Lucinda, Dorien, Sybil, and Etta Mae made their way to the front. Edward Giles stood up with some reluctance and let the other people in the row go ahead of him. I couldn't decide whether he wasn't interested in a free autographed cookbook, or he was just shy.

Sonia certainly knew how to work a room. Olivia asked each guest in line how they would like the book signed, and then scribbled their name on a small card and passed it to Sonia. It was all very streamlined and professional. Sonia signed books for the next half hour, stopping to chat with individual fans, asking questions about their hometown, their children, and their families. She even asked one woman to show her a photo of her Cavalier King Charles spaniels so she could admire them. She never seemed rushed and was happy to allow people to take pictures of her.

At one point, Olivia bent down to ask Sonia if she would like something to drink and Sonia bellowed, "I sure would, honey. And grab me some more of those shortbread cookies. I have to do a taste test." She gave a raucous laugh and aimed a broad wink at the audience. "Let's make sure these are up to snuff," she said teasingly. "I hope these are Sonia Scott classics."

Ali flashed me a look and I hoped Sonia would approve of our efforts.

"These *are* all Sonia's recipes, right?" Olivia leaned close to me, arching her eyebrows.

"Why, yes, they are," I blurted out. "All three of them." The lemon bars and cherry cheesecake tarts were out of Sonia's *Southern Favorites* cookbook, and Lucinda had offered to bring some shortbread cookies that were featured in Sonia's *Easy Desserts* cookbook.

Sonia was about to start signing bookmarks—Olivia had thoughtfully brought what looked like several hundred—when she frowned and started scratching her arm.

"Darn," she said irritably. "Do you have cats in here? I can feel my allergies kicking in."

Ali shot me a startled look. Barney and Scout were safely ensconced upstairs, taking their morning naps on the windowsill. "Not in this part of the shop," she admitted, "although we do have two cats upstairs."

"That must be it," Sonia said, munching on a cookie. I noticed someone had placed a few cookies next to her on a pretty plate decorated with a rooster. The cookies were sand-colored and looked delicious. I decided they must be the shortbread "Sandies" that Lucinda had brought.

"Are you all right, Sonia?" Ali hovered over her.

"I think so; I'm just very sensitive to cats." I noticed a red flush creeping up her throat and was about to comment when she jumped to her feet. "Olivia, find my inhaler right away," she rasped. "My chest feels so tight I can hardly breathe. I need to splash some water on my face. Where's the ladies' room?" She coughed twice and made a strangled gasp as a deep frown line appeared between her eyes.

I jumped to my feet. "It's right down the hall, but do you need—" Sonia ignored me and heaved herself toward the hall. She was clutching her throat but gamely held up one finger in a *just a minute* gesture. She raced down the hall into the ladies' room and I heard the door slam shut. Olivia and I exchanged a look.

"She's terribly allergic to cats," Olivia said, scowling. A touch of annoyance crept into her voice. "I should have said something to you earlier. It never occurred to me that you lived in your shop."

"We live *above* the shop," Ali corrected her. "But I don't understand what happened to her. I've never seen anyone with such a severe cat allergy." I hadn't, either, and I'd been alarmed when I saw Sonia's neck suddenly turn a vivid shade of candy-apple red.

Olivia dug into an oversized tote bag and pulled out an asthma inhaler. "We just need a quick break from the signing. Sonia can take a few puffs on this and she'll be right as rain."

She took off down the hallway with a couple of "Team Sonia" staffers racing after her.

There was an excited buzz in the room, and I saw Sara Rutledge half rise out of her seat. We locked gazes for a moment and she shot me a questioning look. When I touched my index finger to my thumb in an *okay* gesture, she nodded and sat back down.

"What's up? Is Sonia sick?" Sam Stiles had made her way to the front of the room and stood close to me, her body poised for action. Sam is a detective with the Savannah PD and a member of the Dream Club. Unfortunately, her grueling work schedule makes it difficult for her to attend meetings. In her mid-thirties, with an athletic build and a brisk, no-nonsense style, she's a commanding presence. I'd seen her slip into the shop a moment earlier and was grateful she was on the scene.

"I'm not sure." I bent close to whisper in her ear. "Her assistant thinks she's allergic to Barney and Scout, and she believes it triggered an asthma attack. Olivia—the assistant—is in the ladies' room with her right now, along with a couple of other staffers. I'm hoping this will all blow over in a few minutes. People are getting restless."

"Don't worry, folks. Everything's fine." Ali practically had to shout to be heard above the noise. "Sonia will be right back and you'll all have autographed bookmarks. In the meantime, eat up. We have plenty of goodies over there!" She gave a wide, reassuring smile and people started edging back to the dessert buffet on the heart pine table. A couple of minutes passed and I glanced at my watch. I was just about to go check on Sonia when Olivia darted out of the ladies' room, her face pale, her eyes wide with panic.

"Call nine-one-one," she shouted. "Hurry up! Something's terribly wrong with Sonia. She's collapsed. I don't think she's breathing, and I can't find her EpiPen." She went white and I could feel the tension rolling off her. I reached for my phone but Sam Stiles beat me to it.

"We need an ambulance, stat!" Sam yelled into her cell as she pushed past me. Sara Rutledge jumped to her feet, tossing her shoulder bag on her chair. I knew Sara had CPR training, and she darted after Sam. By now everyone in the audience knew something was amiss.

Olivia was visibly shaken. "I thought you brought her the asthma inhaler—" I began. My voice was wobbly, and I clasped my hands together to keep them from shaking.

"The inhaler isn't working." She turned Sonia's green Coach bag upside down on the table. Beads of sweat appeared on her forehead and her voice had taken on a shrill, desperate note. "She needs her EpiPen. That's the only thing that's going to save her now."

An EpiPen? If Sonia needed epinephrine, it must mean that she was going into anaphylactic shock.

"Do you want me to help you look?" I offered. I felt helpless just standing there.

"No, I'll find it. I know she has it with her. I saw it earlier today." Olivia shoved her hands into the pile of lipsticks, gum wrappers, receipts, tissues, bookmarks, and business cards strewn across the table. Little scraps of paper feathered in the air. I remembered that Sonia had a habit of scribbling notes to herself and dropping them into her purse.

"Where is the EpiPen?" Olivia's voice spiraled upward; it sounded like she was bordering on hysteria. She made a pitiful note in her throat, almost a groan of pain. "It has to be here, but where, where?"

"Doesn't anyone have a backup pen?" I asked gently, riffling through the debris from Sonia's purse. I knew people often carried two pens in case one of them malfunctioned.

"I have an extra one, but mine's missing, too!" Now her voice was glazed with panic, and I knew she was seconds away from losing control. She dumped the contents of her tote bag on the floor. "How could they both be missing? That's impossible," she screamed. She was on her hands and knees, palms outstretched, sifting through the items from her bag. I noticed she was much neater than Sonia, and she carried a wallet, a small makeup kit, a pen and pad of paper, a BlackBerry, and a package of tissues. No sign of the missing pen.

"It could be a false alarm," I said, trying to calm her. "The cats are both upstairs—"

"Don't you understand anything? It's not the cats; it's something else. Something much worse." She stood up, let out a deep sigh, and blinked rapidly a few times, as if she was fighting back tears. "I knew this would happen," she said darkly. "I just knew it." With that, she bolted out of the room, heading back to her boss.

I opened my mouth to speak but knew it would be pointless. What had she suspected would happen? And what did she mean by "something worse"? My gaze traveled to the buffet table. Was it the food? What could Sonia have possibly eaten that caused her to collapse? An unpleasant tingling sensation coursed through my body and a knot of cold fear crept up the back of my neck.

"Please stay calm, everyone," I said as people started shouting questions. "Help is on the way. Right now we need to take our seats and clear a path for the paramedics. I'm sure this is a false alarm." *But Olivia insisted that Sonia wasn't breathing. Could that be true?* My voice quavered with emotion and I swallowed hard, taking a deep breath. "As soon as they check her out, we'll be able to continue the book signing. Sit back and relax, everyone." I put on my "game face," as Ali calls it, and spoke with a lot more conviction than I actually felt.

3

The next few minutes passed in a blur. The paramedics burst through the shop doors, pushing a gurney piled high with resuscitation equipment. I noticed one of the paramedics looked to be barely out of her teens, a thin, wiry redhead with a sprinkling of freckles across her nose. She took the lead down the hallway, hoisting a defibrillator off the stretcher as her partner, a middle-aged male with a considerable paunch, hurried inside the ladies' room.

I peeked inside and my breath caught in my throat. There was Sonia, lying very still, on her back, in the middle of the bathroom floor. Both paramedics were now kneeling beside her, working quickly, their expressions intent. They spoke softly to each other as they passed equipment back and forth.

Sonia looked exactly as Olivia had described—like someone who'd collapsed without warning—and I spotted a small bruise on her forehead. She'd probably hit her head on the porcelain sink when she fell. I had the sudden fear that the resuscitation efforts were all in vain. Sonia looked lifeless, her features slack, her limbs splayed at odd angles like a doll's. I noticed she had a scratch on her neck, probably also from her fall.

Sam Stiles ushered all of us back to the center of the shop.

"Let's give the EMTs some space to do their job," she said quietly. "Keep everyone out of the hallway. I'm going back in there to see if I can help."

I felt queasy and took a seat at the signing table, looking out over the audience. I didn't think the fans realized the seriousness of the situation and I heard a woman in the front row tell her friend that Sonia had "fainted."

I knew better, and I was sure I'd caught the words "anaphylactic shock" drifting down the hallway. The EMTs must have been in phone contact with the hospital, and they were giving clipped updates on Sonia's condition. "Edema, impossible to intubate," someone said curtly, and I sucked in a breath. If they were talking about intubating her, then Sonia really wasn't breathing and Olivia's analysis of the situation was correct.

After what seemed like an eternity, the EMTs emerged from the hallway. The younger of the two was talking into a mic pinned to her uniform. "ETA ten minutes," she said brusquely. Sonia was lying perfectly still on the gurney, with an oxygen mask strapped to her face. Her eyes were closed and her face was a mottled red. A soft groan went up from the audience as the paramedics hurried out to the ambulance. Olivia, along with the rest of Sonia's entourage, looked shell-shocked.

"How bad is it?" I whispered to Sam, who appeared next to me.

"Very bad," she said, shaking her head. "No detectable

pulse, the airway's blocked, and epinephrine didn't seem to help."

"But the oxygen mask—?"

"Just standard protocol." She shook her head. "It's probably not going to be enough to turn things around." I remembered Sam had once told me that paramedics often slap an oxygen mask on a patient even if there isn't any medical reason to do so. They want to give the appearance that the person is still alive and that they are making every effort to resuscitate them as they whisk them off to the hospital.

"Oh, that doesn't sound good," I said, surveying the crowd. This was going to be devastating news for her fans.

"They'll have her in the ER in a few minutes, but I think she's already gone. She probably could have been pronounced dead at the scene."

"This is horrible," Ali muttered.

I was silent, watching Sam, who was scanning the room, her eyes narrowed, her body tense. Her arms dangled at her sides, but I noticed she was closing and unclosing her hands as her gaze swept the audience. She was on high alert today, but what—or who—was she looking for?

Then I spotted Etta Mae Beasley in the front row, hugging her autographed copy of Sonia's cookbook to her chest. There was an odd look on her face, an expression I couldn't quite place. If I didn't know better, I'd say she looked almost triumphant.

Etta Mae's lips were twitching in a ghost of a smile, and her expression was gloating. But that was impossible, wasn't it? Why would she be happy that Sonia was seriously ill? Etta Mae had made it clear that she wasn't a fan of Sonia's, but did her feelings go beyond mere dislike? There was something chilling about her expression, and my stomach clenched.

I tried to remember what had happened when Etta Mae had walked up to the table and received her autographed book from Sonia. Had the two women argued or exchanged words? I'd been distracted, pouring lemonade for the guests. I made a mental note to ask Olivia if anything unusual had occurred.

Etta Mae must have felt me watching her, because we locked eyes for a brief moment, and then she quickly arranged her face into a bland expression. I turned and noticed Edward Giles staring fixedly as the paramedics wheeled Sonia away. His expression was thoughtful, without a touch of emotion or a hint of surprise.

Odd. Unless he had such a sanguine temperament that nothing rattled him? Most of the audience members seemed shaken up by the event, and a few women were crying softly into tissues and dabbing their eyes.

"What happens next?" Ali asked, pushing a strand of hair out of her face. Her usual poise had vanished and she looked ready to burst into tears herself. I shot her a sympathetic look when Sam stepped in and took charge of the situation.

"We have to send the crowd on their way," Sam said quickly. "Let's dispatch them quickly and don't let anyone touch the food." She gestured to the long table with half-eaten desserts and piles of plastic plates. "Keep everything exactly as it is. We may need to bag it."

"You're going to take the food?" Ali asked incredulously. "Do you mean as evidence?"

"Possibly. Let's not get ahead of ourselves."

"What exactly do you expect to find?" Sara nudged my shoulder a little as she squeezed between us. Sara's a good friend, but she's first and foremost a reporter, and I wondered if she hoped for an exclusive on what might be a newsworthy—

if tragic—event. If this was foul play it would certainly put her byline on the map if she could file a story direct from the scene. I almost expected her to whip out her pocket tape recorder to capture Sam's remarks.

"Nothing yet." Sam's voice was clipped. "Nothing at all. So let's not make problems where none exist, okay?"

"Of course not. I would never do that!" Sara looked first at me, then at Ali, for validation, her voice ringing with indignation.

"Sam doesn't mean anything by it," I said, leading Sara away from the head table. "She's a detective; it's her job to be suspicious, remember?" Olivia was sniffling and gathering up the bookmarks and the contents of Sonia's purse. The other crew members, a couple of cameramen, a sound guy, and a lighting tech packed up their equipment, whispering to each other. Two women staffers touched Olivia on the arm and then grabbed their purses and headed out the door.

"We're finished here, right?" The lighting tech picked up the last of the klieg lights and nodded at Olivia.

"Absolutely," she snapped. Her eyes were brimming with tears as she scooped up some index cards and dropped them into the bag. I knew she would have to face a tough situation at the hospital. The next half hour might prove to be the most difficult of her life. Would she like some company or would she consider it an intrusion? Olivia was so self-contained, it was hard to predict.

"Ali and I could come with you, if you like," I ventured. "In fact, we could drive you, if you don't feel up to it."

"No, I'd rather go alone. You've done enough." Her voice was as dark and flat as the ocean on a cloudy day.

"I'll call you from the hospital," Sara said to me in a low

voice as Olivia scurried out of the shop. A beat passed between us. "Either way."

"Most of the Dream Club members are here, so we might as well hold an impromptu meeting," Persia Walker suggested a few minutes later. We'd just ushered out the last guest and put a CLOSED sign on the shop door. Sam Stiles had left for the station house to make a report and we'd left the remaining food untouched, as she'd ordered.

"Well, for heaven's sake, let's not hang around here, let's go upstairs," Dorien said. She shivered and rubbed her upper arms. "This place is giving me the creeps. For all I know, we're standing right in the middle of a crime scene."

"A crime scene? Nonsense," Sybil Powers cut in. "Sonia had some sort of major allergic reaction, and it was certainly nobody's fault. None of us could have predicted this would happen. All we did was offer her a warm welcome."

She turned to our new members, Etta Mae Beasley and Edward Giles. "You're going to join us for the meeting, right?" The two new members were hanging back uncertainly, and I had the distinct feeling they weren't the least bit eager to go upstairs to our apartment. Did they really think we had deliberately harmed Sonia? Or was it just a natural desire to escape the unpleasantness of the past half hour?

"I think I should be going—" Edward began, but Dorien grabbed him firmly by the arm. "That's silly," Dorien said, lifting her jaw a little. "You're new to the group, and we have a lot to process here. Whatever happens with Sonia, we all know that something significant took place here today. We need to use our collective energy to learn more about the situation." Her voice was as brittle as glass, her face tense. Dorien's abrasive personality was never far from the surface.

"Collective energy?" Edward's eyebrows shot up. He looked like he wasn't sure what he'd gotten himself into.

"Yes," Dorien said flatly. "And never forget the power of the collective unconscious. That's why we formed the Dream Club. Dreams are the royal road to the unconscious." She shot Edward a meaningful look, and I wondered if he'd get the reference. "I suppose you know that?"

"That's from Freud, right?" Apparently Edward knew his psychology.

"Yes, of course," Dorien added in her blunt way. Edward looked unconvinced but trudged dutifully after Dorien. Etta Mae was as silent as a sphinx, her arms folded across her chest, until Sybil urged her forward.

"Edward and Etta Mae, you're new to the club and you'll be interested to know that we solved a murder once," Persia offered, "just a few months ago." She looped her arm through Etta Mae's and fell into step behind Edward and Dorien.

"Really? I had no idea." Edward brightened a little, his eyes widening with interest. He stopped to take a breath on the landing and then took the final step into the apartment. Ali bustled around the kitchen, grabbing a pitcher of iced tea from the refrigerator. She placed it on a lacquered tray on the coffee table with some cranberry-colored glasses and a platter of brownies, and urged everyone to help themselves.

"Actually, it was two murders," Persia went on, settling herself on the sofa. Edward took a seat across from her and the Harper sisters squeezed together on a settee. Dorien grabbed a comfy upholstered chair, and the rest of us pulled over kitchen chairs.

Persia waited until she had everyone's attention before continuing. "Looking back, we saw loads of hints in our dream material. A lot of imagery and symbolism. They were like premonitions. All we had to do was talk it out, and we came up with some amazing interpretations, didn't we, Ali?"

"Yes, we certainly did," Ali admitted. "That's what dream interpretation is about: analyzing content and trying to pull out the secrets. I think we finally convinced Taylor that this isn't just a lot of hocus-pocus." She smiled at me and I looked at her fondly. We'd certainly become closer since I'd moved to Savannah to help turn her failing business around. And my skepticism about the Dream Club had all but disappeared. I'd seen the group in action and it was hard to not be impressed by their keen insights and their creative approaches to solving a murder.

That caught Etta Mae's attention. "Really? You somehow tapped into your dreams to find the killer?"

Sybil nodded. "We just put our heads together and made a pledge to think about poor Chico every night." Chico, a dance instructor who owned a studio right across from our shop, was murdered a few months ago and the Dream Club was instrumental in solving the crime.

"I've never heard of anything like that," Etta Mae said skeptically. She was sitting on the edge of the sofa, her face rapt with interest. "You actually came up with the killer's name?"

"It wasn't quite that simple," Dorien said testily. "I know you're probably new to dream work, but—"

"As am I," Edward interjected.

"But you have to remember that dream material is symbolic. So it's not all black and white, cut and dry," Dorien continued. She has an angular face, and her asymmetrical haircut had fallen into her eyes. She brushed it away hastily and her voice became more animated. "Everything is a symbol. So, think symbols when you dream. Something means something else. An object can represent a person, for example. A tree can symbolize your mother. Or even yourself." She paused to peer at Etta Mae and Edward. "You really have to dig deep to make any progress in analyzing your dreams. You can't just stay on the surface, because the truth lies hidden somewhere in your subconscious."

"That's true," Ali piped up. "You can't access the information in your waking state. You have to wait until you fall asleep, and then material rises to the surface. The moment you wake up, try to remember as much as you can about your dreams. We recommend keeping a pen and paper on your night table. If you wait until morning, it may be too late to recapture the dream. Just get in the habit of writing down a few key words, if you can. Does this make sense to you?"

"I think so," Etta Mae said slowly. "It's a lot to absorb all at once." I found myself agreeing with her. I had been new to dream interpretation when I moved to Savannah, and I'd learned a lot from the members of the club.

"Just take it one step at a time," I suggested. "No one picks this up immediately. It's a process. Take your time and after a while, it will become intuitive. You'll learn things about yourself that you never knew. All of us have secrets, and dream interpretation brings them out into the open. It makes the information available to us."

"That's good to know," Etta Mae said after a long moment. *She's afraid of something*, I decided, *but what?* A shadow of discomfort darkened her face and she shifted uneasily in the chair. Her eyes were suddenly narrowed, shuttered, as if she was hiding something. The impression flitted by so quickly, it was almost subliminal, but I felt a little tingle go up my spine. Etta Mae set down her teacup very carefully before continuing. "I never thought of writing down my dreams. Usually when I wake up, I can't even remember them, and then something happens during the day that suddenly makes me think of them."

"That happens to all of us," Persia interjected. Persia loves bold colors and was wearing a bright yellow tunic top stenciled with Toucans. Matching yellow earrings the size of Necco Wafers dangled from her ears. "A sound, a song, maybe a sunset—something triggers a memory and suddenly the whole dream comes right back to you." Etta Mae nodded, as if she agreed.

"Sometimes I can even scribble down a few words and then ease right back into the dream," Ali continued. "Not always, but that's a very valuable skill to learn."

"This is all very interesting, but I really don't see how you could gather real evidence from dreams," Edward said slowly. He leaned back in his chair, reached for the pipe in his pocket, and then changed his mind. "If dreams are just re-creations of what a person has seen and experienced, then why would they be any more helpful than just straightforward remembering? Why not just approach the issue logically and write down everything you've seen and heard? That seems to be far more sensible."

He nodded after he finished this little speech, and he reminded me of some professors I'd encountered in graduate school. Not quite smug, but certainly sure of himself. I wondered how open he would be to new ideas. There's a lot of give-and-take in the Dream Club, and everyone is encouraged to voice his or her opinion. Would Edward really be a good addition to the mix?

"I think you're speaking as a researcher," Lucinda said in her breathy little voice. "I used to be an educator, too, and I never thought I'd be able to switch gears and turn off my 'left brain.'" She gave a self-deprecating laugh. "It's all about right brain in the Dream Club."

"Lucinda is right," Sybil said with a touch of exasperation. I could see that Edward was what the group would call a "doubter," someone who was interested in dreams but not convinced of their power. I felt the same way when I first came to Savannah. I was secretly amused at Ali's faith in the Dream Club and had no idea that their insights would prove to be so valuable. "Even if someone had total recall—which most of us don't—dreams offer us new insights into everything our senses tell us. Dreams can highlight important issues for us, things that seemed inconsequential at the time."

"The reason dreams are so difficult to interpret, Edward, is because they're very complex," Persia offered. "It takes real skill to make sense of them, and I learn something new every week."

"I hope I can get some tips, too," Etta Mae said. "All the women in my family have the gift of prophecy, and that's why I wanted to join this group." She helped herself to a brownie, and then she went for a quick change of subject. Was it deliberate? "This is delicious," she said, inspecting it. "How'd you get it so moist?" she asked, taking a bite.

"Kahlúa is the secret," Ali told her. "You can't really taste the alcohol, because it burns off in cooking, but it gives it a very nice flavor." She waited a beat and then said, "You mentioned earlier that you had a bad experience with Sonia. Would you like to tell us more about it?"

Etta Mae's face twisted into a frown and she let out a low, strangled laugh. "Unpleasant? You could say that. She stole something precious from me and my family." She looked around the circle. "She comes across sweet as pie on television, like the next-door neighbor you wish you had, but trust me, it's all an act. The woman's a thief."

"That's a very serious accusation," Lucinda said

reproachfully. There's still something of the schoolmarm about Lucinda, even though she retired from her headmistress job a few years ago. "I hope you have evidence to back up your statement."

"You bet I do!" Etta Mae cackled. She gestured to her tote bag. "The proof's right in there. Her new book proves it. It's a total rip-off of my family recipes. I'm so glad you loaned it to me, Ali. I'll return it to you." She laid it on the coffee table. "I have my own copy from the book signing. And now I have something *really* interesting to show you." She reached into a tote bag and pulled out a battered leather-bound book the size of a scrapbook.

"Your family cookbook," Minerva said. "You carry it with you?"

"I thought we could pass it around," Etta Mae said with shy pride. "It's kind of fragile, so I'd appreciate if you turn the pages real carefully. Some of the recipes were glued in there more than a hundred years ago, so you have to watch they don't slip out. They're hanging by a thread. I'm surprised it's lasted as long as it has."

"You gave this to Sonia?" I asked.

Etta Mae nodded. "I sure did. I sent a copy, of course, not the original, and I mailed it to her headquarters in Chicago." She gave a little snort. "A month or so later, I got a form letter saying they didn't accept unsolicited recipes. The letter wasn't the least bit friendly, and I was miffed. All my original recipes are in here." She laid it carefully on the coffee table. "Have a look, if you like."

"I'd love to!" Minerva said, reaching for the cookbook and laying it carefully on her lap. "Oh, I love the way it's divided up. There's one section just for family celebrations and another for church suppers." She turned the pages and smiled.

"Here's a macaroni casserole that feeds a hundred people. That must have been quite a party."

"What's a 'Repent at Leisure' cake?" Rose asked, peering over Minerva's shoulder.

Etta Mae laughed. "That's sort of a joke. It's for bridal showers." When Rose looked puzzled, she quickly said, "You know the saying, 'marry in haste, repent at leisure'?"

"Oh, I see," Rose said with a bemused expression on her face. "Very clever. And here's Aunt Sally's Best-Ever Funeral Cake and Uncle Jed's Delectable Pork Belly Casserole," she said when Minerva turned the page. "Oh my, such colorful names."

"The recipes are great for family events," Etta Mae said proudly. "I still make some of them, but I've never managed to make the pie crust the way they did back then. And my biscuits aren't as light and fluffy as my grandma's. I don't know what her secret was, but they almost floated off the cookie sheet. Mine are pretty good, but they're like hockey pucks compared to hers. I guess she took that secret to the grave with her," she said glumly.

"Sonia knows what she did. That may be her name on the cover of her shiny new cookbook," Etta Mae said, her mouth suddenly twisted into a snarl, "but the recipes in there? They're mine, all mine."

4

My cell chirped then, and the room fell silent as I flipped open the lid. It was Sara; I heard hospital sounds in the background. I took the phone out to the balcony, still reeling from Etta Mae's surprising pronouncement.

"Sonia didn't make it," Sara said in a wobbly voice. "I don't think she even had a pulse when she was admitted." My heart hammered in my chest. I hadn't known Sonia personally, but sudden death is disturbing, and I felt a chill pass over me.

"I'm sorry to hear that," I said softly. "Whatever hit her, must have hit very fast."

"She looked ashen, almost blue, when they wheeled her into the ER." I didn't realize I'd been holding my breath and blew out a little puff of air. I glanced back inside to the living room, where everyone was looking at me expectantly.

"Sonia's dead," I said quietly to the group. Persia gasped, but everyone else was silent. Etta Mae had a strange, vacant smile on her face. I walked back out on the balcony with the phone still clasped to my ear. "What's the official word?"

"Nothing yet; it's too early to tell," Sara told me. "No cause of death, not a word. Her publicist is rushing to get an obit ready for the paper. I think it will just say she died suddenly and not give any details." She sighed and a long beat passed.

"Do they"—I paused, choosing my words carefully—"suspect foul play?" I realized I was digging my nails into my palm so tightly my knuckles were turning white.

"I think so." Sara had lowered her voice to a whisper. "Sam Stiles is coming back to the shop to gather up all the food and plastic plates as evidence and to take a quick look around. You haven't touched anything, have you?"

"No, of course not. The club members are still here, though. We're sitting upstairs, and Ali is trying to get some clarity on what happened."

"Clarity? Oh, please," Sara said with a note of exasperation. "Forget about clarity." I remembered that Sara was initially skeptical about the Dream Club and our mission. She said it all seemed a little too New Age for her taste, and she preferred to stick to hard facts. She'd warmed up to us a little, but she still remained something of a skeptic. "Here's what you need to do," she said, her voice suddenly stronger. "Taylor, you need get everyone out of the shop before Sam gets there. Send them home, on the double."

"But I told you, we're upstairs. We're not even near the shop." I glanced inside at the group gathered around the coffee table. They were talking in low voices and glancing curiously at me. Now that they knew Sonia had died, there were going to be endless speculations and theories as to what could have happened.

"Doesn't matter," Sara insisted. "You don't have to

explain anything. Just send them on their way. You can have an emergency meeting later in the week if everyone feels up to it. Clear everyone out right now, or it's going to be awkward. Sam will be right over, and she'll have some detectives with her. The scene has already been contaminated; don't make it worse."

Dorien was reluctant to leave, but after I explained the situation, everyone gathered up their things and headed downstairs. I noticed Etta Mae had carefully returned her family cookbook to her tote bag. Edward seemed eager to make his departure and his expression made it clear he was shaken by the day's events.

"We'll meet later in the week," Ali promised.

"You can count on it," Dorien said firmly. I saw her whisper something to the Harper sisters as they walked slowly down the sidewalk toward their flower shop. Probably discussing her theories about Sonia's death, I decided. I poured myself a large glass of ice water and waited for the Savannah-Chatham Metro PD.

When Sam arrived, she was all business. She snapped on a pair of gloves and started issuing directions to the two police officers who accompanied her. "Bag everything you can," she said, pointing to the buffet table. "Don't forget the trash." *The trash?* Ali and I exchanged a look.

"Anything special we're looking for?" a tall cop with a buzz cut asked.

"A missing EpiPen. Maybe two of them. Sift through things carefully; the pen could be broken or crushed."

Or someone could have pocketed it, I thought. It would have been easy to do in all the commotion after Sonia collapsed. I tried to remember who was around Sonia's purse when everything went south, but the only person I could remember was Olivia. And she'd seemed genuinely distraught as she foraged through her boss's purse, desperately trying to find the EpiPen. Olivia said she carried a backup pen for Sonia, I remembered, and I wondered if she'd ever located it. Was it possible that someone had swiped both EpiPens, leaving Sonia to die of suffocation as her throat swelled up?

"And Olivia Hudson mentioned Sonia's necklace is missing, so maybe you could take a quick look around for it," Sam continued.

"Her necklace?" Ali asked. "Is it valuable?" I tried to recall what Sonia was wearing this morning and remembered she was sporting a silk print blouse in bright yellow. It was unbuttoned at the collar and I remember seeing a thin silver chain glinting around her neck.

"I don't think so. She said it's costume but it has sentimental value. The family might want to have it back."

"Why would anyone take it?" I asked. I was standing in the middle of the shop as the crime scene techs made their way through the room, bagging evidence and taking photos.

"Probably no one took it," Sam said. "It might have slipped off when the paramedics were working on her, or maybe someone removed it at the hospital. Olivia says she never took it off. Apparently Sonia was very superstitious and she thought something terrible would happen if she didn't wear it."

"Poor Sonia," Ali said. "Something terrible *did* happen," she added sadly.

I turned to Sam. "Then a necklace isn't really important, right?"

"No, it's just one of those nagging details. You know how

compulsive I am." She gave a rueful smile and walked along the long heart pine buffet table, inspecting the dishes.

I knew exactly what she meant. Sam always says that "the devil is in the details," and she wouldn't rest until every nagging little question was resolved. That's how she managed to close so many cases with the Savannah PD and make detective in a very short time. Once the evidence was collected, Sam asked for the guest book that was kept in the front of the shop. "I'll need to keep this for a few days."

"Not everyone signed in," I said thoughtfully. "I remember seeing a few stragglers who came in late." I opened the book and glanced at the first page of names. Most of them were familiar to me, townspeople or friends of Ali's. "And, of course, there was Sonia's staff, or as she liked to call them 'Team Sonia.' I'm pretty sure none of them signed in."

"That's okay," Sam said. "It will give us a starting point. I'd like to go over these names with you tomorrow. It shouldn't take long." She glanced at the sign-in book, running her finger down the names. "How did you invite people to the signing? It sounds like it was a last-minute event."

"It was," Ali told her. "I sent out an e-mail blast last night to some of our regular customers and, of course, we told all the members of the Dream Club. I suppose a few tourists might have stopped by as well. We didn't really expect a big turnout because we didn't have time to promote it."

"WOW, WHAT did you think of Etta Mae's bombshell?" Ali asked me after the police had finally left. "I'm flabbergasted." She blew out a breath. "There's no way to tell if it's true, of course, but she certainly seemed convinced. I suppose she'll tell us more as time goes on."

We were padding around the kitchen in shorts and flip-flops. We'd closed the shop for the rest of the day, so there were no customers downstairs and the apartment seemed as still as a tomb. I brushed off the morbid image and busied myself making coffee. I think both Ali and I felt at loose ends, mulling over the tragic event at the book signing.

"No one challenged her except for Lucinda, did you notice that?" Ali went on. "They didn't even ask a single question."

"I think it shocked all of us," I said, rescuing the cream pitcher from Barney, who was determined to lap up the last few drops. "Nobody could pull it together to ask a question. Not even Dorien," I noted. "Although knowing Dorien, she's probably saving her questions for the next meeting."

"I'd love to know what Etta Mae said to Sonia at the book signing," Ali said softly. "I couldn't hear a word of the conversation. It looked a little intense, but I don't really think it was confrontational. I wonder if Sonia even knows who Etta Mae is."

"No idea. Who knows, maybe Sonia has run into this sort of thing before. She's a celebrity and I think she meets a lot of people who want something from her. I'm not sure we should have accepted Etta Mae into the club; there seems to be something a little off about her."

I had my doubts about Edward Giles as well but didn't voice them. There was something so reserved and self-contained about the university professor that I doubted he would be a good match for our group.

"I think Etta Mae will settle in," Ali said amicably. "She did seem a bit edgy today, but maybe it was just a case of nerves. This has been an incredibly stressful experience for everyone. Poor Sonia. I still can't believe this happened."

She curled up on the sofa and pulled Scout onto her lap.

She immediately started purring and walking in circles before she finally settled down and began gently kneading. "Ow," Ali moaned as her sharp claws connected with her bare leg. She winced and lifted her off her lap and onto the sofa cushion farthest from her. "She never remembers to keep her claws in," she said ruefully. The vet told us that Scout was probably taken away from her mother too early. The mother cat teaches the kittens to sheathe their claws when they knead, but poor Scout never got the message.

"I wish we'd had more time to hear about it. She certainly got everyone's interest." I paused. "I think it's far-fetched, you know. Not really believable. At least that's my first reaction." Ali reached over to pet Scout, who cleverly was trying to weasel her way back onto her lap via the coffee table.

"You may be right," Ali said thoughtfully. "On the face of it, it seems pretty improbable that Sonia actually stole Etta Mae's recipes. Just from a practical perspective, how in the world would she hope to get away with it? Especially if there were loads of family members who'd had access to the book and would be outraged to think a celebrity had stolen them and passed them off as her own. After all, that's part of their history."

I nodded. "I think it's unlikely. There have got to be thousands of recipes floating around the Internet; why would a famous chef like Sonia have to resort to stealing? She probably has loads of staff to find the best recipes and test them for her. Besides, is it even possible to copyright a recipe?"

Ali shrugged. "I'm not sure. Etta Mae acted like her recipes were special, something handed down from generation to generation."

"If that's true, they'd have to be adapted for modern

tastes," I insisted. "People are into healthy eating these days. Tastes have changed over the years. Not many people cook with lard anymore, and a hundred years ago, people liked to fry vegetables in leftover bacon grease."

"Bacon grease?" Ali, a strict vegan, gave a delicate shudder. "I hadn't thought of that angle."

A while later, Ali went downstairs to begin working on a candy platter for a Fabulous Fifties party, and I decided to do a quick check of the inventory. Since I'd become co-owner of the shop, I'd persuaded Ali to branch out. Selling retro candy wasn't enough to keep the business afloat, and after some initial resistance, she'd agreed to go after catering jobs and had approved my plan to start offering light lunches and desserts. Candy platters—perfect for '50s theme parties—were filled with old favorites like Necco Wafers, Chunky bars, Red Hots, and Boston Baked Beans. I'd been urging Ali to consider doing '50s hors d'ouevres like pigs in blankets, shrimp cocktail, mini meatballs, and fruit kabobs.

We were far from being a booming success, but profits were up for the first time in months and it looked like we had finally turned things around. Street traffic had improved thanks to some creative window displays, and a chalkboard posted on the sidewalk touted the daily specials.

We had a long way to go, but I was happy that we were moving forward and that my sometimes impulsive, flighty sister had settled down and was actually going to run a profitable business. Ali has had a checkered career and a series of failed ventures. The problem is she's never had a specific career goal, and she's always searching for something just out of reach. Since graduating from art school, she'd worked for a graphic designer, done stints as marketing coordinator for a textile museum and event planner for an art gallery, and even run a glass-blowing shop. It seemed as though all her talents had finally come together and merged into a successful business enterprise. I could only hope I was right.

When Noah called me at six, I was taken by surprise. My heart gave a little lurch when his warm, sexy voice raced over the line. I was in the shop, tidying up a gummy bear display, and I pulled over a counter stool, settling down to talk.

"Sara told me what happened," he said quietly. "Are you okay?"

"I think so. I was pretty shaken up at first, but the initial shock seems to have worn off. It was probably worse for Sara because she actually followed the ambulance to the hospital. She's the one who called to tell me Sonia didn't make it."

We talked for a few minutes about Sonia's sudden death and the possibility of foul play. As far as I knew, the jury was still out on whether or not it was a homicide, but Noah seemed to have his suspicions. Noah is a private detective and his mind is razor-sharp, instantly homing in on possible motive, means, and opportunity when he's sizing up potential suspects. When he worked for the FBI, he was part of an elite division at Quantico, the Behavioral Science Unit, and he brings those same skills to his work as a PI.

"Who would have had it in for Sonia?"

"I don't know, and that's what's bothering me. I guess anyone who's reached that level of fame is bound to have made some enemies along the way, but would anyone hate her enough to kill her? Her fans seemed to love her. She employed a whole entourage; the woman had an empire. She was an inspiration to a lot of people because she started out with nothing and worked night and day. One of those rags-to-riches tales that people love to hear about."

Noah snorted. "Someone wasn't too impressed by her. She probably clawed her way to the top. I'm guessing there are some wannabes who might have been jealous of her fame and wealth. I think we should start where we always start."

"By following the money?" I was grateful that Noah seemed eager to help with the investigation, and I knew his protective instincts had kicked in. Until the mystery of Sonia's death was solved, a cloud was going to hang over Oldies But Goodies.

"Exactly." Ali walked out of the stockroom and shot me a puzzled look. I mouthed *Noah* and she nodded.

Following the money is one of Noah's favorite strategies. I was silent for a moment, thinking of who might benefit financially from Sonia's death. Her heirs? Very possibly. Maybe some business colleagues? Certainly not her stockholders; her sudden death would cause stock prices in Sonia Scott, Inc., to plummet.

And now that Sonia was gone, who was left to carry on the brand? The cookbooks, the television show, the video cooking lessons, the friendly, down-home blog? Women thought of

Sonia Scott as being open and approachable, someone you could share a cup of coffee with at your kitchen table. She was friendly, folksy, and an awesome cook.

It seemed sad to think she'd spent decades building up her fan base, acquiring corporate sponsors, creating a whole line of cookware and table settings, and now it was all gone in a flash.

"I don't know enough about her yet. Sara said she's going to look into the financials—"

"I know, Sara is digging up information right now. I've already made reservations for the four of us to go over the case tonight." *Reservations?* My pulse went up a notch. "Dinner at Marcelo's at seven. Can you and Ali make it? Sara has already said yes."

I didn't hesitate. Marcelo's is my favorite Italian restaurant in Savannah. "We'll be there." I flipped my phone shut and then glanced at my watch. I'd have to hustle. Just time enough to dash upstairs, take a quick shower, and pull on a sundress. I called to Ali over my shoulder, "Don't defrost anything for dinner. Noah is taking us to Marcelo's."

"Won't three be a crowd?" she teased. "I'm sure he'd rather dine solo with you."

"Not tonight," I shot back. "Sara's coming, too. We're going to be discussing what happened to Sonia. He's just concerned because she was murdered here; it's not a date."

"If you say so," she said, raising her eyebrows just a tad. "But from what I remember, Noah has trouble separating business from pleasure."

I could understand her suspicions. Noah Chandler and I have had an on-again, off-again relationship since I moved to Savannah. We have a "history," as folks are fond of saying. I first met Noah when we both worked in Atlanta, where we spent an intense two years together. I was working as a strategist for a consulting firm and Noah was an FBI agent with the Atlanta field office. It was love at first sight, but not the type of love that's sustainable. The timing was off. I was traveling nonstop, we were both workaholics, and neither one of us had the time or energy to devote to a relationship.

Noah moved to Savannah shortly after I arrived to help Ali with the shop. He has family in town—a couple of elderly aunts, along with a cousin on the police force—and he's always loved the South. He said he'd had enough of the Bureau, that's why he decided to set up his own detective agency. He's quickly built a reputation for being smart, tough, and honest. I ran into him at a dinner party when Ali and I were investigating Chico's murder a few months ago, and now we've started seeing each other again.

This time, we're taking it slow. It's not a red-hot romance like in the old days, just a warm friendship that will stand the test of time.

We're both different people than we were when we were younger. Now that Noah's in Savannah, he seems happier and more relaxed than I've ever seen him. He tells me I'm more laid-back since I gave up my corporate job in Chicago. It makes me wonder what would have happened if we'd both stepped away from our stressful lifestyles back in Atlanta. Would we have been kinder and gentler with each other? Less obsessed with our careers and more committed to our relationship?

Water under the bridge, as Noah would say. Noah always tells me I spend too much time on might-have-beens and insists I need to focus on the moment. I tell him I'm working on it but old habits die hard.

"What do we know so far?" Sara said, whipping out her notebook. Sara, a green-eyed blonde, is as a bright as she is beautiful. She went to journalism school at Emory and won every journalism award the school offered. We were friends back in Atlanta, and I knew how much she wanted to be an investigative reporter. I was delighted to find her in Savannah and hoped she would find her niche here.

Journalism is a tough field, and at the moment, she's working as a stringer for the local paper. She covers whatever stories they assign her—everything from basketball games to city council meetings to the police desk—but I know she'd like to specialize in crime reporting. I think someday she'd even like to write true crime novels like her idol, Ann Rule. Sonia's murder had all the hallmarks of a major celebrity case, and if the story turned out to be as big as I thought it would be, this could be a game changer for Sara.

"We know that Etta Mae thinks Sonia stole her treasured family recipes," I said. "That much is definite."

"Do we have any solid evidence that it really happened?" Noah cut in. "Could Etta Mae just be someone who's disgruntled and maybe even a little jealous of Sonia's success? It's been known to happen, you know. Remember the guy who said Stephen King ripped off his unpublished novel? When the lawyer asked him how Stephen King could have had access to it, he insisted that Stephen King had read his mind. Now, that's really far-fetched."

I shook my head. "I remember that case." I thought for a moment. "And the answer is, I guess I have no way of knowing the truth about Etta Mae's accusations. Etta Mae doesn't seem like a nut job, and she insists she has rock-solid proof. Apparently she sent the recipes to Sonia and was rebuffed. The company sent her a form-letter rejection and said they never use recipes from outside sources."

"I'm sure that's true," Ali added. "I read up on Sonia's company. Supposedly they pride themselves on developing everything in their test kitchens. They guarantee that they use all original recipes. Why would they need Etta Mae's recipes? She's taking this way too personally, and I'm not sure why."

"I don't know why she's so offended," Sara said. "She sounds overly sensitive to me. I bet loads of people approach Sonia about using their recipes. She probably gets hundreds or even thousands of requests every year. You can't really expect her to take the time to reply individually to every single person who writes to her."

I paused to take a sip of sangria. "You're right. But the story didn't end there for Etta Mae. To her surprise, her recipes turned up in Sonia's new cookbook. At least that's what she claims."

"Is she sure about that?" Noah asked. "Does she have any proof this is what really happened?"

I peered at Noah over the rim of my sangria glass. "Well, the names of the recipes were altered, but Etta Mae says she recognized them right away. All the ingredients were the same. They even used the same measurements. Etta Mae feels it's a clear-cut case of theft." Noah's eyebrows inched up. I could tell his original skepticism was melting and he was starting to think that there might be more to Etta Mae's story than meets the eye. I was still having trouble deciding if Etta Mae was credible. She seemed so outraged and emotional, I didn't quite know what to believe.

"So Sonia used Etta Mae's recipes and changed the names of the dishes? Why would she do that?" Sara cocked her head to one side, reaching for a breadstick. Usually I ask the servers to remove the bread basket from the table so I won't be tempted, but Sara is as thin as a swizzle stick, so she can afford the calories. I took a longing look at the crunchy breadsticks—a house specialty—and forced my attention back to the story of Etta Mae and her family cookbook.

"It could be the names were a little folksy, or they had too much of a down-home flavor," I said, recalling some of the recipes included in the book.

"Folksy can be good," Ali mused. "I like it when cookbook writers include a little bit of history about the recipe and where it came from. It makes it seem more personal, like sharing recipes with a friend."

"I'm afraid these were a little *too* folksy," I said ruefully. You know, 'Aunt Sally's Best-Ever Funeral Cake.' And 'Uncle Jed's Delectable Pork Belly Casserole.'"

Sara chuckled. "I see what you mean. Pork bellies and funeral cakes don't sound too appealing."

"Maybe Etta Mae's feelings were hurt by the company's reaction," Ali offered. "It still doesn't mean she would do anything to harm anyone."

"You're probably right," Sara said. "And killing Sonia wouldn't solve anything. It would make more sense to seek legal redress if the company really did steal her recipes and try to pass them off as their own."

"But if it isn't Etta Mae, where does that leave us?" I asked. Deep down, I felt it was very unlikely that Etta Mae would murder anyone, especially over a bunch of family recipes. I made a mental note to see if I could find any of her "treasured family recipes" online, using a few of the names I remembered. Who knew, maybe one of Etta Mae's relatives had a blog. I'd make it a point to ask her at the next Dream Club meeting.

"Where does that leave us? Back at square one, the money trail," Noah said. He tipped his glass of sangria to me.

Sara nodded. "I've got a little bombshell for you. I've done some work on the financials, and one person who would really benefit from Sonia's death is Olivia Hudson. As far as I can tell, she's bright and ruthless and sick of being the power behind the throne. She could run the company starting tomorrow if she had to. She's clever enough and ambitious enough to make it work. All she'd have to do is get the approval of the board of directors, and I think they're in her corner."

"Olivia the devoted assistant?" I asked, surprised. I hadn't seen this one coming.

"Olivia the unappreciated employee," Sara retorted. "She may not be as devoted as you think. I found out some juicy gossip about her. She started to file a lawsuit against Sonia years ago, and someone high up in the company talked her out of it. They ended up settling out of court for an undisclosed amount."

"A lawsuit?" This was intriguing. "On what grounds?"

"It was a contractual disagreememt and the records are sealed," Sara said, glancing at Noah. "Something about Sonia's company not living up to the terms of their contract with Olivia. They hushed it up as fast as they could because Olivia was threatening to go to the Labor Relations Board."

"Unless you have a friend who can get us access . . ." She let her voice trail off with a winsome smile. Sara has an uncanny ability to get people to dig up long-buried records for her.

"I may know someone who can help us. Can you give me a little more to go on?" Noah was passing a bread basket around the table and I managed to resist them once more. I knew I'd be stuffing myself with lasagna for the main course, plus I wanted to leave room for Marcelo's famous tiramisu.

Sara was dipping a piece of Italian bread in a saucer of seasoned olive oil. "Not really. But the fact that it was settled so quickly is probably significant." "So does that mean she really had a case?" Ali asked. She paused while a waiter refilled our glasses of white sangria. "And if the details had come out, it could have embarrassed the company?"

Noah nodded. "It doesn't necessarily mean she had a case, it just means she could cause a lot of trouble for the company. If she made a formal complaint to the Labor Relations Board, they'd be obligated to investigate it. This would definitely affect the brand image Sonia tried to promote."

"That's true," I interjected. "The last thing she'd want would be a hint of scandal or unfair labor practices. Sonia liked to project the idea that her company was just one big happy family."

"Sounds like one big dysfunctional family," Sara offered. "So, you'll try to follow up on the potential lawsuit angle, Noah?"

He nodded. "Absolutely. I still have some friends at the DOJ." Our eyes locked for a moment and I felt a familiar little tug at my heart.

"Any news from the Savannah PD?" Sara asked, breaking the mood. We both knew that even though Noah was a private investigator he had strong ties to the police and he'd helped us out before in our investigations.

"They found the missing EpiPen," he said casually.

Sara stopped with her fork to her mouth. The server had placed chilled salads in front of us. "You're kidding! Olivia looked all over for that thing. I saw her myself."

I remembered the frantic scrambling as we all searched for the EpiPen. Olivia had tossed the contents of Sonia's purse on the floor in a panic. Then she'd turned her own tote upside down. There wasn't a trace of the pen and she seemed genuinely panicked. Had it all been an act?

"It was in the trash. They went through it with a fine-tooth comb."

"You mean in the trash bins outside the shop?" I pictured someone pocketing the EpiPen from Sonia's purse, or Olivia's purse, and then tossing it in a Dumpster.

"No, it was right in the shop. In the wastebasket near the kitchen area."

"I don't know how we missed it." I was flummoxed. We keep a wicker trash basket at the end of the counter, and everyone had access to it. I tried to think if I had seen anyone lurking around the trash basket during the book signing. I think I would have noticed it. Everyone in the audience stayed in their seats until it was time to approach Sonia for the signing. So that meant that someone on her own team had thrown the EpiPen away. Or did it?

"The salads here are delicious," Ali said, breaking my train of thought. "They chill the plates—that's a nice touch, isn't it?

Sara snapped her fingers in a Eureka moment. "Wait a minute, the plates! I nearly forgot about them. What about the plates?" she said, her green eyes blazing.

"Plates?" I said blankly.

"Plates, trays, serving platters, whatever you call them," Sara said, her voice rising in excitement. "The serving plates with all the pastries on them. Does anyone know what happened to them?"

"If you mean the serving plates for the desserts at the book signing," I said, suddenly understanding, "they're gone. When the cops arrived, they scooped everything up as evidence and I haven't heard anything about them."

"Anything else on the money angle?" I asked hopefully. There seemed remarkably little to go on, unless Noah or Sara had a new bombshell. "Did anybody find out about the will?"

Noah flipped open a tiny notebook and glanced inside. "No, not yet. It's still in probate."

We were silent for moment, mulling over what we knew so far. I felt we had uncovered only a small part of the puzzle and we needed some major pieces to fill in the gaps. Did Sonia have an enemy in her ranks? Was there an outsider holding a grudge? Could someone at the book signing have plotted to kill her? Worst of all, could it be Etta Mae from the Dream Club?

"I've heard a bit of gossip," Sara said. "Sexual hijinks at the highest level of Sonia Scott, Inc." She paused dramatically before breaking a breadstick in half. "It seems Sonia was a little too close to her marketing director, Jeremy Watts."

My mind flew to Jeremy Watts and the cozy scene I'd witnessed at the taping. Except it was Olivia who'd been having a tête-à-tête with Jeremy, not Sonia. "You're better than TMZ," I told her. "How did you dig up this little tidbit?"

"It's an open secret that Sonia and the very-married Jeremy have been an item for years."

Ali looked surprised. "Lucinda thought he and his wife, Leslie, were such a happy couple. But Lucinda is such a dear, she always thinks the best of everyone."

Sara shook her head. She dug into her tote bag and pulled out a grainy newspaper photo. "Here's Jeremy with Sonia at a luncheon in Tampa that was sponsored by a civic group.

I printed this out last night." The photo showed a smiling Sonia with her arm around Jeremy Watts. The couple definitely looked cozy, and Sonia had her face turned up to him in a rapturous smile. *Was Jeremy playing the field and involved with two women, one his boss and the other his colleague? Or did I misinterpret their conversation outside the studio?*

"And you're sure Sonia's seriously involved with him?" I asked. "It's not just a fling?"

"It's serious," Sara said solemnly. "Sonia has been after him to divorce his wife and marry her. He seems to be on the fence about it; he has little kids. The gossip magazines are all over it."

"I don't think her fans would be too keen on that," I said thoughtfully. "She likes to project such a wholesome image. Being labeled a home-wrecker would definitely show a darker side of her personality."

"But would it really hurt her cookbook sales? Or her TV ratings? That's all that matters in the long run: the bottom line," Noah chimed in. "I think her fans would have been loyal to her, no matter what. What else do we know about Jeremy's wife?"

"She was one of Lucinda's students at the Academy," I offered. "She and Lucinda chatted at the studio, and Lucinda introduced her to us. Lucinda was so glad to reconnect with her, she invited her back to her house after the taping." I paused. "Poor Leslie. I wonder if she knows about her husband's affair."

"She must," Sara offered. "She'd have to be an idiot not to. I think we should look at her as a suspect."

"We need to look at everyone. The sooner the killer is brought to justice, the better," Ali said.

"Amen to that," I agreed. "When the story hits the news,

Oldies But Goodies could be in for some bad publicity. The reporters are bound to mention the place that Sonia died—"

"Not only died, was *poisoned*," Sara cut in. "That's what they'll say."

Ali's cheeks flamed. "She may have been poisoned or it may have been an allergic reaction. But everyone in Savannah knows it wasn't our food that killed her."

"Don't be so sure about that," Noah said mildly. "You don't know what sort of twists and turns the story will take when it hits the national news. We have to wait and see."

We were silent while the server cleared our plates and brought the entrees. I didn't want to alarm Ali, but I knew Noah was right. The sooner this case was solved, the better for us all.

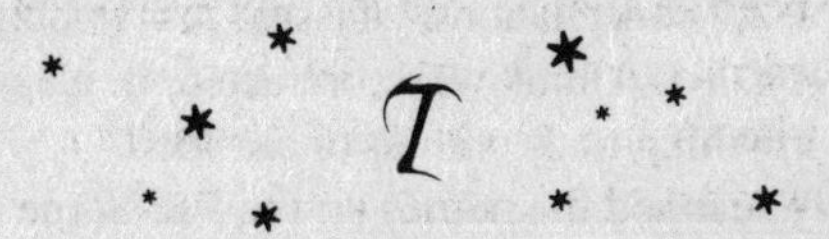

The message light was blinking when we returned from dinner and Ali settled down at the kitchen table. "Let's hope those flyers helped," she said cheerfully. "We could use some new business." Last week, we'd handed out flyers and coupons for our new Handheld Dessert Menu around town, and we hoped we'd made a splash. The menu items included everything from caramel cake pops to tiny jars of mini-desserts like key lime pie and bourbon-pecan rice pudding.

The mini-desserts were Ali's idea, and I was sure they'd be a hit. Each mini-dessert was served in a baby food jar decorated with a swatch of gingham. Customers could grab a plastic spoon and be on their way, exploring the city. We have tables and chairs at Oldies But Goodies, both indoors and on the patio, but the handheld desserts seemed to strike a chord with tourists. They were eager to buy a quick snack and be off, exploring the beauty of Savannah.

I watched Ali's face crumble as she sat with the phone

clasped to her ear, shaking her head and taking notes. When she finally hung up, I pulled out one of the ladder-back kitchen chairs and sat down across from her. "That bad?" I asked sympathetically.

Ali pushed her notepad toward me. "It's worse than bad; it's a nightmare. All cancellations," she said in a wobbly voice. "I can't believe it. You'd think we'd contracted the plague. People don't want anything to do with us or our food."

I quickly scanned the names on the list. Some were new customers who'd ordered catering jobs for special events. We'd invested a few hundred dollars handing out samples and developing a free "tasting menu," hoping it would pay off with local businesses and civic groups.

It looked like our efforts had been a dismal failure. "Even the Little Miss Chef contest?" I frowned. "I paid a sales call on the pageant organizer last week and gave her fifty free mini-desserts for the girls." *And a thick wad of coupons for free half pounds of our retro candy. And a generous donation to her nonprofit*, I thought grimly.

The organizer—a prominent civic leader here in town—had been so appreciative and friendly. How could she pull the plug on us? It felt like a betrayal of the worst sort. She'd said she loved the food and candies at the shop and had promised to recommend us to all her friends. What had happened? There was only one explanation, and Ali and I both knew what it was.

"Sonia," Ali said bitterly, as if she had read my mind. "Sonia happened."

I started to contradict her and then stopped. The truth was staring us both in the face and there was no way to sugarcoat it. I had thought inviting Sonia Scott to sign books at the shop was going to be a fantastic boost to our struggling business, and instead it may have killed us. At the very least, we'd taken a major hit, and I had no idea how to turn things around.

"If only we hadn't served food," Ali said, her face creased with despair. "It's the food that did it—at least that's what people will think. If only we had stuck to the book signing, none of this would have happened."

"It was inevitable," I reminded her. "The food was a big part of the promotional effort. It did draw a crowd," I said, remembering the fans eagerly munching on goodies from Sonia's cookbook. "Ali, we both thought it was the right thing to do, and there's no sense in second-guessing ourselves now. Hindsight is always twenty-twenty."

"I know you're right," she said, scooping Scout onto her lap. She began idly stroking Scout's thick fur and her features relaxed a little. Barney and Scout have the ability to sense when either one of us is upset, and they always seek us out for a little cuddling. A few soft purrs and head nuzzles can do wonders. The cats are highly sensitive to our moods, always ready to offer their own brand of feline comfort. "I guess we need to develop a game plan." She blew out a little puff of air and her voice was stronger.

"That's the spirit." I was glad to hear the new note of resoluteness in her voice. The old Ali would have crumbled in the face of adversity or simply closed the business, but my sister had grown in so many ways in the past few months. I felt a rush of pride. Ali was showing a strength of character that I'd never seen before; her fighting spirit was an inspiration to me.

I'm the one with the MBA and the business background, but I was stymied at what we should do next. If people really believed that our food had something to do with Sonia's death, it was going to be hard to turn this around. I made a mental note to ask Sara if she thought running a piece in the local paper would help. Or would that just make it worse? This was a tough call.

And I needed to find out from Noah when the autopsy results would be back. What really had killed Sonia? I drew a mental picture of the buffet table, loaded with lemon bars, tiny cherry cheesecake tarts, and shortbread cookies. Was it possible that peanuts had been lurking somewhere in there? These recipes were all straight out of Sonia's cookbook. And Ali and I had made two of the desserts ourselves.

"Ali," I said abruptly, "do you remember when Sonia shouted for more cookies?"

"I sure do," she said, nodding her head. "She practically bellowed across the room. She said she had to do a taste test, so she needed a refill. She was joking, of course, but yes, I remember her asking for a refill on the pastries."

"Who handed her the plastic plate with the cookies, do you remember? And what did they put on it?"

She squinted her eyes and scrunched her face in thought. "I just can't remember," she said finally, putting Scout back on the floor. "It's funny, I can see the blue plastic plate with the red rooster. I can see it piled high with goodies, but I don't know who made the selection and who handed it to her."

"It might have been two different people," I told her. "That's a good point."

"You're right; it could have played out that way. Sonia never got up from her seat, and that means someone filled the plate for her at the buffet table." She paused. "And then somehow the plate got passed up the line to her. This is a mess," she added, resting her forehead on her hands for a moment. "Do you think we'll ever figure it out?"

"Of course we will," I said with more optimism than I really felt. "We have to," I muttered under my breath as Ali heated a pan of milk on the stove. Even in the hot summer months, Ali is fond of a cup of hot chocolate before going to bed. I think it's more of a nostalgia thing than anything else. We used to have hot chocolate on cold winter nights in the Midwest, during that golden time when our parents were alive and all was right with the world.

"I think we have to put it out of our minds for tonight," Ali said a few minutes later, heading down the hall with her mug of cocoa.

"This will all look better in the morning. That's what Mom used to say, remember?" I said. She gave me a wisp of a smile, and I felt a catch in my throat. There were times like this, with her face scrubbed clean and her soft hair curling around her neck, that she looked like a teenager. And I was her big sister, always looking after all, trying to protect her from her own devil-may-care personality.

"Of course I remember. And she was right. Sleep well, sis. We'll tackle this together in the morning. C'mon, kitties, bedtime." Barney padded dutifully down the hall after her, and Scout quickly followed. I smiled, realizing that I was still a "visitor" in their eyes and Ali was the one they adored. She was their "special" human and the dispenser of hugs and cat treats. I would have to earn my way into their little furry hearts. I bet a handful of cat treats every day would do the trick.

Ali had left the cancellation list on the kitchen table, and my spirits sank as I looked over the familiar names. Friends, acquaintances, neighbors—these were people we had counted on, some new customers and some old ones. All of them were rejecting us and it stung. One thing was certain. We had to solve Sonia's murder, and we had to do it fast.

8

It was barely 9:45 a.m. when the rapping on the shop door shattered my morning coffee-and-croissant break. I'd made sure everything was shipshape downstairs early that morning and then had retreated back to the apartment for a quick cup of java before officially starting my workday. Ali was taking a yoga class and wouldn't be back till noon. I'd be managing the shop by myself, with the help of Dana Garrett, our college intern, who spent several hours a week with us, learning the ropes of running a small business.

"Hold on, I'm coming!" I skipped down the steps, wearing what had become my business uniform. A white polo, embroidered with the Oldies But Goodies logo in navy blue, and a pair of tan cargo shorts. I was puzzled by the early-bird customer. Was someone picking up a special order? That seemed unlikely. Most of our special orders had been abruptly canceled, I thought sadly, lifting the shade. I flinched when the rapping turned into a burst of staccato pounding, making my head throb. The noise was metallic, as if someone was hammering at the door with a set of keys.

"Honestly, what's the rush . . ." I began and then swallowed my words when I recognized a familiar face. Olivia Hudson stood on the stoop, dressed to the nines in a chic black linen shift with exquisite gold jewelry. I raised my eyebrows, unlocked the door, and she marched in as if she owned the place. Just as I'd guessed, she was clutching a set of keys in her hand, threading them through her fingers as if they were brass knuckles. Practically a lethal weapon, I noted with amusement.

"Finally," she said, exhaling noisily like a racehorse. "I wasn't sure what time you opened, but I was guessing it was nine. I took a quick power walk around the square to kill some time and then I decided I couldn't wait any longer." *A power walk?* She was impeccably dressed, but she had a fine film of moisture above her lips and her hair was curling around her neck. She probably hadn't realized the Savannah sun can be intense, even in the morning hours. Her stiletto sling-backs weren't exactly made for hoofing it, and it occurred to me that her feet were probably killing her.

"We open at ten," I said pleasantly, biting back my irritation. I gestured to the sign in the window. "But we're always happy to open early for our guests. If you had called ahead of time, I would have been downstairs to greet you."

"Well, I'm here now, and I suppose that's all that matters," she snapped. She stepped back, eyes flashing as she took in my casual outfit. Her lips curled in disapproval. I was glad I'd taken the time to jam my feet into sandals instead of my usual flip-flops. From the way Olivia was raking me head to toe with her icy gaze, I could see she didn't appreciate my choice of business attire. We tend to be informal in the shop, and wearing shorts is cool and comfortable when I have to unload items from the stockroom and unpack heavy boxes of candies.

"What can I do for you?" I asked, forcing a pleasant note into my voice. I pulled two pitchers out of the refrigerator: one held icy cold lemonade and the other, sweet tea. "Perhaps something to drink?"

"Well, some tea would be good," she said, whisking out a hanky and blotting her forehead. She accepted a glass of sweet tea and drank thirstily, her gaze wandering around the shop. "It feels strange being back here," she said, her tone softening. "After what happened." She glanced at me helplessly and gave a little shudder. Her gaze kept going to the area in the back of the shop where we'd staged the book signing for Sonia. Maybe she was more devoted to Sonia than I'd realized. She seemed genuinely upset.

I nodded. "This must be a very difficult time for you." I gently guided her toward a seat at the counter. "How are you doing?" I was still puzzled at her visit but found myself feeling sympathetic toward her. At the very least, Sonia's passing must have created an enormous upheaval in both the company and her personal life. I wanted to ask her who was running Sonia Scott, Inc., but couldn't think of a polite way to do it.

"I'm doing okay. *We're* doing okay," she amended. "The Sonia Scott brand will go on forever," she said flatly. Her voice was oddly robotic, like a talking press release.

"I'm sure it will," I agreed. I started to sit down next to her and to my surprise, she suddenly guzzled the rest of her tea and stood up. If I thought she'd come for a gabfest about Sonia's death, I was clearly wrong. "Is there something I could help you with?" Now I was really baffled. She started pacing the shop area, glancing at the items on the shelves and low tables as if she was searching for something. She had a deep frown line between her eyes, and I doubted she was looking for Necco Wafers.

"I left something in here the other day," she said in flat tones. "When Sonia"—she winced—"had the book signing."

"I'm so sorry, but I don't recall seeing anything," I told her. I trotted along behind Olivia, feeling the tension rolling off her. What was missing and why was it so important? She appeared to be walking aimlessly, letting her fingertips trail along the glass candy case, idly touching gallon jars of sweets. "I'd be glad to help you look," I offered.

She suddenly stopped in her tracks and wheeled around, nearly bumping into me. "Do you remember when I tossed my tote upside down, trying to find the EpiPen?"

"Yes, of course. It was missing, and then they . . ." I caught myself just in time; I nearly revealed that it had been found in the trash can inside the shop. "I don't understand. Are you still looking for the EpiPen?" I asked, puzzled.

"No, of course not." She shot me a disgusted look. "I don't care about the EpiPen. I'm looking for my day planner. It's tan leather, about the size of a paperback." She spread her hands in the air to show me the size. "It was in my tote," she said. "I must have lost it when I dumped everything on the table." She swallowed hard. "It's nothing important," she said with a too-bright smile, "but it's just something I'd like to have back."

She was lying, I knew it. Lying or hiding something. The planner must be important or she would never have come back for it. Her voice had taken on a false note, thin and high-pitched, and she was speaking too rapidly. "Who knows, it might have gotten mixed up with all the publicity materials I was lugging around that day," she said vaguely. She bent down to examine some magazines on a coffee table. "I just thought I might have left it here, that's all."

Should I tell her the police had already been through the shop, taking everything that looked suspicious? Surely she'd figured that out for herself, hadn't she? I didn't recall seeing a tan day planner, either on the day of the book signing or when the police had processed the scene.

"I can help you look for it," I said, "but I'm not really sure where to start. As you can see, we've tidied everything up." It was true. After the police had left, Ali had made a quick sweep of the shop and dusted and polished everything in sight.

"I see that," she said, starting her pacing again. "But I know I left it here," she said, a hard note creeping into her voice. She was making me uncomfortable, and I wished she'd relax and sit down so we could have a normal conversation.

"I'm something of a Luddite," Olivia confessed. "I know most people keep track of their appointments on their computer, but I just like to have a hard copy in my hands. My assistant transcribes everything onto her computer for me, but I'm so paranoid, I always think that the computer might crash." Olivia gave a rueful smile. "Most people don't agree with me; they say I'm making double work for myself."

I thought of Minerva Harper. "I have a friend who feels exactly the same way. She likes to jot down ideas and appointments in her date book." We were silent for a moment, Olivia still sweeping the shop with her keen-eyed gaze.

"It looks like the planner isn't going to show up," she said after a moment, biting her lip.

"I can ask Ali and Dana to be on the lookout for it," I suggested.

"No, that's okay. Don't bother with it." She waved her hand in the air like she was batting away a pesky fly. She suddenly seemed to have zero interest in the missing planner.

Was she trying to throw me off guard, convince me that it wasn't important?

What secrets lurked inside? Some sort of inside information about her competitors? Something that she wanted to keep to herself? I was getting more intrigued by the minute, but I didn't want to tip off Olivia.

"I'll do my best to find it for you; just make sure you leave me your contact information." She turned to leave and my memory jogged into gear. "Olivia, I saved some things for you from the book signing." She turned in surprise. "I found a couple of extra copies of Sonia's cookbook and I thought you'd like to have them back." I reached under the counter and handed her the books.

"Thanks," she said stuffing them into her Louis Vuitton tote bag. Judging from Olivia's jewelry and shoes, I felt pretty sure it was the real deal and not a knockoff.

I was just about to offer Olivia a sample of one of the handheld desserts to take with her when Etta Mae walked into the shop, holding a gaudy piñata. "I want to fill this with candy for my nephew's birthday party," she said with a grin. "He's turning four today, and he loves gummy bears." She stopped dead in her tracks when she spotted Olivia.

"Olivia," she said, her voice low and raspy. "What are you doing here? I hoped I'd never have to see you again." Her lips thinned and she narrowed her eyes, facing her opponent.

"Oh, for heaven's sake, Etta Mae, can't you let bygones be bygones? Sonia is dead, or have you forgotten that? How long are you going to hold a grudge against the company?"

"This has nothing to do with holding a grudge," Etta Mae said. "This is about justice."

"Well, if you think we did something illegal, you can have your day in court," Olivia said blithely. "And good luck with that." She snorted. "People pester us all the time, trying to pawn off their favorite recipes on us. Then they get insulted when we don't use them. I tried to explain to you that all our recipes come out of our test kitchens. We don't need any more recipes for 'Mom's Favorite Meat Loaf,' trust me."

Olivia slung her tote bag over her shoulder and made tracks for the door, but not before glaring at Etta Mae. If looks could kill, Etta Mae would be in her grave. Then she turned to me. "Thanks for the tea, Taylor," she said with a thin smile. "I hope we meet up again someday." She gave Etta Mae another hard look. "And you, my dear, need psychological help. I sincerely hope you get it."

With that, she made her exit, leaving a sputtering Etta Mae in her wake. "Do you believe the nerve of that woman?!" she demanded. Her voice shook with indignation. "What was she doing, showing her face here again?"

"I had a few books left over from the signing," I said mildly. "She was here to pick them up, that's all." I took the piñata out of Etta Mae's hands and led her to the candy counter. "Now, what kind of gummy bears do you think your nephew would like?"

When Ali returned home a couple of hours later, I told her about the confrontation between Olivia and Etta Mae.

"At least it didn't come to blows," she said, sinking into the chintz sofa upstairs. Dana was downstairs, working in the shop, and it was nice to take a noontime break with my sister. One of the joys of owning your own business is that you can set your own schedule. At times, it feels like we're working way too many hours a week, but we love the flexibility of being our own bosses.

In the corporate world, I was a slave to my BlackBerry, my electronic calendar, and my never-ending travel schedule. Running the shop with Ali was a new way of life for me, and I'd been learning that it had definite perks as well as risks.

"Olivia stopped by to look for her missing day planner," I said.

"What did it look like?" Ali said, sitting up straighter.

"Olivia said it's small, tan leather, about the size of a paperback book." I gestured with my hands, as Olivia had done.

"But we *do* have her planner," Ali said. "It got swept under the counter, and I rescued it." When my jaw dropped, she added, "I left it down in the shop in the Lost and Found cabinet."

I smacked my forehead in frustration. "I didn't even think to look in there."

"I forgot to tell you about it," Ali said apologetically. "There's not much in the cabinet," Ali said. "A couple of binkies, a decoder ring, and some grocery coupons." She laughed. "Plus a dog-eared copy of *Fifty Shades of Grey*. No one has come back to claim it; maybe they're too embarrassed."

I was already on my feet, running down the stairs with Barney and Scout at my heels. For some reason, whenever I run, they feel compelled to gallop after me. Maybe it's a herd instinct, going back to the days when their ancestors hunted wildebeest on the savannah. Or maybe they remember that Ali keeps a big glass jar of cat treats for them down in the shop.

"Is it in there?" Ali said, peering over my shoulder. She'd come dashing down the stairs after me while I searched the cabinet. "It has to be! Unless someone swiped it, of course, and why would they?"

"You can relax; it's here," I said, pulling out the tan

leather planner. I sat at the counter and as I flipped it open, a thin sheet of paper slipped out I quickly scanned the first few lines, written in a girlish, loopy handwriting in violet ink. "Here's a note Olivia wrote. No wonder she wanted to find the planner."

"Really?" Ali plunked herself on the stool next to me. "What kind of note?"

"A very personal note. It's a love letter"—Ali's eyes widened—"and it's addressed to Jeremy Watts." I folded the note, tucked it back in the planner, and carefully placed it in the small safe we keep in the storeroom.

"So Jeremy was having affairs with two women at once? Sonia and Olivia?" Ali asked when I'd returned to the counter. When I nodded, she gave a little sigh, her mouth turned down at the edges. "The plot thickens, doesn't it. What's going to happen next?"

"I'm turning the note over to the police," I told her. "It could be evidence."

"And motive," she added. Ali looked unhappy at this new development, her eyes clouding, her expression downcast. If Jeremy was having an affair with Olivia, Olivia might want to get Sonia out of the picture. I decided it was time to call in the Dream Club.

9

Noah called me the following evening, just minutes before the Dream Club was to meet above the shop. My thoughts were swirling around the note I'd found in Olivia's planner. I'd sealed it in a manila envelope and dropped it off with the desk sergeant at the Savannah-Chatham Metro PD earlier in the day. It was evidence, but I didn't know if it was significant to the case.

We expected a full turnout, and Ali and I had readied the upstairs living room for the group. Ali was serving homemade cider—a new recipe—instead of the usual sweet tea, and I'd been experimenting with a recipe for "haystacks" with mixed results. The finished product didn't look quite as attractive as the one in the picture, and I wasn't sure I'd judged the amount of chocolate correctly. And I'd used high-fiber breakfast cereal instead of Chinese noodles. Sometimes you can fiddle with a recipe so much it bears no resemblance to the original dish. I've learned the hard way that some dishes are classics and it's better not to tamper with them.

"The autopsy results are in," Noah said. His voice was low and thrumming with energy. "They're just the preliminary studies, but I thought you'd like to be the first to know."

I had Noah on speakerphone so I could continue to pry the frozen haystacks off the wax paper–covered tray as we talked. I felt a little frisson of excitement. "Any surprises, or is it what we thought?"

"Sesame seeds were found in Sonia's stomach contents. If she had a severe nut allergy, the sesame seeds would be enough to do her in. The ME said there's no sign of any other trauma, so we have to assume she died of anaphylactic shock. She didn't have a heart attack, a stroke, or a seizure. She ate sesame seeds and her throat became so swollen, her airway collapsed. Without the EpiPen, she didn't have a chance." I winced, remembering the paramedics saying they'd found it impossible to intubate her. It seemed shocking that she could die so quickly, but I knew allergies—whether peanuts or sesame seeds—could be deadly.

"So it's just what we expected," Noah went on, "but it still doesn't get us any closer to solving the murder."

"Have they definitely classed it as a murder?" I was grateful that Noah had a close friend with the Savannah PD and could get inside information for us.

"There's still some debate about that," he admitted, "but the PD wants to treat it as a homicide and launch a full investigation. But the ME thinks Sonia could have accidentally ingested the sesame seeds, so he's not ready to call it a homicide, at least not just yet. Of course, that could change as new information becomes available. We'd have to find some evidence that someone deliberately planted the sesame seeds in one of the desserts." I pondered this for a moment. I was sure that none of the recipes called for sesame seeds.

"What do you think really happened?" I trusted Noah's instincts.

"I think it looks suspicious," he said without hesitation. "But it doesn't matter what I think; we need evidence." He waited a beat and then said, "How's business at the shop? Any repercussions?"

"Things aren't so good," I said glumly. "Nothing like a little murder scare to drive away customers. I think everyone believes Sonia died from food poisoning and not an allergic reaction." I wanted to tell him about Olivia's surprise visit, her quarrel with Etta Mae, and the love note we'd found, but decided to save it for another time. I could hear voices and footsteps on the stairs as the Dream Club members made their way up to our apartment. I blew out a little sigh.

"You sound discouraged," Noah said.

"I think things are at a stalemate. I have no idea what to do next."

Unless we could prove that someone deliberately introduced sesame seeds into one of the dishes at the book signing, the investigation would be over. Sonia's death would be chalked up to natural causes, and no charges would ever be filed. Ali and I were just managing to turn the business around with a positive cash flow, and I felt like someone had thrown a monkey wrench into the works. Would we ever be able to clear the shop's name, or would a cloud of suspicion hang over us forever?

Noah laughed. "Don't give up just yet. This is usually the time something big breaks and turns the investigation in a new direction. I've seen it happen before."

"Hope you're right," I told him. I quickly wound up the

conversation with Noah just as the first guests made their way into the living room.

Etta Mae, predictably, was still smarting from her encounter with Olivia. "I told Rose and Minerva about that dreadful woman," she said, throwing herself onto the sofa. "She was positively rude to me!"

"I'm sure she's still upset over Sonia's death," I said soothingly. "After all, the two of them worked together for years and years. It must have been a terrible shock to see her collapse like that. And don't forget she was with her at the hospital when she died. That was probably traumatic for her."

"Not to speak ill of the dead, but I hope Olivia realized there were two sides to Sonia." Etta Mae's voice was bitter as she glanced around the circle. "Maybe she was upset, as you say, but I think it was just the shock of the moment. I doubt there was any love lost between those two. Olivia was probably angling for Sonia's job. Sonia bossed her around like she was a lowly assistant, not an important executive of the company. I saw it myself." She nodded her head. "I Googled Olivia, and all the business magazines say the same thing. The word on the street is that Olivia was the brains and the energy behind the organization. Without her ideas and her hustle, Sonia Scott, Inc., would have stayed a little local company, with Sonia doing cooking displays in department stores and catering barbecue dinners at the local firehouse."

I remembered that Sonia had come from humble beginnings and had created her empire with very little capital, relying mainly on sweat equity. In the early days, she'd delivered homemade pies and cakes to her neighbors, catered potluck suppers for church groups, and never turned down a job. She had earned every bit of her success, but could there be someone out there jealous enough to snatch it away?

I made a mental note to check out what Etta Mae was saying about Sonia and her treatment of Olivia. It would certainly take suspicion off Etta Mae if she could point a finger at her disgruntled employee. After all, Olivia had means, motive, and opportunity to knock off her boss. Etta Mae was right about a Sonia-Olivia rivalry; at one point, Olivia had actually sued her employer. Both the *Wall Street Journal* and *Forbes* had covered the lawsuit, and Noah discovered it was settled out of court. Sonia and Olivia had refused to discuss it in the media and both women claimed it had been settled amicably. But did bad feelings remain?

"If that's true, maybe that's why Olivia came off as so abrasive," Sybil Powers said mildly. "She probably wasn't happy in her job and felt undervalued. I suppose it's only normal to lash out when you're stuck in a situation like that." Sybil, dressed in a vibrant red-and-yellow cotton dress, was sitting with Persia Walker on the love seat, Dorien was sitting alone on a kitchen chair, and Lucinda Macavy had pulled up a wicker rocker. I could hear Sara Rutledge deep in conversation with Edward Giles as they walked up the stairs.

Almost a full house tonight. I quickly pulled over two of the ladder-back kitchen chairs and started pouring cider for everyone. Sam Stiles, our resident detective and club member, had called to say she was on duty and wouldn't be able to make it, but everyone else had confirmed.

"I don't even know where to start tonight," Ali said, once the group had settled down and helped themselves to cider and pastries. She'd made some delicious apple cider donuts, which were an immediate hit. Several people asked for the recipe and she promised to e-mail it to them. "We need to include these on the dessert board downstairs," she said to me in a low voice. I nodded as I bit into a cider donut. It was delicious, both tart and sweet at the same time. The donuts were so good, they were practically addictive.

"I hope everyone has tried to process what happened to Sonia," Dorien said in her abrupt way. I knew when Dorien said "process," she was referring to dream work. People involved in dream work believe you can come to a deeper understanding of an event, especially a trauma, if you allow your subconscious mind to explore the event in a dream. Dreaming is a safe way to open a window to our innermost thoughts and feelings.

It seemed that outspoken Dorien was hijacking the meeting once again. I bristled a little. Ali is too kind to speak up for herself and always worries she'll offend someone. I don't think she realizes Dorien has a hide like a rhino.

"What a shock." Dorien blew out a little sigh. "I was almost afraid to let my head hit the pillow last night." She locked eyes with the two newcomers, Etta Mae and Edward Giles. "I never know where my dreams will take me," she said self-importantly. Dorien is a self-proclaimed psychic and often makes predictions about the future. Sometimes her predictions are so oblique it's hard to know if she's really on target, but no one ever dares question her. Dorien can be prickly and is known for her sharp tongue.

"I feel the same way," Sybil cut in. "I'm a little apprehensive myself. I don't really relish the idea of hopping into the head of a murderer." She gave a little shudder.

"I think we need to approach this in an organized way," Persia said, reaching for a lemon tart. Ali had tried a new recipe, and I was eager to see the group's reaction. Almost everyone in the group prefers the old classic "Southern" recipes, and I've learned that we shouldn't go too far afield.

No one was sampling my version of the classic haystack recipe, and I decided I must have missed the mark this time.

"What would you suggest?" Ali said politely. She tossed me a tiny eye roll and she probably realized she'd already lost control of the evening's agenda. Luckily, I knew she'd be a good sport about it and play along with whatever the group wanted.

"Well, I think we should go around the room and try to get a handle on any unusual imagery that popped up in last night's dreams. Why don't we start with the two new members, Etta Mae and Edward?" Persia leaned forward, her bangle bracelets clacking together.

Ali nodded and sat down. "That's a great idea. Go ahead, Etta Mae. You can be the first one up tonight."

Etta Mae flushed and seemed to lose her composure for a moment. "Well, I don't want to go first," she said weakly, casting me a pleading look. "Couldn't someone else take the lead?"

"Why in the world don't you want to start?" Dorien asked, a sharp edge in her voice. "You have some pretty strong opinions on Sonia, and I bet you've come up with a theory of what happened."

"You'd be wrong if you thought that," Etta Mae shot back. "Dead wrong." She was showing a touch of her usual fire. "I have ideas, all right, but did it ever occur to you that maybe I'd like to keep them to myself? Don't you ever play poker? If you did, you'd know it's not a good idea to show your hand right off the bat." She sat back and took a big swig of apple cider. "I'd like to just listen tonight and put in my two cents at the end, if there's time. If that's okay," she added, turning to Ali. I nearly laughed out loud. Dorien had finally met her match in the feisty Etta Mae.

Ali tried to smooth things over, like a good hostess. "Of

course that's all right, Etta Mae. Please don't feel you have to share anything you don't want to. That's not what this group is about. We try to keep it loose and friendly here."

"A little *too* loose and friendly, if you ask me," Dorien muttered under her breath. I glared at her, but she refused to meet my eyes. Dorien is definitely a passive-aggressive type, throwing in little digs whenever and wherever she can. Usually I just ignore them, but I was feeling edgy tonight and I found it hard not to show my annoyance.

"Edward," Ali said brightly, "why don't you tell us about your dreams?"

Edward flushed and set his pastry dish down on the coffee table. "I'm not exactly sure how this works," he began. "Do I just tell you what I recall about my dream, like I'm telling a story?" He paused, looking more uncomfortable by the minute. "And then what do I do? I'm afraid I'm a bit lost here. And I should warn you that usually my dreams are just bits and pieces. I don't think they'll be easy to interpret."

"Don't worry about that, Edward. You just describe your dream and then we'll chime in with some interpretations." Lucinda Macavy was giving Edward a wide smile, perching on the edge of the white wicker rocker. In fact, she was leaning forward so much, I was afraid she might topple forward. Edward and Lucinda are single and about the same age. Was shy little Lucinda thinking of Edward as a possible beau? She led a very restricted life during her years as the headmistress of a girls' boarding school, and now that she's retired, I think she's in the mood for a little fun. And that might include some male companionship. She tried a national online dating site, with disappointing results, and we've encouraged her to look for a new relationship right here in town. "Don't be intimidated, Edward," she went on. "We all share our dreams. Sometimes when someone offers an interpretation, it resonates with us, and sometimes it's completely off target. We're all friends here, so anything goes."

I nearly chuckled, thinking of Lucinda's first night at the Dream Club. She'd regaled us with a dream about finding herself stark naked in the freezer aisle of the local Publix. That certainly had sparked a lively discussion. I doubted Edward, a conservative university professor, would have anything so entertaining to tell us, but I've learned never to prejudge people or their dreams. In dream work, as in everything else, still waters run deep.

"I don't think this is relevant," Edward began, patting his pocket. I knew he usually smoked a pipe, but in deference to our no-smoking rule, he was abstaining tonight. "I'm afraid I didn't dream about anything important. Last night, I dreamt about the trade routes that brought exotic goods to the New World in the nineteenth century."

"Trade routes? Exotic goods? Why in the world would you dream about something like that?" Dorien asked. "Isn't that a little abstract?"

Edward flushed. "I told you it wouldn't be exciting." Edward looked as if he was tempted to bolt from the room, and I decided I'd better intervene.

"Edward, if you could just tell us about the images you saw in your dream, that would be helpful," I said. "And maybe talk about whatever emotions you were experiencing."

"Yes, Taylor's right," Lucinda said eagerly. "That would give us something to work with." She was smiling brightly at him, and I was convinced she was hoping this might be the start of a budding romance. "We need some pictures, something visual."

"All right, then. This is what I remember. I saw Savannah Harbor," he began, "back in the late nineteenth century."

He stopped and looked around the group. I nodded enthusiastically, urging him to continue. "In the dream, it was stretched out before me, like a panorama. It was a bustling place; the wharf was teeming with people. The ships had just arrived—they were amazing vessels, filled with exotic fruits and vegetables, nuts and seeds. Only the very wealthiest people in town could afford them."

"I saw a painting of the Riverfront in the old days, and it looked just like that," Dorien cut in rudely. "In the old days, people had never seen anything like a pineapple or a banana, and they tried to figure out ways to use them in desserts."

"That's probably where the idea for Bananas Foster came from," Sybil chimed in. "I have a wonderful recipe for that, if anyone wants a copy."

"What do you think made you dream about the Savannah Harbor?" Ali asked. I could tell she wanted to get back on topic and not interrupt the thread of Edward's story.

"We're covering the history of trade in one of my classes this semester," Edward replied. "So I suppose it was on my mind when I went to sleep. I'm afraid I didn't have any emotional reaction to the harbor and the ships. It was like watching a scene in a movie." He cast a worried glance at Dorien. "I'm afraid my dreams won't be too revealing and will probably just reflect my academic interests." Edward seemed so apologetic, I was worried he was going to drop out of the group.

"Did you see the Waving Girl in your dream?" Persia said suddenly. I knew the Waving Girl was Florence Martus, because there is a statue erected to her in Emmet Park. According to local legend, Florence would wave a welcome and farewell to each ship that visited Savannah Harbor in the late nineteenth and early twentieth centuries.

Edward smiled. "No, I'm afraid there was no sign of Florence," he said. "It's an interesting story, though. Her brother was rumored to be the lighthouse keeper on Tybee." He reached for his apple cider and I could tell he was eager to stop talking and let someone else take center stage. "I'm afraid that's all I have for tonight."

10

"Anyone else have anything to add?" Ali said after a long pause. "Would someone like to go next?"

"I have something to report," Sybil said. "I tried lucid dreaming for the very first time yesterday, and I think I'm a believer!"

"Lucid dreaming?" Sara asked. "Isn't that like being half awake and half asleep?"

"When you have a lucid dream, you know you're dreaming," Sybil said. "It's an amazing experience. It's a lot like dreaming, but it's more powerful."

It's also more vivid and realistic, according to some of the club's members. Some researchers and neuropsychologists say different areas of the brain are activated during lucid dreaming than during regular REM dreaming. It's a fascinating field, and there's still a lot to learn.

"Yes, and you'll never believe what happened." Sybil lowered her voice. "I was dreaming that I was looking at myself in the mirror and suddenly the image shifted. I positively had chills." She let her gaze wander around the group, and I could feel goose bumps rising on my arms. "A very strange feeling came over me, as if I was transported back to a different time."

"Did you feel like you were awake or asleep while you were in this state?" I asked.

"I felt like I was awake, but not wide-awake, if you know what I mean. I knew I could direct the dream. That's the advantage of lucid dreaming. I knew I could stop or start it any time I wanted. So I just took a deep breath and told myself there was no need to be frightened. I could bow out at any time."

"Who did you see in the mirror, my dear?" Rose Harper asked.

"Well, first I saw myself, of course, and then the image changed. I was staring at a woman with a kerchief on her head. I couldn't tell if she was from the present day or from the past. She was holding out a basket to me, and she kept nodding her head as if she wanted me to take it. It seemed like she wanted to tell me something or help me understand something."

"The woman in the dream," Persia said, reaching for a tiny cherry tart, "is it possible she was trying to tell you something about Sonia's death?"

A look of understanding flooded Sybil's face. "Yes, I think she may have been. But for the life of me, I don't understand the message. She wanted me to look at something in the basket. It doesn't make any sense, does it? The only thing in the basket was some sort of seed or nut. They were tiny and cream-colored; that's all I can remember. The woman held some up in her hands and let them sift through her fingers as they fell back into the basket. She was watching me intently the whole time. There was something strange about her, and I felt uncomfortable."

"Were they pistachio nuts?" Minerva asked.

"Oh no, they were nothing like that. They were very small, smaller than a grain of rice. They had to have been seeds." Sybil was looking over our heads toward the front windows. The sun was bleeding on the horizon, sending bright ribbons of scarlet and gold over the sky. I couldn't tell if she was admiring the sunset or was momentarily transported back into her dream.

"What happened next?" I asked. Seeds? Sonia's stomach contents had contained seeds. Could the dream offer any insight into her death?

"The scene shifted and the woman faded. I realized I was standing on a dock. It was Savannah Harbor, I think. I don't know what year. The ships looked different, sort of old-timey, so it must have been in the past."

"Just like in Edward's dream," Lucinda said excitedly. "You both dreamt about the same place and time period. What do you suppose this means?"

"I have no idea," Sybil said slowly. "The whole thing seems very unusual. It's almost as though I were dream-hopping." Sybil insists that all the women in her family have this ability.

Sybil has been privy to a great number of "secrets" by dream-hopping, but she feels duty bound not to share them unless someone's life or safety is at stake. She was giving Edward a keen look, and I wondered if she'd try to enter one of his dreams.

"There must be more to the story," Lucinda pressed on. "This is fascinating." I had the feeling she wanted to turn the floor back to Edward, or at least give him a chance to comment. I glanced over at the professor. He was sitting ramrod straight in his chair, his elbow on the armrest, his chin in his hands. He was studying Sybil as if she were a bug under a microscope, and I wondered what he was thinking. Edward is surely a man who plays his cards close to his vest, as my Granny used to say.

"Edward, do you have any thoughts on this?" Dorien asked.

Edward rubbed his hands together and took a deep breath. "I'm afraid I don't." I had the idea he didn't like being the center of attention and didn't enjoy being put on the spot.

For a moment, we all were silent. Then Ali said, "Can you tell us more about the woman? Somehow I think she's the key to the dream."

Sybil looked down at her lap and played with the bright rings she sported on nearly every finger. I had the feeling she was stalling for time, choosing her words carefully. I wondered if the memory might be hazy, but when she spoke, her voice was clear and strong. "I think she was speaking to me in Italian. I remember hearing the word '*bene*.'"

"Bene?" That got Sara's attention. "Are you sure about that?"

Sybil gave a vigorous nod of her head. "Yes, she kept saying it over and over. '*Bene, bene*,' and urging me to look into the basket. I have no idea what she meant."

"'*Bene*' means 'fine,' or 'good,' or 'all right,'" Sara said. "Maybe she meant whatever she was selling was good." No one said anything, and I wondered if we were all thinking the same thing. Sybil had dreamt about seeds, and we knew that Sonia had ingested seeds. Was this too much of a stretch? Dream interpretation is more of an art than a science, and it's difficult to pin down the meaning that floats up from our subconscious. Dreams are very personal, and I've learned that what the dreamer brings to the story is just as important as the words and events in the dream. It's what you read into it, your emotional reaction, that counts.

"It's a mystery," Ali said after a moment. "I'm afraid I don't know what to make of it." She smiled at Etta Mae. "Shall we move on?"

Etta Mae sat back, crossing her hands over her chest in a classic "closed" body-language position. She even swung her legs to one side, in the opposite direction of Ali. Her intentions were crystal clear. She was literally and figuratively tuning out the group. "I told you I'd like go last," she said peevishly.

"Of course," Ali said agreeably. "Anyone else?"

"I dreamt about jewelry," Lucinda said eagerly. She glanced over at Edward to see if he was listening. Since Lucinda is a voracious shopper of a home shopping network, it's not surprising that she dreamt about jewelry, I thought wryly.

"Jewelry again?" Dorien said snidely. "More cubic zirconia, I suppose?"

"Why, no, that wasn't what I dreamt about at all," Lucinda said, her smile fading. She had been so enthusiastic about sharing her dream, and now her expression made me think of a deflated balloon. All the energy and passion had been sucked right out of her by Dorien's thoughtless remark.

I made a note to speak to Ali after the meeting. Surely there was some way to curb Dorien and her sharp comments. No one ever had the gumption to do it before, but things were getting out of hand. I noticed people were starting to glance at her before they began talking, as if they were censoring themselves. This couldn't continue, and I vowed to do something before the next meeting.

Everyone should feel free to openly discuss dream content without being criticized or mocked. That belief is at the heart of the Dream Club. I idly wondered if Ali and I should try to come up with some rules for the club, although knowing Dorien, she would never think that they applied to her.

"Tell us about your dream," I said encouragingly. "I want to hear about the jewelry."

"Well, it was the strangest thing," Lucinda said, warming to the story. "Someone gave me a very valuable piece of jewelry. It was a necklace. A pendant on a thin silver chain. I knew it was precious, and I wore it when I was strolling around the grounds of a mansion. There was a little pond, and when I stopped to look at some koi fish in the pond, the necklace slipped right off my neck and disappeared into the water. I looked for it, but suddenly the water turned very dark, almost black, and I realized it was gone forever." Her shoulders slumped and she looked dejected. "It's odd how a dream can evoke strong emotions, feelings that are still with you the next day. Logically, it makes no sense. You know the events in the dream weren't real, but the feelings seem real."

"I think everyone here can relate to that," Ali piped up.

I've had the same experience myself. I had night terrors when I was younger. Whenever my dreams evoke strong emotions, they seem to linger in my mind for hours after I wake up. When I argue with someone in a dream, I find myself feeling angry and out of sorts with the person the next day. It makes absolutely no sense, but feelings are feelings and they take on a life of their own.

"How do you feel right now, Lucinda?" Ali's tone was gentle.

"I feel so sad, like I've lost something precious and can never get it back." Her gaze swept the group. "What do you think the dream means?"

"Dark water can mean death," Minerva said. Her sister Rose nodded in agreement. "I remember when our aunt Tabitha passed, Rose and I had dreams about the ocean at night. They were so vivid and disturbing. The scene was bleak, with no moonlight shining on the waves. The water was black and forbidding. I still feel queasy just thinking of it. Do you remember that, dear? We both had the same dream."

"I do," Rose said. She gave a little shudder. "I have that dream when someone in my family is very sick or close to passing on. And I'm afraid at our age, that happens all too frequently." She gave a rueful smile, and Minerva reached over and patted her hand. The sisters were devoted to each other and had lived together for decades. I always wonder what would happen if one of them passed away. It would surely be devastating for the remaining sister.

"Do the dreams go on for a long time?" Sara asked.

"No, they're very powerful for a few days and then they're gone. After the loved one has died and we've all grieved for them, the dream changes."

"In what way?" I found myself intrigued and had a vague memory of dreaming of water before my parents died in a car crash. I wondered if Ali recalled having similar dreams. We were both hit hard by their passing, and sometimes I think Ali has never really recovered. This is one of the reasons I feel so protective of her.

"I still dream about water, but now there's sunlight dancing on the surface. The dream has a totally different feel to it; it's filled with light, not shadows. These dreams make me happy because I know my loved ones have moved on to a better place."

We just had time for two more dreams, and Ali described a classic anxiety dream, probably because she's worried about the future of the shop. She told us how she'd found herself alone on a train, in the dark of night and unsure of her destination. After the train sped out of the station, she realized she had no ticket and had left her luggage and purse on the platform.

So there she was, on a speeding train in the pitch dark, feeling more alone and vulnerable by the minute. Where was she headed? What would happen when she got there? It sounded terrifying, and her voice shook as she told the story. Dreams about a journey to an unknown destination commonly occurred when people were under a great deal of stress.

When she finished recounting the dream, Rose Harper reached over and rested her hand gently on Ali's shoulder. "There, dear," she said in a comforting tone, "all this turmoil will pass and everything will be all right. You'll see."

"Yes, buck up, my dear," her sister Minerva added. "We're all here for you and we're not going to let anything happen to your shop."

Ali smiled her thanks and started to ask Etta Mae if she'd like to share anything, but Etta Mae quickly pressed her lips together and shook her head.

The meeting wrapped up shortly after Minerva Harper reported dreaming about a rose garden, which wasn't unusual since she and her sister own a flower shop right down the block. It was a light, happy dream and didn't seem to lend itself to any particular interpretation. Dorien offered an interpretation involving "roses and thorns," suggesting that danger lurked behind beauty, but she didn't make any headway. Minerva insisted there were no thorns in her rose garden and there was no hidden agenda. Dorien gave a loud sigh, not at all happy to see her interpretation dismissed so readily.

As the group made their way down the stairs, I was surprised to see Edward huddled in a conversation with Persia on the landing. He was leaning close to hear her, and he seemed more animated and engaged than he'd been the whole evening.

I skipped down the stairs to the shop and grabbed a package of root beer licorice off the shelf for the Harper sisters. One of their great-nephews loved licorice and I always tried to set some aside for him. We have a new distributor in Atlanta who sends us wonderful licorice selections, including some new flavors I was eager to try—peach, grape, and candy apple.

I noticed Edward and Persia were continuing their conversation in the foyer. As I drew close, I heard Edward say, "Are you absolutely sure it was '*bene*' that you heard?"

"Yes, of course I'm sure," she insisted. "*Bene*—that's exactly what I heard." She threw me a puzzled glance as Edward shook his head and took a step backward, a look of astonishment on his face. I could feel the sudden, subtle charge in the atmosphere.

"Is something wrong, Edward?" I asked. I watched as a muscle jumped along his jawline.

"No, of course not. I just realized I overlooked something," he stammered. A look of consternation flitted over his face, and he quickly said good night and left.

"I wonder what that was all about." Persia seemed amused with the mild-mannered professor and his abrupt departure. "He's an odd duck, isn't he?"

"I think he's just uncomfortable with people he doesn't know very well," I told her. "I've heard he doesn't get out much, apart from his classes at the university." Edward might be socially awkward, but that wasn't the whole picture. I tried to make sense out of Edward's reaction. He had seemed shocked; his face had gone pale for a millisecond when Persia had repeated "*bene*." There was definitely something going on here, but what?

"The word '*bene*' doesn't have any particular significance, does it?" Ali was showing some more guests out the door but moved close to talk to us.

"Not to me, but it certainly got Edward's attention," I said. I wondered what he was holding back. "In fact, more than interested—I think he was intrigued." I was having trouble getting a handle on Edward, and I still wasn't sure he'd be a good match for the club. We never exclude anyone who applies for membership, but we insist on a personal recommendation from a current member. Etta Mae, for example, was recommended by the Harper sisters. She was a frequent customer in their flower shop, and they'd been chatting over the power of dreams. Edward had been recommended by Sara Rutledge, our reporter pal, who met him at a university function and thought he would be an interesting addition to our group.

From time to time, a new member decides not to continue with us. In any case, we like to keep the group small because it makes for a livelier discussion and a more intimate gathering. I think people might be hesitant to share if we let the meetings get too big. A dream club requires a high level of trust among members, if it is to be successful. That's probably the only ground rule we have: strict confidentiality. Anyone who breaches that is automatically expelled, and I'm happy to say that has never happened.

"'*Bene*' can mean a lot of things," Rose Harper said as I handed her the bag of candy.

"It's supposed to mean 'fine' or 'all right' in Italian," I said, wondering if she hadn't followed the conversation we'd just had upstairs. Rose is slightly hard of hearing but refuses to admit it.

"That's one meaning, my dear," she said, resting her hand lightly on my arm. "But there's another." She leaned closer, watching as the last guest departed. "She might have been referring to benne chips."

"Benny chips?" I was drawing a complete blank. "Benny, like the name?"

"No, not the name Benny. It's *b-e-n-n-e*," her sister Minvera chimed in. "Back in the day, everyone made cookies with benne chips," she said. "Take a look in any vintage cookbook and you'll see loads of recipes using benne chips."

"Really? I've never even heard of them."

"Today they call them sesame seeds."

"Sesame seeds! Do you suppose that's really what Persia was dreaming about?" *Maybe Persia had misunderstood. She thought she'd heard the Italian word* "bene," *but maybe what she really heard was "benne."*

"It's very possible," Rose said. "Another area to investigate, you know."

"It certainly is," I agreed. I mentally ran down tonight's dreams. Lucinda had dreamt about a missing necklace and dark water. Could the necklace be the silver chain with a pendant that Sonia always wore? And we know that dark waters can symbolize death, so no surprise there. Edward saw ships bringing exotic foods to Savannah, and Persia met a woman offering her a basket of benne bits, which are actually sesame seeds.

And sesame seeds are what killed Sonia.

I walked back upstairs to make myself a cup of soothing chamomile tea. No doubt about it; something deadly was afoot in dreamland.

11

After spending a restless night tossing and turning, I jumped out of bed at 7 a.m., listened to my one voice mail message, and called Sara Rutledge. I knew she'd be up and sitting at the computer. She's been hard at work on a true crime novel, blocking out a couple of hours each morning to meet her goal of writing a thousand words a day.

"I hate to disturb you," I began, and she quickly cut me off with a laugh.

"Disturb me? Don't be silly; you're doing me a favor. I'm beginning to wonder why I ever decided to write true crime. I'm so tempted to chuck the whole thing, but that would mean forty thousand words down the drain." She groaned. "I could have written a dozen feature articles instead of wasting my time on a true crime novel. How did I get myself into this mess? I'm so stressed out, I can't decide what to do."

"Then I'm glad I caught you in time," I said hastily.

"When you're so undecided, it's better not to do anything. The right course of action is to take no action at all. You've got to trust me on this." She was silent and I pushed the button on the coffeemaker. In a few moments, the kitchen would be filled with the delicious aroma of hazelnut latte, and I was practically salivating at the thought. "You may have hit a bump in the road with your book, Sara, but you can't toss it down the drain. It would be better to step back from it. Take a wait-and-see attitude before doing anything so drastic."

"It's more than a bump in the road. I feel like I've fallen into a black hole," she said with her usual flair for drama. "And I'm so ready for a break this morning. What's up?"

"I had an idea about the case in the middle of the night," I told her. Barney and Scout were winding around my legs, eager for their breakfast. I managed to open a can of Beef Bits with one hand by tucking the receiver under my chin. When I set the two dishes on the floor, the cats pounced on them as though they hadn't eaten in days.

"A new lead?" Sara asked. She immediately jumped into high gear, and her voice crackled with energy.

"It could be. I'm thinking of calling on Jeremy Watts today. Would you like to come along?"

"Jeremy Watts." A long beat. "Sonia's married lover. That's not a bad idea, but how will we track him down? Do we even know what city he's in?"

"He's right here in Savannah, at the Red Lion Inn."

"Really? How did you find him?"

"Minerva Harper rises at the crack of dawn, and she left a message on my cell. She had a dream about Jeremy last night. She said a strange feeling came over her and she thinks he could be the key to Sonia's death. She also had a strong sensation that he was close by, and I took that to mean right here in Savannah." I trusted Minerva's insights, and she'd been helpful before when we solved the murder of dance instructor Chico.

"That's interesting that she feels that way, but it's not exactly the hard evidence we're looking for," Sara said. "What did you have in mind?"

"Let's meet for breakfast and we can talk it over. They have a nice coffee shop at the Red Lion Inn. It's on the right as soon as you go into the lobby." I glanced at my watch. "The Red Lion at eight? That way we can catch him before he goes out for the day."

"I'm in," Sara said.

The buzzer on the coffeemaker dinged, and the fragrant aroma of hazelnut coffee was so enticing, I couldn't wait to taste it. I figured Ali was still sleeping, but I planned to leave a cup of coffee on her night table and then jump into the shower.

When I walked down the hall, Ali's door was cracked open and she was sitting up in bed, stretching. She reached happily for the coffee and cradled the mug in her hands. "No eggs Benedict?" she teased. "Not that I'm complaining; coffee in bed is enough of a treat."

"No time for eggs Benedict," I told her. "I'm meeting Sara for breakfast this morning; do you want to come along? You'll have to hustle, because we need to leave in half an hour."

"I can do it!" she said, jumping out of bed. Ali is blessed with blond good looks that require very little maintenance. A touch of lip gloss, a hint of mascara, and she can turn heads, especially when she wears her hair flowing loosely down her back. She usually sweeps it into a French braid in the shop, but when she's in casual mode, she likes to wear it in a high ponytail. Either way, she's gorgeous.

"Tell me again why you think Jeremy Watts is registered here," Ali said as we hurried into the Red Lion. It's a small hotel near the Riverfront, popular with business travelers.

"Minerva Harper saw it in a dream. But I wanted to be sure, so I called and pretended I had a message for him." I grinned. "He's here, all right. Room two-oh-six. When the desk clerk offered to put me through, I hung up."

"Minerva saw Jeremy at the Red Lion Inn in a dream?" she asked doubtfully.

"Well, it wasn't spelled out specifically in the dream; it was symbolic. But the key elements were right there, and all I had to do was put them together."

"What kind of symbolism are we talking about?"

"In Minerva's dream, she saw Jeremy Watts at a red-carpet event. She didn't know what to make of it, but she figured it had to be important, so she jotted down what she could remember and called me early this morning."

"A red-carpet event? You mean like a Hollywood awards show?"

"Yes, exactly. I know it sounds unlikely, but she was very clear on what she'd seen." I stepped up my pace. I was wearing a new pair of espadrilles and nearly tripping in them. I hardly ever wear heels since I've moved to Savannah; I tend to wear flip-flops or ballet flats in the store. "And he was standing under a huge poster of the MGM lion and photographers were snapping pictures of him. So I put it all together. Jeremy, the color red, and a lion." I snapped my fingers. "Only one place in Savannah could fit the bill. The Red Lion Inn."

"Wow, I'm impressed." Ali nudged me. "My sister, Nancy Drew."

"Well, it was all due to Minerva. She led us here. I'll have to call her later and tell her the dream was right on target. Except for the photographers, of course," I added as we hurried into the lobby.

We spotted Sara sitting at a booth in the coffee shop as we passed an elaborate breakfast buffet along the far wall. Breakfast is an important meal of the day in Savannah, and the Red Lion is known for two signature dishes: French toast crusted with coconut and bread pudding with candied pecans.

Ali and I slid into the booth across from Sara, who was scrolling through her phone messages. She flipped the lid shut and smiled at us. "I picked this booth because it gives us a good view of both the elevator and the revolving doors. If Jeremy comes in for breakfast or if he just wanders through the lobby, we can nab him."

"We're not going to really nab him, are we?" Ali looked alarmed and I laughed.

"Just a figure of speech," I told her. "We're going to have a friendly conversation, that's all. As far as he knows, we're running into him accidentally. He won't suspect a thing."

"I still don't know how you tracked him down," Sara said. "That was good detective work, Taylor."

"Not at all," I said modestly, flipping open the menu. "I'm afraid all the credit goes to Minerva Harper. Like I said, she's convinced he had something to do with Sonia's death."

Sara raised her eyebrows. "Well, there are some other leads that seem to have more potential, don't you think?" I tried to look noncommittal. I knew she was referring to Etta Mae Beasley.

"Do you mean someone a little closer to home?" Ali asked. I could feel Ali tense as she sat next to me. Ali was upset at the idea that some people might consider Etta Mae a suspect. Ali was tenderhearted and believed Etta Mae was simply someone who was wronged and was seeking justice, not revenge. I'm sure she didn't think Etta Mae was capable of murder, although Sara clearly felt differently.

Sara made a zipping motion with her finger across her lips. "My lips are sealed. I shouldn't prejudge anyone. I just think, well"—she paused and sipped her ice water—"I can think of someone with a really strong motive, and I bet you can, too."

When the server came to our table, we all decided to forgo the breakfast buffet and ordered hot tea and scrambled eggs on wheat toast. The buffet looked tempting, but it could easily add up to a day's worth of calories. There was a wide selection of bacon, sausage, hash browns, buttered grits, rolls, and pastries, plus an omelet station and trays of fresh fruit. I vowed to come back someday when we had time for a leisurely brunch.

"So we're just going to pretend this is a coincidence if we see Jeremy?" Sara asked. "How will we engage him in conversation? I'm not even sure I'd recognize him."

"He was at the television taping, but not the book signing," I reminded her. "I think you met him but it was very brief and there was a lot going on."

"What if he doesn't want to be interrogated?" Sara asked.

"Oh, it's not going to look like an interrogation," I said. "We're just going to offer our condolences and see if he's planning a memorial." Would Jeremy take the bait and tell us something helpful? Or was this going to be a total waste of time?

12

Jeremy Watts appeared just as we were finishing up breakfast. We'd ordered another pot of coffee and Ali and Sara were deep in conversation while I kept an eye on the French doors that led into the lobby. I watched in astonishment as a local television reporter and her photographer marched up to the front desk. The photographer was checking out the hand-painted murals and architectural details as if he was trying to find a good shot for background. *Photographers!* Just as Minerva had predicted.

"What are they filming?" I asked our server.

"Oh, they're doing a feature on haunted hotels here in Savannah." She lowered her voice. "The Marshall House is really supposed to be haunted, but my boss hopes they'll include us in the piece. He's probably telling her he's seen ghosts walking up and down the corridors at night." She grinned. "I don't believe any of it, but the tourists love this stuff. It's good publicity."

A couple of minutes later, Jeremy Watts strolled into the coffee shop with a copy of the *Savannah Tribune* tucked under his arm. He was heading for a small table in the back when I jumped to my feet, blocking his way.

"Jeremy? I didn't know you were still in town." I stretched out my hand and he clasped it, a look of pure bewilderment on his face. "I'm Taylor Blake. We met at the studio when Sonia taped her show." He still looked blank. "My sister and I own a candy store. Sonia had a book signing with us?"

"I'm afraid I don't recall—" he began hesitantly.

"Oh, that's quite all right," I cut in. "You met a ton of people at the studio." I quickly introduced Ali to Jeremy and then insisted that he sit with us.

"I'm really in rather a rush," he said tightly. I was sure he was lying. He'd strolled into the coffee shop like he'd had all the time in the world and had even bought a newspaper. I think he'd been looking forward to a nice leisurely breakfast without a pack of noisy women to disturb his peace.

"Sit right here," I said, squeezing over on the red leather banquette to make room for him.

"But I was just going to have a quick cup of coffee," he protested, and this time Sara broke in.

"That's perfect," she said heartily, "because we just ordered a fresh pot." She signaled to the server for an extra cup and Jeremy eased himself onto the seat, looking decidedly uncomfortable. "This is our friend Sara," Ali added. "She's writing a feature on Sonia for the local paper."

"It's so sad," Sara said demurely, lowering her eyes. "The whole thing—I can hardly believe it happened," she added. "I don't think you were there for the book signing Ali and Taylor hosted . . ." She let her voice trail off in a question.

Jeremy waited until the server poured him a cup of steaming coffee before replying. "No, I wasn't. I attended the taping, but then I had some pressing things to do in Atlanta for the company." He paused and arranged his features in a look of abject sadness. "I was as stunned as anyone else when I got the news from Olivia."

"So it was Olivia who told you that Sonia had passed away?"

"Yes, she had just come out of the ER. I'll never forget that call." He stopped and wiped an imaginary tear from his eye. "It was such a shock to all of us. She can never be replaced." There was a false note in his rendition, something odd and off-key. I think Sara sensed it, because she exchanged a glance with me, her eyebrow arching a tiny bit.

"No, of course she can't be replaced. She was one of a kind," Ali said, her voice warm with sympathy. She waited a moment and then said, "But life goes on, and the company will go on. What will happen to Sonia Scott, Inc., without its leader at the helm?"

"That's a good question," Jeremy said, his mouth twisting. "I've never even considered it. I don't think anyone else did, either. It was her company, her brand. She tested every single recipe, she approved every piece of advertising . . ." He stopped and sipped his coffee. "We'll just have to muddle through without her; we owe that much to the stockholders."

"Ah yes, the stockholders," Sara said dryly. "It always comes down to that, doesn't it? Money, profits, the bottom line."

"It's what Sonia would have wanted," Jeremy said piously. "She was really concerned about her employees. She arranged the most generous benefits you can imagine, and her door was always open if there was a problem." I tried to keep my expression neutral. Jeremy's description was at odds with the temperamental diva I'd seen at the taping. "It's a personal loss for me," he said solemnly.

I bet it is! I thought cynically. I tried to think of a way to delve into Jeremy's rumored romantic relationship with Sonia, but I couldn't think of anything that wasn't downright offensive. "Tell me," I said finally, "did you work with Sonia for a long time?" An innocent question and I could only hope it would lead to some reminiscing on his part.

"Since the beginning," he said, eyeing me with sudden interest. I wondered if he knew where my thoughts were headed. "We started out as colleagues and became"—just a hint of a telltale pause—"very dear friends."

"I see," Sara said. She pulled out her notebook and scribbled in it. "Very dear friends," she repeated. She shot me a quick glance. It was obvious she didn't believe a word of it.

Jeremy was immediately on guard. "Hey, is this an interview or something?" He smiled to soften the comment, but there was an edge in his voice. "I'm speaking as one of Sonia's friends, not as a representative of the company. You'll have to check with the press office if you want an official statement."

"Oh, you don't have to worry. This isn't official," Sara said, her eyes clear, her voice soothing. "I just thought I might write a human-interest piece for the paper about Sonia and how the public loved her. And her cooking, of course. I loved the way she took vintage recipes and gave them a modern flair." I wondered if she was goading him, hoping to get him to comment on Etta Mae and her family cookbook. But Jeremy wasn't taking the bait. She gave him a big, guileless smile, and he suddenly took a big swallow of coffee and glanced at his watch.

"Well, that sounds very nice, but I really should be going," he began.

"Are you planning on staying in Savannah for a while?" I asked. "Maybe we could meet up again. You could give Sara some more background details for her article." He hesitated, so I added, "Think about it, Jeremy. You were probably closer to Sonia than anyone else—one of her inner circle. You must know wonderful stories about her that you could share. It would be a tribute, a way to memorialize someone we all admired."

I was afraid I was laying it on a little thick, but Jeremy seemed to have run out of objections. At least for the moment. "Well, I am leaving town today, but I guess I can stay for a few more minutes," he said peevishly. He looked directly at Sara. "What exactly would you like to know?" His tone was blunt, exasperated. No more Mr. Nice Guy for Jeremy.

"Just a couple of questions about your role in the organization," Sara said sweetly. For the next few minutes, she peppered Jeremy with questions about the company, how it all began in Sonia's home kitchen, and his role in her empire. He was vague about his duties but admitted that he often traveled with Sonia "to deal with the press and make her life easier."

I noticed he kept glancing toward the lobby. I followed his gaze but couldn't figure out what he found so intriguing. The camera crew must have moved to an upper floor. I couldn't spot them from the booth, and I had an excellent view of the lobby.

"It must be hard for you to travel so much," Sara was saying sympathetically. "You still have young children at home, don't you?"

This time he didn't bother to hide his annoyance. "Yes, I do," he said curtly. "Luckily my wife is a full-time homemaker, and she takes excellent care of them."

"Your wife," Ali said slowly. "We enjoyed meeting Leslie at the taping, and one of our friends, Lucinda, was so happy to see her there. Lucinda used to be one of Leslie's teachers at the Academy."

Jeremy's eyes flickered in surprise and then he nodded. "I remember Leslie introduced me to her former teacher from the Academy. Leslie is a big fan of the show and she tries to attend the tapings whenever she can. She always enjoys them. And now I really must go," he said. "Thanks for the coffee." He popped up like a jack-in-the-box. His movement was so abrupt the bench on the banquette wobbled dangerously and I nearly tumbled forward into my coffee.

"Are there any funeral arrangements in place?" I spoke quickly, afraid Jeremy was about to fly the coop.

"Nothing is firmed up yet; you'll have to check back with me." Again I saw him glance toward the lobby, and this time I spotted something furtive in his look. Maybe there was more going on than just the camera crew, but what? He was definitely edgy, and he was drumming his fingers on the tabletop.

"I'll make sure we check back with you. We'd love to be there to honor Sonia," Ali told him. "After all, we were the last ones to see her alive," she added, and I was sure he winced. "Could we have one of your business cards?"

"Here, knock yourself out," he said ungraciously. He reached into his pocket, tossing a few cards on the table. His fingers were trembling. He was as twitchy as a drug addict. I picked up a card and saw he was listed as director of communications—a lofty title. I wondered if that could be significant. Was that really his job description? He'd told Sara to contact the press office if she had further questions. But wouldn't he be the one running the press office? If so, he should be the one answering our questions. It must be an honorary title, I decided. Designed to make him feel important.

Maybe Jeremy was actually a well-paid gofer, sleeping with the boss. That sort of situation was bound to cause a lot of resentment with other employees, and I wondered if we could find someone at Sonia Scott, Inc., who would be willing to talk to us. There must be someone—somewhere—who had the inside scoop on Jeremy and would be willing to dish.

"Just one more thing," Sara asked as Jeremy was preparing to make his getaway. She reminded me of Columbo, the famous television detective. Asking "just one more question" was one of his favorite shticks, and he loved to catch his suspects off guard. "Did Sonia always wear a silver chain with a pendant?"

He blinked. "A silver chain? I have no idea." He waved his hand in the air like he was batting away a gnat. "Why do you ask?"

"No reason." Sara smiled and closed her notebook. "Just wondered."

He glanced at his watch and bit back a sigh. "Is that it?"

"How is Olivia regarded in the company?"

"Olivia?" He shook his head. "She came on board long before I did. She was very close to Sonia, I think." Sara started to interrupt him, but he held up his hand, palm out, like a traffic cop. "We have completely different responsibilities. As far as I know she has a good reputation in the company. What will happen now, that's not for me to say. Olivia seems to be a loyal employee; that's all I can tell you."

When Jeremy left, Ali turned to me. "I think we're getting somewhere," she said eagerly. "He admitted he spent a lot of time traveling with Sonia."

"And he seemed annoyed when you mentioned his wife's name," Sara pointed out.

"He did. I don't think he wants us to have any contact with his family." Ali looked pleased, as if we had garnered some key pieces of information. I was less convinced.

I'm not sure how significant it was that the two of them frequently traveled together. What did it really prove? It certainly would have given Jeremy and Sonia some serious time for hanky-panky, if they were so inclined, but that didn't lead to a motive for murder. It looked like we were back at square one. Without a solid motive, Jeremy couldn't possibly be considered a suspect.

"He didn't give us much information about Olivia," Sara noted. "Either he's telling the truth, or he doesn't want to say anything positive about her. I wonder if the two of them could be rivals, as well as lovers."

"What do you think, Taylor?" Ali asked. "You're looking kind of somber. Don't you think the meeting with Jeremy went well?"

I rallied and managed a tiny smile. "I don't think we got much new information out of him, but it wasn't a total waste. He seemed a little uncomfortable when we mentioned his wife." I thought back to the lingering looks he had exchanged with Olivia at the taping and the steamy note she'd written to him. Of course, it was possible she had feelings for him and they weren't reciprocated. "And he's obviously not going to say anything negative about Sonia. He's playing his cards close to the vest, and we're going to have to meet with him again."

Noah had always told me that he'd solved many a case when the suspect felt threatened and made a blunder. We still didn't have a motive, unless he was being edged out of the company. But we didn't have any evidence of that, and no one was talking.

As far as his affair with Sonia, it seemed to be common knowledge, and there was no way his wife wouldn't have heard of it. So if Sonia had issued some ultimatum to Jeremy, threatening to go to his wife, it wouldn't have mattered to him. Did Jeremy have any reason to kill Sonia? Was there any monetary advantage to Jeremy in having Sonia out of the picture?

If I had Ali's trusty Magic Eight Ball, it would say, *Try again later.*

After we finished our second pot of coffee, Ali and I headed south, back to the center of the city, and Sara decided to follow up on a lead for a story she was working on. She was covering a local political race where there was some controversy over voting irregularities. "It makes a nice change from soccer games and flower shows," she said teasingly. "You know what they say about power and corruption."

"I do. Just be careful; we don't want to lose our star investigator," I told her.

"No danger of that." She smiled and hurried away, her blond hair gleaming in the sunlight.

We were halfway to Forsyth Parkwhen I realized I'd left my wallet on the banquette seat in the coffee shop.

"Are you sure?" Ali looked stricken. "Why didn't we see it when we left?"

I stopped dead in my tracks and looked in my tote bag. I always keep it in a separate zippered compartment, and my heart dropped when I saw it was empty. "I don't know, but let's hope it's still there." We immediately retraced our steps, my heart thudding with anxiety. They say women carry their lives in their wallets, and I'm no different. I keep telling myself to scale down and carry one credit card, a few bills, and my driver's license, but somehow I never get around to it.

I raced inside while Ali stayed outside to make a quick call to Dana about an incoming order. I'd pushed through the double glass doors, vaulted through the lobby, and zipped into the coffee shop when the hostess looked up and recognized me.

"Ms. Blake," she said cheerfully. "Don't panic. We have your wallet right here. The busboy turned it in when he cleared the table."

"Thank goodness," I said, nearly giddy with relief. "I *was* in a panic." She had my wallet neatly stashed in a manila envelope under the counter at the front, and I gratefully accepted it.

I was about to turn to leave when I saw a familiar face out of the corner of my eye. I quickly ducked behind a pillar and peeked out to take another look. *Hah!* Just as I thought. There was Jeremy Watts, sitting with a well-dressed woman in the back of the restaurant. He had his head bowed, looking over some documents.

His companion turned to talk to the server, and I got a full view of her face. Olivia Hudson! I quickly jammed my wallet into my tote bag and hurried onto the street. Maybe we weren't back at square one after all. I could feel a big grin spreading across my face and couldn't wait to tell Ali the news.

13

"Jeremy and Olivia?" Ali asked, as I grabbed her arm and pulled her down the street. "I had no idea they'd be so open about their relationship. Not very discreet, are they?" I wanted to get away from the Red Lion as quickly as possible, in case Jeremy glanced out the bay window and spotted us. "What were they talking about?"

"I told you, I was at the cashier's station. I couldn't hear a word they said."

"But how did they act? What was their body language like? Did they look like they were a couple?" We stopped at a crosswalk and I inhaled the soft air. It was a beautiful day in Savannah: not too humid but warm enough to know you were in the South.

"Do you mean, were they canoodling over the French toast? I really can't say." I thought back to the scene I had just witnessed. It was impossible to figure out what sort of relationship they had. Business? Pleasure? Or maybe both.

"Canoodling?" Ali raised her eyebrows.

"I got that expression from Minerva Harper. She used it the other day," I said, slightly embarrassed. I don't know why the expression had popped up in my head, but it had.

"I've never heard anyone under eighty-five years old use that term."

I grinned. "Whatever." The light changed and we hurried across. We didn't have any particular destination in mind. My thoughts were scattered and I tried to make sense of what I'd just seen.

"Do you suppose they were staying at the hotel together?" Ali said after a moment.

I stared at her. Ali has the uncanny ability to read my mind when I least expect it. I've heard that sisters can do that sometimes, and I find it fascinating.

"That was why I caught him looking past my shoulder and staring into the lobby from time to time," I said. "I bet he was afraid Olivia would suddenly show up and spot us. It all makes sense now." We were walking fast toward the center of town, and the streets were crowded with tourists. The sunlight was filtering through the banyan trees, and it was good to feel the balmy air against my skin.

"But does that mean he'd arranged to meet her for a business meeting over breakfast"—Ali paused—"or does that mean they were sharing a room and he happened to go down to breakfast first?"

I shook my head. "No idea. And don't forget he said he had almost no contact with her. I wonder why he thought it was important enough to lie about."

"He could have lied because he wanted to mislead us, or maybe he lied because he's a sociopath and that's what they do. They lie just for the fun of it. It's part of their nature; they like to feel they're putting one over on us." Ali prides herself on being an amateur psychologist and loves to read books on the criminal mind.

"Maybe," I murmured. Another thought zinged into my brain. "If they were sharing a room, it certainly gives Olivia a motive for getting rid of Sonia." *Could both women be fighting over Jeremy?* He wasn't Johnny Depp, that was for sure—not heartthrob material by any stretch of the imagination. But sometimes women made odd choices, and it never ceased to amaze me. Two intelligent, ambitious women smitten with Jeremy, who seems like the ultimate hanger-on? It boggled the mind.

"I can't imagine anyone committing murder over him." Ali frowned. "Maybe it isn't a romantic relationship between Olivia and Jeremy. Maybe they're coconspirators."

"Coconspirators?" Ali's also a great fan of shows like *CSI* and *Criminal Minds* and was warming to her new theory.

"Yes, I can see that happening," she said, her voice spiraling upward in excitement. "Think about it; it makes sense. Both Olivia and Jeremy have the inside track at the company. What if they figured out some way to swindle Sonia Scott, Inc., and they're going to split the rewards? Maybe Sonia got wind of it, so she had to go. Either Olivia or Jeremy could have done it."

"That's not a bad theory," I told her. "It works, up to a point. In fact, it might even explain why Jeremy wasn't present at the book signing. Why did he say he missed it?" I struggled to recall his exact words.

"I think someone said he had to get back to Atlanta," Ali reminded me. "That could mean anything. He could have set up the whole thing ahead of time. Did you notice he flushed a little when Sara asked him about the silver necklace?"

"He seemed uncomfortable," I agreed. "He obviously wanted to get off that topic as fast as possible."

"I think it fits," Ali said. "It's the best theory so far."

"You're right on that one," I told her. "Now it's time to bring in the big guns."

"The big guns?"

"The Dream Club, of course."

"We called this emergency meeting," I explained a few hours later, "because things are moving slowly with the investigation into Sonia's death and we need to put our collective energy to work." It was nearly four o'clock, and I hoped we could get right to the point.

I didn't mention that profits had plummeted at the shop; even some of our most loyal customers were canceling orders and hardly any new people were dropping by the store. A cloud was hanging over us, and the only way to dispel it was to find the killer. As far as the general public knew, we were somehow responsible for serving tainted food that caused Sonia's death. The local paper had reported it as a "severe allergic reaction," but I knew a few gossips thought otherwise.

"You know we'll help you any way we can, dear," Rose Harper offered. Her sister Minerva, sitting next to her, nodded vigorously. Since it was before dinnertime, Ali and I decided not to serve desserts to the group. I made a pitcher of iced tea with fresh lemon and Ali pulled a container of homemade cheese straws out of the freezer. Cheese straws are a popular treat at Southern gatherings, and they are deliciously addictive. Like potato chips, it's very hard to eat just one.

"What exactly do you need us to do?" Dorien asked.

"I'm not completely sure," I admitted. "I feel like we're stalled and need some prodding to go forward." I looked at

Minerva. "I want to thank you for your phone call this morning. I found Jeremy Watts, and everything was just as you said it would be."

"Really?" She clapped her hands together with delight. "I'm so glad, my dear. I was afraid you would think I was a foolish old woman, but the dream was so vivid, I just knew it meant something. You thought so, too, didn't you, Rose?"

Rose nodded, reaching for another cheese straw. "I knew you were on to something. I felt a little chill when you told me about your vision. But tell us how the meeting went," she said to me. "I bet Mr. Watts was surprised to see you."

"I'll say," Ali piped up in a wry voice. "Stunned was more like it."

I quickly filled her in on our meeting with Jeremy at the Red Lion. When I mentioned having spotted Olivia at the same hotel, she lifted her eyebrows.

"The plot thickens," she said archly.

Minerva nodded. "That it does, my dear."

I'd debated calling this emergency meeting but had decided to go ahead with it after talking with Ali. I knew only a handful of the Dream Club members were available in the late afternoon, but I thought it was important to get their take on where we stood. I was disappointed that Sam Stiles was absent again. I hadn't seen her since the day of Sonia's murder.

"I have something I want to run by you," I said, pulling out pages I'd copied from the sign-in register before Sam took it to the police. "These are the people who signed in that day. I think it's a good starting point." Dorien Myers leaned close. "I recognize most of the names," she said, going down the list with her finger on the page. Most of them were longtime customers, people from the neighborhood who knew us socially.

"But you don't recognize all of them, right?" I prodded. It was a long shot, but we had to try a different tack. What if the person responsible for Sonia's murder was present that day and signed in? And at this point, we couldn't afford to ignore any lead, no matter how far-fetched.

"Read the names to us, dear," Minerva said. She had leaned over, peered at the pages, and then sat back in her chair. "My eyes aren't what they used to be."

I read out the names of familiar customers, friends, and Dream Club members. Several minutes passed while people contemplated the names, and I drew a blank.

I thought of another angle. Sam Stiles had told Noah they'd found a silver chain and pendant in the bags of evidence they'd collected at the shop. Presumably it was the one Sonia had worn at the signing. It was engraved with the name "Trudy."

"This is a long shot, but does the name 'Trudy' ring a bell with anyone?" I quickly explained about the pendant. It must have been significant if Sonia wore it every single day.

"Trudy? Could it be Trudy Carpenter?" Lucinda broke in. "I think she was a student at the Academy. I'll have to check the records to be sure." Lucinda still had friends on the faculty of the school where she had worked and participated in some of the school's events. "And if I'm not mistaken, she may be related to Sonia." She took a delicate bite of a cheese straw.

"She's related to Sonia?" This took me by surprise.

"I believe she's her niece." She thought for a moment. "I can check the school yearbooks, but Minerva and Rose are the experts on genealogy. I bet they could come up with something more definitive."

"Was she a local girl?" I asked.

Lucinda nodded. "She was definitely from Georgia. As I

recall, her parents lived in Valdosta, and she may have moved to Brunswick when she graduated." She frowned. "I seem to remember she was a very sweet girl, but she fell in with the wrong crowd." She shook her head sadly. "Sometimes all it takes is one wrong turn, and your life spins off in a different direction." There was so much emotion in her voice I wondered if she was talking about herself, not a student from years ago. I've always believed that Lucinda is a woman with secrets.

"Yes, we can check it out for you, too," Minerva said eagerly. "We can work on it tonight."

"If you wouldn't mind, we'd really appreciate it," I told her. Minerva and Rose have an amazing amount of genealogy knowledge at their fingertips. I might spend hours laboring over something they could find in a few minutes, so I never hesitate to ask them for help.

"Glad to do it!" Rose beamed. "We've finished all our flower orders for the rest of the week, so we were just going to watch the *NCIS* marathon. I'd much rather work on a project and feel productive." She looked genuinely happy at the prospect of working on the case, and I certainly wasn't going to dissuade her.

"I can check legal records for you," Persia offered. Persia works as a paralegal and has access to all sorts of interesting commercial transactions, real estate deeds, and state records that have helped us in the past. It's amazing to me that everyone leaves a paper trail. Sometimes the past catches up with you, in spite of your best efforts to hide it.

"It's shocking how much information is out there," Lucinda said. "Either online or in courthouse records or newspaper clippings. My grandmother taught me that a proper Savannah woman is mentioned in the newspaper only three times in her life: when she's born, when she's married, and when she dies. Of course, she was from a different generation." She sipped her tea and a shadow crossed over her face. "In some ways, life seemed simpler, you know. Fewer choices, I suppose." She gave a sad little smile. "I don't suppose we'll ever go back to those times, will we?"

"I'm afraid not," Ali told her. "The genie's out of the bottle." Barney and Scout awoke from their naps and strolled lazily into the kitchen, looking for their dinner. They liked to eat at 5 p.m. sharp, and you could set your watch by them. "Oh," Ali said, jumping up. "I didn't realize how late it was. I think we should stop for tonight, unless someone else has something to discuss?"

"I think we've covered everything," Persia said. "Let's all get to work. We'll touch base with you in the morning."

"Good idea," Rose agreed. "Maybe we can have a conference call," she said eagerly. "I've been doing that for some of my crowdfunding projects and it's been really effective." *Crowdfunding?* I smiled. As an octogenarian, Rose is the oldest person in the Dream Club, but she has embraced technology in a way that would put younger members to shame.

14

"One thing I don't understand," I said to Noah the next morning, "is why Sonia didn't make it a point to invite her niece Trudy to the book signing and the TV taping. She never said a word to Ali or me about her niece. You'd think she'd be glad to have family show up. I just don't get it."

"Maybe Sonia was close to her niece but not to other members of the family," Noah said mildly. "There could be jealousy on Trudy's side, or maybe some old family feud, who knows? Another possibility is that Sonia didn't want to share the limelight. Sometimes these celebrities are pretty self-centered."

Noah passed me a cup of fresh-brewed coffee. I was touched that he remembered hazelnut was my favorite flavor, and he even added some fat-free half-and-half and a packet of sweetener. Noah is a stickler for details. "Families can be the key to understanding the victim," he said wryly. "I hope I've taught you that much."

I smiled at him. He was sitting behind his desk, the sunlight slanting in the window and dancing over his finely chiseled features, his smoky eyes sparkling with enthusiasm. Now that he wasn't with the Bureau anymore, he was wearing his hair a little longer, and it suited him. He also seemed more relaxed, less tightly wired. Leaving the Bureau and all his friends behind was a gut-wrenching decision for him, but the right one.

"Yes, you've taught me well. And that's why I'm looking at family and employees right now. The case is complicated because Sonia's company is so vast and her entourage was enormous. The trouble is, I'm still trying to figure out who's who in the inner circle and who's on the fringes."

"Start with the key players," Noah advised.

"That's part of the problem. Sonia surrounded herself with so many people it's hard to know who was a friend and who was a foe. And who was just a hanger-on," I added. "I called a meeting of the Dream Club yesterday to regroup. I figured it was time to decide what to do next."

"What did your fellow dreamers come up with?" Noah always looked mildly amused when I mentioned the Dream Club, but he knew enough to keep an open mind—or at least the appearance of one. He'd started out as a complete skeptic, and now he'd warmed up to the idea that dreams can send powerful messages.

So much material is hidden in dreams. Sometimes a little nagging thought will unlock a fragment of a forgotten dream. That happens to me all the time. The message might be buried deep in symbolism, and our job is to dig it out and decipher it. I've been surprised at how many times my dreams have offered me insight on an issue I've been struggling with. Sometimes I don't see the connection immediately, but it's there.

Some of the more seasoned Dream Club members, like Sybil and Persia, will get to the meaning very quickly. I'm new at the game, but I'm making progress. It takes a lot of skill to interpret dreams, but I think I'm on the right track.

"We all agreed we need to start close to home. That's why I want to find out everything I can about Trudy Carpenter. She's Sonia's nearest relative, as far as I can tell. I figured I'd start there and expand the circle outward."

Noah taught me the importance of learning everything you can about the victim when you begin an investigation. And leaving nothing to chance. This advice came in handy when the Dream Club solved the murder of Chico, the dance instructor who owned a studio right across the street from Oldies But Goodies. When you look at the family, you can discover new leads and the investigation can go off in a totally different direction.

"Do you want me to run a background check on her? I can do it right now."

"Yes," I said, surprised. "It wouldn't hurt to see what turns up." I remembered that Lucinda had said that Trudy had fallen in with the wrong crowd, but that was years ago, when she was a schoolgirl. As far as I knew, she was now a respectable Southern matron, married with children, who happened to be related to a celebrity.

"Trudy Carpenter? From Savannah?"

"No, she's originally from Valdosta. And she may have moved to Brunswick, if that helps." I remembered what Lucinda had told me. "But she attended the Academy, right here in Savannah, for high school."

Noah spent a few minutes at the keyboard and looked up in surprise. "Well, if it's the same Trudy Carpenter, she's had a few arrests for DUIs, and she's living with a convicted felon in a run-down section of Brunswick. His name is Reggie

Knox. He's listed as being at the same address. He's out on parole. Does the name ring a bell?"

"Reggie Knox? No, I've never heard of him. Why was he in prison?" My mind leaped ahead and I wondered if Trudy could be living with a murderer.

"Drugs, possession and dealing. Robbery and assault." Noah shook his head. "Domestic violence and a few bar fights. He sounds like a piece of work."

"Wow." I was stunned. "That could explain why Trudy didn't attend the book signing. No wonder Sonia wanted to distance herself from her niece and her lowlife boyfriend." I gave a little shudder.

It would be interesting to see where all that money was going. I hoped Persia would get a copy of the will as soon as it went through probate. Wills are a matter of public record, and I knew Persia could get the details for us. Who stood to inherit Sonia's fortune? An interesting question!

"The truth is, we actually don't know much about Sonia's family," I went on. "She had a longtime lover, Jeremy Watts, and that's all I know about her personal life." I told Noah about our meeting with Jeremy at the Red Lion and my surprise at spotting Olivia having breakfast with him. "Sonia's never been married and has no kids. Her whole life was devoted to her career and building her brand."

"Interesting from an inheritance point of view," Noah offered.

"That it is," I agreed. "There's a lot of money involved, a huge estate."

"Speaking of money, how are things at the shop?" Noah said, topping off my coffee. "I've been worried about you and Ali. Has there been any fallout from Sonia's death?"

"I'm afraid so." I bit back a little sigh. "Business is way down. It doesn't matter that Sonia died from an allergic reaction; people seem to think we poisoned her. They're not interested in the facts, and you how gossip spreads down here. Like wildfire."

"I was afraid this would happen," Noah said. "Perception is everything. You're going to have to do a marketing blitz to get things back on track. Let the public know that Oldies But Goodies is safe and reliable."

He was quiet for a moment, with his elbow on the desk and his chin cupped in his hand, staring out the window. I took the opportunity to look around his office. It's exactly what I thought Noah would choose. Sleek modern furniture in rich teak, a creamy Berber carpet, vintage drawings of old Savannah on the walls. Noah's taste ran to classic styles and subdued colors. The office inspired confidence, and it fit his personality. He'd rented a small suite with two offices and a reception area. I wondered if he might take on a partner if his business took off. At the moment, it was a one-man agency. No assistant, no secretary.

I stood up to inspect a lovely drawing of the Savannah Harbor when he asked, "Do you like my new digs?"

"I love them." The only jarring note was that his desk was piled high with papers and he had to move a stack of file folders off the upholstered armchair for me to sit down. It was controlled chaos, as Ali would say, but I think the office would look better with some organization. "You're doing this all on your own?" I asked. "Isn't it hard being a one-man show?"

"It is, and I'm going to hire a secretary this week. Just part-time for now, and if it works out, we'll go to full-time. In fact, I'm interviewing a few people today." He glanced at his watch and frowned. "The first one should be here in a couple of minutes. A lot of people replied to my ad"—he opened a desk drawer and pulled out a sheaf of papers—"but

I've narrowed it down to six candidates. I'd like to hire someone with a background in law enforcement or legal issues. Plus I need someone I can trust to keep things confidential. Whoever I choose will have to deal with a lot of sensitive material, so discretion is key."

I nodded. "I think you'll find just the right person," I told him. "I won't keep you." I reached for my bag. "You have a lot on your plate right now, and I don't want to take up any more of your time."

"I always have time for you, Taylor." His voice was low and husky as he moved close and wrapped his hand around mine. I felt a delicious little thrill at his touch. "Try not to worry about the shop. Tell Ali we'll solve Sonia's murder and things will get back to normal. You'll see." I smiled at his optimism. Noah always has a way of making me feel safe and secure. He leaned in closer and our faces were almost touching. It could have been a romantic moment, but it was ruined when we heard the door to the reception room open.

"Your interview," I said softly.

"Awful timing," he said, gathering me for a brief hug. His eyes were warm and dark and full of feeling.

"We can get together later," I murmured.

"Count on it," he promised. "I'll call you."

When I got back to the shop, I saw Dana and Ali huddled together at a small desk in the back where we do the accounts. Ali was riffling through a pile of brochures and looked up with a bright smile on her face. "Taylor, I'm so glad you're here. Dana has come up with an awesome idea to drum up business."

Dana flushed. "Ali and I came up with it together," she

said modestly. "You know what they say about great minds running on the same track."

"Really? That's terrific." I poured myself a cup of spicy gingerbread tea and pulled up a chair. It was one of our most popular flavors, and I made a mental note to place a bigger order next time. "So what's this project and how can I help?"

I was glad to see that Ali was taking action to turn things around instead of wallowing in despair. The truth is, I was worried that the business might not survive the sudden downturn after Sonia's death, but I couldn't seem to come up with a plan. Sometimes I wish I'd taken more marketing courses and fewer financial classes when I was doing my MBA.

Dana's a marketing major in college, and her nonstop energy and enthusiasm are two of her most important assets. As our intern, she gets credit for helping us at the shop; in return, we promise to give her a taste of what it's like to run a small business. We also send regular evaluations to her professors. So far, they have all been sterling. Dana's a gem, and I'll be sad when she graduates and leaves us.

"Well, here's what we came up with. See what you think." She pushed a yellow legal pad across the desk to me. It looked like a sketch for a newspaper ad, and I was surprised. We have almost no advertising budget, and newspaper ads are pricey.

I read the headline and was stunned. "We're offering cooking classes?" And free ones, I noticed wryly. Not even income producing. What in the world was she thinking?

"Yes, isn't it wonderful?" she said happily.

"Cooking classes." I tried to keep my voice neutral. "Ali, are you sure this is the right direction to take?" I ventured. I didn't want to rain on her parade, but seriously, cooking classes? We'd be paying not only for the ad but for the supplies.

"And this is the ad you want to run?"

Ali nodded. "Dana designed it. She's really talented, isn't she?" She grinned at our young intern, who was beaming with pleasure.

"But how will we pay for it?" I said, deciding it was better to just dive right in with my concerns.

"We hadn't really gotten that far yet," Dana admitted. I glanced at Dana, trying to read her expression. Her sunny smile had been replaced by a wary expression as she realized a storm was brewing. Ali and I have had our share of disagreements over how to run the shop, and this might be the biggest one yet.

"Ali, ad space is expensive, and you know we have zero in the promo budget right now."

My worst fear was that the store would slowly slip back into the red. Ironic. A few months ago, the shop was bleeding red ink when I flew in to help Ali turn the business around. And now it was dangerously close to coming full circle—in a couple of weeks, we could be right back in the red again. This time might be the death knell for the store. How could I convince Ali that we needed to cut back on expenses and not toss our money away on foolish projects? At this point, every penny had to count. Our bottom line had taken a big hit with Sonia's death, and who knew if it would ever recover.

"Oh, we won't pay for it—or we won't pay very much." Her tone was light and casual, and I tried not to bristle. She gave a little wave of dismissal, and it was obvious she wasn't taking my worries to heart. "We'll just run it in one of the neighborhood shopping circulars," Ali said blithely, "not one of the major newspapers. You can buy ads for almost nothing in these little fliers. I've already called to get an estimate. And I'm thinking maybe we can work out a co-op arrangement with another store." She jotted a note on a Post-it. "That way, they'd be footing half the bill for the ad. Although, if we get a really good deal, we could probably pay for it ourselves."

"A co-op ad," I said slowly.

"Yes, it will cut our expenses in half. All I have to do is find someone who wants to go in with us on the ad, fifty-fifty. It's a win-win situation." She thought for a moment. "In fact, I was just thinking that this might be something you'd like to follow up on, wouldn't you, Dana?"

Dana nodded and immediately whipped out her own notebook. She was superorganized and kept a list of her daily tasks; it made it easy for us to give her professors a detailed description of how she spent her time.

"I guess I'm not clear on something," I piped up. I shook my head, wondering where she was going with this. "What's our end of the deal? What can we offer another business that would make them want to split an ad with us?"

"Well, we could pick a specialty store, maybe a cheese store. We'll feature some of their products in our recipes. And we'll put up a poster in the shop, telling customers where they can get ingredients for all the recipes. That would really be good advertising. I bet a lot of businesses would like to take advantage of the opportunity."

I shook my head. "I'm not at all sure about that."

"Of course they will. Don't you see?" Ali raced on, her eyes alive with excitement. "It will be a way to generate new business. Everyone loves a free cooking class, and as you can see"—she reached over and flipped the pad to a new page—"we're offering them for all age groups."

"Indeed," I said, at a loss for words. "All age groups."

"We even have Toddler Chef classes," Dana said brightly. "That was Ali's idea. There's something for every age group." Her voice was spiraling upward, and she was now practically vibrating with enthusiasm. "I think the Toddler Chef class is going to be my favorite. We can have little aprons printed up with the name of the shop on the front and maybe even go for those cute white hats that chefs wear."

"Toques," Ali said helpfully.

"Yes, toques," Dana agreed. "There must be a specialty store somewhere that makes them in children's sizes."

Toddler Chef? Ali loved kids of all ages, but I could just picture the shop being overrun with out-of-control toddlers in toques and their doting moms. It sounded nightmarish.

"You like the idea, don't you?" Ali's voice suddenly wavered for a moment. She shot me a keen, questioning glance, and I knew this was the moment of truth. If I dashed her hopes about the cooking classes, it would be a huge setback for her. And for the shop, I wagered.

"Like it?" I reached across the desk to bump fists with her. "I love it!" I managed to keep a grin plastered on my face even though my spirits were sinking and a cash register in my head was going *ka-ching, ka-ching* at the thought of all the money we'd be spending that we didn't have.

"There's more," she said eagerly, pointing to the legal pad. "Keep going. It gets better."

I flipped over the next page. *Oh no!* It seemed we were also offering *Master Chef* classes. At no charge, of course. So that made a total of three classes: the regular, The Magic of Cupcakes, presumably aimed at adults; the dreaded Toddler Chef class for mothers and toddlers; and the Master Chef class for people who were seasoned cooks. My mind reeled at what this would entail.

I conjured up an imaginary expense sheet. Ali often tells me I have the soul of an accountant, and she doesn't mean it as a compliment. The expenses for the supplies would add up exponentially, unless we offered the finished products for sale at the end of the class. And wouldn't that defeat the whole purpose? In most cooking classes, the participants are allowed to bring the goodies home with them. Of course, most cooking school students pay for the privilege of attending class. With Ali's plan, we were giving away the store. Literally.

Another objection reared its ugly head. Would we have to suspend normal business hours while the classes were in progress? I looked around the already crowded shop, with its narrow aisles and overflowing display cases. As far as I could tell, we'd have to widen the center aisle and hold the classes there. Of course, business wasn't exactly booming, so losing a morning's sales might not make much difference either way.

"And guess what the best part is?" Ali asked.

I shook my head. I literally couldn't come up with a single thought.

"We'll be teaching the classes together."

"We? We, as in you and me?"

"Yes, of course." Ali grinned. "It's time for you to get your hands dirty, Taylor. You can't just sit around and crunch numbers all day long. C'mon," she teased me, "you're up for a challenge, aren't you?"

"Well, I'm game, I guess." I swallowed hard. Cooking is not my forte and Ali knows it. Ali has always been in charge of making the luscious pastries, and my sole contribution has been defrosting them and serving them at Dream Club meetings. This was a game changer, and I didn't know what to make of it.

"I can picture it now," Ali said dreamily. She had her chin in her hand, staring at the front of the shop, with the bright window display that Dana had designed. Dana had displayed copies of Sonia's dessert books on a white wicker table and had placed a platter of frosted cupcakes in front of them.

Balloons and confetti added to the festive air. "Just think about it, Taylor. The whole shop will be filled with happy customers, all enjoying homemade treats they've baked themselves. And all the cute little kids—they'll be so happy decorating cupcakes, and we'll give them helium balloons to take home. I can see it all in my mind's eye." She gave a happy sigh. "It's perfect, isn't it?" she murmured.

I took a deep breath and let it out slowly. "Perfect," I agreed. "Absolutely perfect." Really, there are some situations in life when a little white lie—or a whopping big lie—is called for, and this was one of them.

15

"Things are getting stickier," Persia Walker said ominously. It was 8:15 the following morning and she was calling from the law firm. "You'll never guess who inherited Sonia's fortune." She sounded out of breath, and I wondered if she'd just run upstairs. Her law office is on the fifth floor of a downtown office building, and Persia's doctor has been urging her to take the stairs instead of the elevator in the hopes of losing a few pounds.

"Don't keep me in suspense," I pleaded. Ali padded into the kitchen with Barney and Scout trotting behind her. I quickly switched the call to speakerphone and motioned to Ali, who took a seat at the round oak table. "Persia, I'm putting you on speaker," I said quickly. "Ali's here."

"Are the two of you sitting down?" Persia teased, drawing out the moment for all it was worth.

"Yes!" we chorused, and I heard a throaty chuckle at the other end of the line.

"Well, here's the big news. It's Trudy Carpenter, Sonia's niece. Trudy is Sonia's sole heir, outside of a few bequests here and there to some of her longtime employees."

"Most of her fortune went to Trudy? What about Jeremy Watts and Olivia Hudson?"

My mind was reeling at the news, and I tried to make sense of it. This was the last thing I'd expected. If Sonia wasn't close to her niece, why did she leave everything to her? And Sonia wore a necklace with Trudy's name on it. That certainly suggested a strong relationship. Did Sonia know that Trudy was living with an ex-con, a real lowlife? I wondered if Trudy had any children and if Sonia had really intended the money to go to them. I made a mental note to ask Noah the next time I talked to him.

"Nothing," Persia said flatly. "Not a penny to Jeremy or Olivia." She waited a beat and then went on, "I was really surprised at that, because she left a fairly generous amount to some of her favorite employees. Did you happen to meet anyone named Charlotte Cross at the book signing?"

Ali looked at me and shook her head. "No, I'm sure I didn't, and her name wasn't in the guest book. Ali doesn't know her, either. What's her connection with Sonia?"

"I'm still trying to figure that out," Persia replied. "Sonia must have been fond of Charlotte, because there's a bequest for Charlotte's daughter, Annabelle, to attend the Academy right here in Savannah. Sonia even left enough money for her to attend four years of college, too. Anywhere she wants to go."

"That's interesting," Ali mused. "Remember when Lucinda said that Sonia was once a student at the Academy? She must have had warm feelings toward the place if she left a bequest like that. It's a very pricey school."

"I do remember that." The whole thing was baffling to

me. A sudden thought zinged in my mind. "Persia, this is all in the public record, right?"

"Yes, anyone can look it up if they want," she replied.

"And the media?"

"The news services haven't caught on yet, but I know they will. Once the story breaks, I'm sure it's going to be big."

"Has anyone tried to contact Trudy?"

"I heard from the grapevine that someone from the *Tribune* tried, but they haven't had any luck. I don't know what it would take to lure her out," Persia said. Her voice dropped a notch. "I better run. My boss is here and I'm supposed to sit in on a deposition. I'll text you the most recent address for Trudy. Later, guys."

"This is getting more and more interesting," Ali said when the connection was broken.

I made a quick call to Sara while Ali fed Barney and Scout and made herself a strawberry smoothie for breakfast. Sara agreed to contact Trudy and see if she would agree to a brief meeting, and I decided to try another tack.

"Ali, how would you like to take a quick ride with me this morning?" It was almost 9 a.m., and Dana had just arrived to help out with things at the shop. The freezer was stocked with soups and I'd made biscuits and muffins the night before, so I was sure she could manage on her own for a couple of hours.

"Sure, where are we headed?" Ali was already pinning her hair on top of her head, ready to jump into the shower.

"Trudy Carpenter's parents. Clare Carpenter is Sonia's sister." She raised her eyebrows. "Assuming they haven't moved. Lucinda Macavy gave me their old address from the days when Trudy was a student at the Academy." I glanced at my watch. "We can be there in an hour or so. We might learn something interesting."

"Just give me five minutes," Ali said, zipping down the hall.

She was true to her word, and after she poured her smoothie into a travel mug, we jumped into the car and headed south out of Savannah.

"Shouldn't we have called them first?" Ali asked as we zipped along a country road toward Brunswick.

"I think we need the element of surprise," I told her. "Besides, they have an unlisted number, and we need to strike while the iron's hot. In a day or so, they'll be fending off reporters, and they might leave town or barricade themselves inside their house. This could be our only chance to talk with them."

"How did Lucinda happen to have their address? Was she friendly with them?" Ali asked.

"She had their address from the school records, but that's a good point." I heaved a sigh. "I should have asked her how well she knew them; that might have given us a foot in the door. I could have asked her for an introduction." I was kicking myself for not thinking of this earlier.

"Who knows?" Ali shrugged. "It was a long time ago. We might have to take our chances and play it by ear. Let's just do the best we can. I have a good feeling about this," she added. *My sister, the optimist.*

When we pulled off the main road and headed up a narrow lane overgrown with crepe myrtle, I was already regretting my decision. Why had I thought Trudy's parents would be interested in talking with us?

Some of Ali's impulsiveness must be rubbing off on me, I decided. I was acting in a way that was completely out of character for me. I never do anything spontaneously, and I weigh my options carefully. This time I'd jumped in feet first, and I had no idea why.

Then my thoughts screeched to a halt because the house loomed into view, an imposing white brick affair tucked behind towering black wrought iron gates.

"Wow," Ali said softly, "I wasn't expecting this."

"Me, either," I said, shaking my head. "It's spectacular." The house reminded me of a Hollywood version of a Southern mansion. Lush foliage, weeping willows, a sprawling veranda, and a long second-floor balcony running the length of the house. I almost expected to spot the Tarleton twins lounging on the front porch sipping mint juleps, waiting for Scarlett to join them.

It appeared the Carpenters were not only wealthy, but "one percent" wealthy. The richest of the rich. I was fascinated by the estate. What in the world was Trudy doing living in a seedy part of town when her parents were living in splendor? Maybe Noah's instincts had been right when he suggested that Trudy might be the black sheep of the family. I needed to know more, because nothing made sense to me. Questions for the Carpenters were zinging through my brain. But would they answer them? And why should they talk to us at all?

There was a video surveillance box by the gate, and Ali hopped out to pick up the phone. The screen suddenly jumped to life, and I knew someone was checking her out. She put on her most winning smile, said a few words into the microphone, and jumped back in the car.

"Well?" I asked.

"Abracadabra, open sesame," she said as the massive gates parted. She held her arms straight out in front of her, palms up, like a wizard.

"Ali, you are amazing. What did you tell them?" I pulled

through the gates and headed up a curvy driveway framed by live oaks.

"I said we were here to pay a condolence call. People in the South still do that, you know." She frowned. "We should have brought muffins, or a fresh apple strudel. That would have been a nice touch. People expect it down here; it's the way they do things."

"I think you did a brilliant job," I told her. "With or without pastries. You must have sounded pretty convincing."

Minutes later, we were seated at a white wicker table on the veranda, which was dotted with pots of lush ferns and tea roses. A uniformed maid served us fresh-squeezed lemonade and assured me "the missus" would be with us shortly. From this vantage point, the grounds were spectacular.

I leaned back in my rocker and admired the wide expanse of green lawn, the neatly kept flower beds filled with impatiens and begonias. I glimpsed a tennis court off to the left and the sparkling blue waters of a kidney-shaped pool to the right. Southern living at its finest.

"Who says money doesn't buy happiness?" Ali murmured. She tilted her head back, catching some rays.

"Can I help you?" A soft, cultured voice with just a hint of a Southern accent brought me out of my reverie. Ali rocked forward so suddenly she nearly catapulted out of her chair.

"I'm Ali Blake," she said, jumping to her feet, "and this is my sister Taylor."

The woman nodded politely but looked puzzled. "I'm Clare Carpenter." She held out a jewel-encrusted hand, and I noticed she was wearing a diamond the size of a walnut. "Do we know each other?"

"No, ma'am," Ali said quickly, "but we own the candy store in Savannah where Sonia"—she paused delicately—"passed away. We had invited her for a book signing."

"Ah yes, the candy store. Oldies But Goodies," Clare said, sinking into a wicker chair. "I read about it in the news. What a terrible thing that was." She didn't seem the least bit upset by her sister's death, and I wondered what their relationship had been like. Had they been close? It didn't seem likely. She poured herself a glass of lemonade, her blue eyes flickering. I had the feeling she was stalling for time, planning what she was going to say.

"Yes, ma'am, it certainly was terrible, a real tragedy. We just stopped by to offer our condolences," Ali said, taking the lead. "We're so sorry for your loss. Sonia was such an amazing person, and we feel privileged to have known her, even for a brief time. No one could have predicted this, and we're just so upset about what happened." She glanced at me and I gave a tiny smile. She had said exactly the right thing.

Clare nodded and brushed a lock of hair back from her porcelain forehead. I figured her to be late fifties, but her skin was so smooth and unlined, I was sure she'd had a series of Botox injections. Or maybe she'd even gone under the knife and had "a little work" done.

Of course, her sister Sonia was well preserved, too, so maybe it was just good genes. I remembered that Sonia was a couple of years older than Clare. There was a remarkable similarity in the two women, except for the hair color. Sonia was a striking redhead and Clare was a platinum blonde.

I had no idea how to bring the conversation around to her daughter, Trudy, and hoped inspiration would strike. When she'd settled herself back in her chair, I took a good look at our hostess. She was wearing a pale lemon-yellow silk blouse with tailored white slacks and espadrilles. Her jewelry was classic, the kind that's handed down for generations. A triple set of pearls, with pearl button earrings, and her streaky blond hair was swept back into a neat chignon. Her makeup was simple and understated, and she shifted in her chair to guard her face from the sun. With her white-blond hair and pale skin, she looked ethereal.

"I hope you know that I don't hold either of you responsible in any way," she said finally. I blinked. I wasn't sure where she was headed with this. "Sometimes things happen that are out of our control, and as a woman of faith, I believe there must be a purpose to everything that happens in life. There are certain things that are beyond our understanding."

Ah. So she didn't blame us for the fatal pastries. I wondered if she'd read the autopsy report or the ME's findings. Did she really think Sonia's death was unforeseeable, an act of God? Skeptic that I am, I found that hard to believe.

"Yes, ma'am," Ali said politely. Ali shot me a look. She obviously wanted me to chime in.

I was at a loss for words and struggled to think of something appropriate to say. "That's good to know, Mrs. Carpenter. We were all so excited to have Sonia visit our shop, and what happened was just tragic." I waited a beat. "We don't know what plans you've made for Sonia's funeral, but we'd certainly like to pay our respects."

"Well, that's very kind of you, but I'm afraid that's not possible. The funeral will be private." She looked out over the vast expanse of green lawn as if she was gazing into infinity. It was perfectly still; the only movement was a hummingbird hovering over a red bird feeder filled with sugar water. I remember the Harper sisters telling me the best way to attract the little birds was with water sweetened with sugar.

A long beat passed and I exchanged a look with Ali. Now what? I was about to break the silence when she turned to face me. "We're having just a few close relatives and friends.

I'm sure you understand." She sighed. "Sonia made her own funeral arrangements, and she was very clear on that. She didn't want a big production; I'm not sure why." She gave a wry smile. "Maybe because she was surrounded by so many people all her life? She couldn't even walk down the street without someone asking for her autograph."

"The price of fame," I said quietly.

Clare nodded. "Yes, indeed. A heavy price. Sonia didn't talk about it much, but sometimes I think she would have been happy to chuck it all and move to a little town in Georgia and have a garden. She was a country girl at heart, you know. She never wanted fanfare."

"Then her wishes must be honored," Ali said solemnly. "As you say, just a handful of relatives and friends."

My ears had perked up at the word "relatives," and I wondered if I could swing the conversation around to Trudy.

"There's something you could help us with, Mrs. Carpenter," I said. "We'd like to send a condolence card to Trudy, but we don't have an address for her. Is there some way we can get in touch with her? And we'd love it if she could stop by the shop and see our window display. We've featured Sonia's latest books."

"How did you hear about Trudy?" Clare's lips tightened into a thin line and her voice had taken on a sharp edge.

"One of our friends was the headmistress at the Academy before her retirement," I said smoothly. "I understand that both Sonia and your daughter, Trudy, attended the school, and she happened to mention it." I kept my voice neutral and ignored the fact that a deep red flush was creeping up Clare's face. She was either embarrassed or angry, I decided.

"Yes, Trudy did spend four years at that pricey school," Clare said. "Fat lot of good it did her." I must have looked shocked because she added, "I shouldn't have said that. I'm not myself today. But the truth is, if you met Trudy, you'd know what I'm talking about."

I pretended to be puzzled and she went on, "Trudy had all the advantages in life, and she's made some horrible choices. We rarely see her. I do have a phone number for her, and sometimes she actually takes my calls. I don't even have a current address for her." She gave a short, bitter laugh. "I can tell her that you'd like to contact her. Just call me in a day or two." She took out a tiny gold pencil from her pocket and scribbled a number on a napkin. "This is my private line."

"That's very kind of you," Ali interjected. I exchanged a look with my sister. Could it be that Trudy no longer lived with Reggie Knox? In any case, I was eager to speak with Trudy as soon as possible.

"But I can't guarantee she'll even get back to me. She lives with some lowlife who seems to control her every move. She's thrown away everything because of him." *The lowlife must be Reggie Knox*, I decided.

Ali nodded sympathetically. "It must be very hard for you. Such a difficult situation."

"It is." She reached up and undid a gold locket she was wearing. She flipped it open and showed us a photo of a young woman with classic features and flaming red hair. "This is Trudy. She was just nineteen when this picture was taken. I like to think of her as a teenager, instead of the way she is now." Her breath caught in her throat and her eyes welled up with tears. "Sometimes you do your best and it's still not good enough."

"Is Trudy your only child?" I asked politely.

"Yes, she is." A frown crossed her doll-like features. "And that makes it all the worse."

Ali murmured how pretty Trudy was and passed me the

locket. I took a look and was so startled, I nearly fell back into my seat. Trudy was looking right into the camera, her eyes shining with happiness, her mouth curved in a wide smile. She was a beautiful young woman with a heart-shaped face.

Trudy looked exactly like Sonia.

16

"I wasn't expecting that," I said as soon as we were back in the car.

Ali put on her sunglasses and tossed me a wry look. "Trudy is a dead ringer for Sonia. She doesn't look at all like Clare, not even remotely." She gunned the engine and took off down the long narrow driveway. "I wish we'd had a chance to chat with Clare's husband. It might shed some light on what's really going on here."

"I think we know what's going on," I said mildly. "The question is, can we prove it, and more importantly, does it have anything to do with Sonia's murder?"

"It could," Ali said. "I wonder if Lucinda knows more than she let on." She gave me a speculative look. "If Trudy is actually Sonia's daughter, Lucinda wouldn't have any reason to keep it a secret, would she?"

"I don't think so. She probably doesn't suspect anything. If Clare and her husband raised Trudy as their own child, no one would have any reason to doubt they're the parents. Especially if they've had her since she was a baby. And offhand, I can't see how it makes any difference, except it explains why Sonia left her fortune to Trudy."

"A fortune that will be eaten up by that ex-con she lives with," Ali said. "No wonder Clare is upset. First she loses her sister and then she realizes Trudy and the ex-con stand to inherit millions."

"And now we have a new suspect. Reggie Knox is a known criminal and he has a motive to kill Sonia. I'd put him at the top of the suspect list. Can't the police bring him in for questioning? I'm going to ask Sam Stiles about it. If he's on parole, I think they can bring him in without much of a reason; at least I hope so."

I stared at the marshlands as we drove past. The air was warm and balmy, and I saw whole stretches of forest overgrown with kudzu. Everything is fresh and green in Savannah, and after living in a concrete jungle in Chicago, it feels like paradise to me. I enjoy every new sight and sound and never tire of looking at the landscape.

"The first thing we need to do is run this new development by the Dream Club," Ali said. "Do you suppose anyone else suspects that Trudy was Sonia's daughter, and not her niece?"

"We'll soon find out," I promised.

"We paid a condolence call on Sonia's sister, Clare, and told her we'd like to contact her daughter, Trudy." Ali waited for a reaction from the group.

"That was the right thing to do," Lucinda murmured. "Although I'm not really sure how close Sonia was to Clare. They may have been sisters in name only."

"Why do you say that?" Minerva's blue eyes were keen with interest.

Lucinda looked flustered and gave a little cough. "Well, I'm not in a position to say," she said vaguely. Her cheeks took on a flush of pink and I had to bite back a smile. Lucinda really is a terrible liar.

I made a note to circle back to that remark. Just as I suspected, Lucinda knew more than she was letting on.

"Interesting," Minerva Harper commented. She lifted her eyebrows and pressed her lips together. It was obvious she didn't believe a word of what Lucinda was saying. She and her sister Rose were sitting side by side, as usual, wearing nearly identical flowered cotton dresses, their wispy white hair framing their faces. "Sonia and Clare might be closer than you think. In the end, I've always found that blood is thicker than water." She leaned forward to help herself to a tiny cherry tart. Ali had defrosted them as soon as we'd returned from Brunswick, and they were still warm from the oven.

"Delicious, my dear," Minerva said approvingly. "I hope you add these to the menu."

"Well, I certainly will, if you like them," Ali said, passing a tray of lemon bars.

"That's a lovely tray," Rose said, admiring the hand-painted lacquered tray from a century ago. "Very colorful."

"Speaking of trays," Dorien cut in, "is there any news about the cookie platter at the book signing?"

"You mean the one with the shortbread cookies?" I asked.

"Yes, of course that's what I mean," Dorien said, allowing herself a tiny eye roll.

"That's the one I brought," Lucinda piped up. "I would

have preferred to use a nice china platter, but you told me not to," she said reprovingly.

"We wanted to keep things casual," I said lightly. Our two plastic platters were stamped with the shop logo (we order them in bulk, online) and Lucinda's cookies were on a blue plastic tray festooned with a bright red rooster. We decided to use high-end plastic dishes and forks that day to make cleanup easier. When the event was over, we'd planned on sweeping everything up into Hefty bags and dumping them into trash bins. I think plastic dishes and utensils bothered Lucinda's sense of propriety, but she'd gone along with it.

"I believe the police are still examining everything," Sara said. "I don't think everything's turned up yet."

"I know that I saw a platter with a rooster on it," Persia said firmly. "I had a pretty good look at it. It was right there in the middle of the table. I can still see it when I shut my eyes." She snared a couple of Kahlúa brownies, one of our most popular pastries. "It couldn't have just disappeared, could it? I don't understand why it hasn't turned up."

"Don't forget, there was that period of time when the shop wasn't considered a crime scene," I said patiently. "When the paramedics arrived on the scene, all they knew was that Sonia was in the throes of some medical emergency. There wasn't any reason to preserve the evidence. It's a shame it worked out that way."

"It certainly is," Sybil said. "If only we knew then what we know now," she said darkly.

"I have the feeling the rooster platter will show up eventually," Persia said. "I dreamt about it last night."

"You did?" I moved my hand so quickly I nearly sloshed my iced tea over my plate. "Please tell us about it." I leaned forward, eager to hear any details Persia might divulge.

"Well, I saw a roasted chicken being shoved into a brown paper grocery bag, and then it was tossed into a bin. When I went to retrieve it, the bin was empty."

"And you think this relates to the missing plate, the plate the police are looking for?" Edward Giles asked. He gave her an impenetrable look and I wondered what he was thinking.

"Of course it's related," Persia retorted. "It's only a hop, skip, and a jump from a roast chicken to a plate decorated with a rooster."

"Surely some of these connections could just be coincidence?" Edward's tone was mild.

"This isn't a coincidence," Persia said, clearly ruffled. "What I saw is relevant." Edward, looking chastened, sat back and stared at the rug. I had the sinking feeling that he wouldn't speak up again for the rest of the evening.

"Do you remember any other details?" Sybil asked. When Persia shook her head, she went on, "How I wish I could hop into the mind of the murderer and see his dreams."

"Or *her* dreams," I pointed out.

"Yes, of course," she agreed. "If only I could will these things to happen," she said fervently. "Unfortunately, it doesn't work that way."

Sybil has no way of controlling which dreams she has access to, so it's totally unpredictable. Sometimes her talent comes in handy, and occasionally it has nothing to do with the case. It's a toss-up, like flipping a coin.

Some dreams have no particular meaning or symbolism and are simply "the residue of the day," a collection of images we've seen or remembered during our waking moments. Dreams are like a collage, composed of thousands of potential images. Who knows what will float to the surface on any given night?

"So you can't pick and choose whose dreams you want to visit?" Etta Mae Beasley asked.

I was glad to see that Etta Mae and Edward had decided to attend tonight's meeting. I wasn't sure whether they planned to continue with the Dream Club. Etta Mae seemed totally focused on the issue of the "stolen cookbook," to the exclusion of everything else, and Edward seemed skeptical about dream work. At some point, I'd have to talk to them privately and see if the club was really a good match for them.

"No, I've never been able to master that art," Sybil said. "There are some very famous people in the field who manage to target certain dreamers, but I don't have that ability. I need to attend more conferences and work on my technique. It's a skill and supposedly it can be acquired, with practice."

"Well, this dream-hopping business is all so random, it hardly seems worth bothering with," Dorien said in her caustic way. "I like dreams that are straightforward, you know. I prefer to get right down to things and not waste time." She was tapping her foot impatiently and casting eager looks around the group as if she was dying to tell us something important.

I knew from experience we needed to address it right away. Otherwise Dorien would prove to be such a distraction that no one else would have the floor.

Ali must have sensed it, too, because she said gently, "Dorien, I think you have something to share. Would you like to go ahead?"

"Well, yes, I would," Dorien said, taking a quick swig of iced tea. "I dreamt about a baby last night, and I have no idea why that's significant." *A baby!* Ali and I exchanged a look.

"Tell us more," Ali urged.

"I just know it's connected with Sonia's death, but I don't

know how. That's the part that's driving me crazy. I can't put the pieces together." Dorien seemed especially keyed up and edgy tonight. She was blinking rapidly, the way she does when she's excited, and she was lacing and unlacing her fingers.

"I think you may be on to something," I said softly. My hope was that I could get Dorien to relax enough to get into a meditative state where she could recall more details of the dream. "Try closing your eyes," I suggested. "Sometimes you'll see the dream like a movie running in your head."

"No, that doesn't help me," she snapped. "I just have to set my mind to remembering and it will come back to me, I know it will. Here's the funny thing. I dreamt about the baby and then I woke up briefly because a car backfired outside. I was only awake for a couple of minutes and I willed myself to get right back into the same dream. And it worked. Weird, isn't it?"

I nodded. I had heard this from several other club members. Some people are so in touch with their dreams, they can slip right back into them, even when the dream has been interrupted. It takes a certain skill to do this, and I've never mastered it.

"You say you willed yourself to get back into the dream," Lucinda said. "Somehow you sensed the dream about the baby was important, but what other details struck you? I'm just curious about what you hoped to discover when you slipped back into the original dream."

"Well, the baby was part of a celebration, I know that much. People were happy and dressed up and exchanging presents."

"Like a party?" Etta Mae asked.

Dorien nodded. "Sort of. But I had the feeling it was bigger than a party, maybe a major event. And a baby was involved."

"A christening?" Rose Harper suggested. "I do so love christenings, don't you? Minerva and I went to the McNamaras' christening last week. Their baby Charlie is only a month old and he's just the sweetest thing." She clasped her hands together and said, "There wasn't a dry eye in that church at his baptism. They'd waited for a baby for so long, you see."

Minerva reached over and put her hand on top of her sister's. "We need to stay on topic, Rose." She gave me a gentle eye roll and I smiled gratefully. I hated to cut Rose off, but she did tend to ramble.

"You don't suppose your dream was about a christening, do you?" Rose asked Dorien. "Because I had a very similar dream about a baby. I figured it was because we attended little Charlie's christening."

"What happened in your dream?" Dorien asked. Her dark eyes were flashing and she'd scooted to the edge of the sofa.

"Well, the dream started out as a celebration, exactly like yours. And then"—Rose shook her head—"the dream veered off a little. There were people smiling and talking and boxes and boxes of presents—"

"Yes, that's just like my dream," Dorien cut in. "What happened next?" The room was deadly still and everyone was focused on Rose as she struggled with her recollection. I felt a little chill go through me as my mind darted back to Trudy and Sonia and Clare.

"Now, this is the part that seems a little crazy." Rose chuckled. "Someone had painted a triangle on the floor. And in the middle of the triangle was a bassinet. A really pretty wicker one—it looked vintage, the kind they used to make in the old days." She shut her eyes tightly and then opened them. "Two women at the party tried to step into the triangle, but only one was successful. She pushed the other woman aside."

"You saw the woman who stepped into the triangle?" Ali asked. "Who was she?"

"No, dear, I never got a look at her face. She was tall and blond; that's all I can tell you."

"What happened next?" My mouth went dry and my voice was hoarse. A triangle. Two women and a baby.

"She walked right up to the bassinet and scooped out a baby! The loveliest little baby you've ever seen, with bright red hair, and crying for all she was worth. She held the baby close to her and just smiled and smiled. But the other woman started to cry. Then she turned around and left the party. It was very sad and my heart went out to her. She hung her head and put her hand to her heart as if she was devastated." Rose sat back and rested her hands in her lap. "And that was the end of the dream," she said softly. "I have no idea what any of it means. What do you all think?"

"The baby was the present," Dorien said in an awed tone. "Both women wanted the baby, but only one woman could have it."

"It certainly seems that way, doesn't it?" Rose answered. "It reminds me of the story of Solomon in the Bible."

"Two women and a little baby." Dorien blew out a breath. "But how does this relate to the case? I was thinking hard about Sonia Scott before I went to sleep. I asked my subconscious to send me a dream message." She shrugged and gave a helpless gesture with her hands. "But the message makes no sense, no sense at all."

And Dorien has no idea that her prayers were answered, I thought.

Ali and I exchanged a look. "I think it's time to tell everyone exactly what happened today when we visited Clare Carpenter," she said. "And what we saw."

17

The room was eerily silent as Ali recounted every detail about our visit to Clare Carpenter and what we suspected about Trudy's birth. I chimed in with Noah's revelation about Reggie Knox, the ex-con who was living in a seedy neighborhood with Trudy. All that would change, I assumed, as soon as Trudy had access to Sonia's enormous fortune. But that meant Reggie Knox would have access to it as well, and I found myself fearing for Trudy's safety.

Persia gave a long exhalation that ended in a sigh. "The whole story is so sad. How could a girl from a good family end up like that? It just doesn't make sense."

"We're not here to judge Trudy and the choices she's made," Sybil said slowly. "We need to focus on how it fits into the bigger question of who killed Sonia."

"Well, we certainly have a new suspect," Sara pointed out. "Reggie Knox is at the top of the list, as far as I'm concerned. He certainly had motive, and now we have to figure out if he had means and opportunity. We need to track down where he was and what he was doing the day of the book signing."

"That's a good idea, but there weren't many men at the book signing," Ali pointed out, "and I think we would have noticed him. He sounds like a thuggish type. He would have stood out like a sore thumb."

I had to admit, Ali was right. Everyone at the book signing was so polite and well mannered, it was impossible to think of an ex-con in our midst. If Reggie Knox had a credible alibi for that date and time, then he was in the clear. We would be able eliminate him from the suspect list very quickly. Unless he had an accomplice, of course.

"Lucinda," Sybil said suddenly, "I'd like to hear more about Trudy. Do you remember what she was like at the Academy? Maybe she was troubled back then and no one noticed. Did she seem lonely, or maybe sad and confused?"

"Not as far as I know, but I don't recall too much about her," Lucinda said in her diffident way. "I certainly never heard any complaints about her from the teachers. From what I remember, she was a shy girl who kept to herself. She didn't have many friends and was something of a loner."

"But she may have been troubled?" Sybil persisted.

Lucinda hesitated. "You know, in those days, we didn't know much about depression or mood disorders, and I suppose Trudy could have needed help. We used to think teenagers were just moody and we hoped they'd grow out of it." She sipped her iced tea and put it down carefully on a coaster. "But now that I think of it, yes, I suppose Trudy might have been depressed. We just didn't recognize the signs back then. No one bullied her, I'm quite sure of that."

I thought of Trudy and her DUIs and the fact that she lived with a known criminal and drug dealer. That certainly fit the profile of someone who'd had a troubled adolescence and had never received counseling or medication for depression.

"Can you recall anything specific about her, something that stands out?" Ali asked.

Lucinda frowned, a faint line appearing between her eyebrows. "She liked to write; I remember that much," she said. "She showed real talent. In fact, one of her stories was published in a regional newspaper and was reprinted in the yearbook. Would you like me to look it up? I saved a complete set of yearbooks when I left the Academy. A bit sentimental of me, but the Academy was such a big part of my life," she said apologetically.

"Of course it was," Ali said warmly. "I'm sure you have a lot of fond memories of those years. Do you think you'll be able to locate the yearbook with Trudy's story?"

"I know I can," Lucinda replied. "I'll look it up tonight. Do you think it might be helpful?" she asked eagerly.

"I do," I told her. "Any light we can shed on Trudy would be good at this point."

The rest of the meeting went smoothly. Etta Mae took the floor briefly to announce she was having what she called "angry" dreams with flashes of red and black. "I see a lot of jagged lines," she said in her abrupt way. "I'm opening my mouth to scream at someone. I'm absolutely furious with them. But when I open my mouth, no sound comes out." She paused and took a deep breath. "I'm so angry and then I start to feel panicky. The other person is just standing there laughing at me. I see red and black shards of glass everywhere. They make a crunching sound under my feet. And there are also shards of glass hanging from the ceiling. I can feel myself getting madder by the minute, and finally I'm so upset I wake myself up." She shook her head as if to dispel the dream. "I sat up in bed trembling and my heart was beating like a rabbit's. It took hours to go back to sleep."

"Talk about 'seeing red,'" Sybil murmured. "That's a classic image, both in real life and in dreams."

I nodded. What Etta Mae was describing sounded like an anger-aggression dream. Sometimes the dreamer is so caught up in a red haze of rage she feels engulfed, as if flames are leaping around her.

"Did the person make you feel like you were talking to a brick wall?" Sara asked. "I've had dreams like that, and it's usually when I'm on the outs with someone and they're not listening to a word I say. It happens when I feel really helpless and vulnerable about a situation in my life. It could be a job or a relationship. Maybe you feel the same way," she said sympathetically.

"That's it exactly," Etta Mae said. "You hit the nail on the head. I feel like I have no power with the executives at Sonia Scott, Inc., and when I wake up, I'm just exhausted, really drained."

"You're still thinking of the family cookbook," Minerva said, "and I can imagine how much it means to you. It's your heritage. I'm not surprised you're upset over this, my dear. Is there anything new on that front?"

"Not that I know of," Etta Mae said glumly. "They're keeping me in the dark, and that's the truth." She set her glass down with considerable force and Barney jumped off his windowsill perch, looking annoyed. "I doubt they'll even bother to respond to my letter, and I bet I'll have to hire a fancy lawyer to get any results." She paused. "With no guarantee I'll even win," she said sadly. "How can one person go up against a whole corporation? It's like David and Goliath."

"This might be a difficult time to find resolution," Persia

suggested. "I work for a law firm, as you know, and we handle a lot of corporate issues. When a CEO dies suddenly, sometimes the whole company is thrown into disarray. I've seen it happen, and it's utter chaos. There's juggling for power among the key executives, and business suffers. Even routine matters get pushed aside, and something like your plagiarism charge might be buried on someone's desk. The problem is, no one is going to consider it a priority at a time like this. The company might be going through a crisis. Sonia's death could have enormous financial repercussions. I wonder how the stock is doing. If it takes a tumble, you can be sure they'll be hearing from their investors."

"I see what you mean," Etta Mae said sadly. "I think you're right that my complaint is probably stuck on the back burner. Let's face it, it's small potatoes compared to everything else they're dealing with right now. But what's the answer? The more time that goes by, the more likely it is they'll get away with it. I have to act now if I want to get any justice. That Olivia knows all about it, but she's definitely not on my side."

Persia helped herself to a thumbprint cookie and chewed it appreciatively. "If you like, I can ask someone at the office about the best way for you to proceed. It sounds like Sonia's company might not be taking your complaint seriously, and you should probably seek legal counsel before going any further. The lawyers at my firm don't charge for an initial consultation, if that helps."

"It sure does, and I appreciate your offer," Etta Mae said, brightening. "Sonia sure didn't take me seriously, and I guess I was just plain naïve to think anyone else at the company would step in and do the right thing. I'll call your office tomorrow and set up an appointment," she said. "That's mighty kind of you."

"Glad to help," Persia told her. "It never hurts to explore your options."

I wasn't even sure if Etta Mae had a case against Sonia Scott, Inc., but I'm no lawyer and she was wise to consult with one.

I glanced at Etta Mae. She seemed an honest, forthright sort of woman, even though she could be volatile and would probably hold a grudge. Still, I couldn't really picture her as a cold-blooded murderer. There was something so down-home and ordinary about her, I just couldn't imagine her serving anyone a plate of deadly cookies.

And deep down, the thought that a Dream Club member might be responsible for someone's death was appalling. These were our friends and neighbors, people we welcomed into our home every week. Was it really possible I could be sitting across from a killer and not even realize it? Wouldn't there be alarm bells going off in my head?

I wasn't even sure who the police were looking at in Sonia's death. Sam had avoided coming to the Dream Club meetings because she either was busy or felt it better to distance herself. After all, Etta Mae was a member of our group. It was a touchy situation.

Would anyone be indicted for Sonia's death? The evidence was all circumstantial and a grand jury would have to decide if someone should be charged. At this point, it was up in the air and I couldn't even hazard a guess.

"I brought my family cookbook in case anyone wants to take another look," Etta Mae said shyly.

"I'm so glad you did. I bet it's a gold mine," Minerva said. "I just love these old family recipes." Minerva reached for the cookbook and carefully flipped through it while the rest of us refilled our plates. Suddenly she gave a little gasp of surprise. "Why, Etta Mae," Minerva said, "did you know there's a recipe for benne biscuits in here?" She exchanged a knowing look with her sister Rose, who leaned forward to read the recipe.

"No, I didn't," Etta Mae said, widening her eyes. "Have you heard of them? I don't seem to recall that recipe at all."

Dorien cleared her throat. "Benne biscuits are sesame seed cookies," she said flatly. "You didn't know that, Etta Mae?"

"Well, I just told you I didn't," Etta Mae retorted. Then the significance of Dorien's comment hit her. An angry flush began to creep up her neck, and her face suddenly was mottled with red patches. "If you think these cookies had something to do with—" She broke off suddenly. "Well, what exactly are you implying?" Her lips had thinned into a hard line and her eyes were as dark and cold as river rocks.

"Nothing," Dorien said, shrugging. "It's just a coincidence, that's all."

"Sales are way up," Etta Mae said bitterly. "The sales of Sonia's cookbook," she added when Minerva shot her a puzzled look. "Ironic, isn't it? All it takes is a dead author and a book shoots its way to the top of the *New York Times* list."

"I think all Sonia's books have been bestsellers," I said gently. I didn't want to add fuel to the fire, but Etta Mae seemed intent on throwing herself a pity party, and we were all reluctant guests. I tried to think of a way to bring the conversation back to more neutral topics but drew a blank.

"Well, her latest cookbook is the best she's ever had because she stole my recipes," Etta Mae insisted. "It was like a gift from heaven."

"That may be true," Persia said in her calm voice. Persia is often the voice of reason when the Dream Club conversations grow heated. "But who knows, you may have your day in court, after all. Wait and see what the attorney says when you come into the office. You may be pleasantly surprised."

"Do you really believe that?" A flicker of hope flashed on Etta Mae's broad face.

"You never know." Persia's tone was gentle. "Most of the time, right prevails. Justice is blind, you know."

Etta Mae snorted. "At least she's supposed to be," she said, her brashness back. "Sometimes I have to wonder, though."

"Just don't be in too much of a hurry to have your day in court," Persia cautioned. "The wheels of justice move slowly, I'm afraid."

"I'll keep that in mind," Etta Mae said with a glint in her eye. Etta can be abrasive, but she seemed genuinely grateful for Persia's help.

18

"Any more dreams to report?" Ali said brightly. She sneaked a peek at her watch. She likes to bring these meetings in under two hours, and we were running late tonight.

"I had an anxiety dream," Edward Giles said suddenly. He gave a sheepish smile, as if he was embarrassed by what he was going to relate.

"Why don't you tell us about it." Ali gave him an encouraging smile and passed a plate of buttery springerle cookies to Persia. She'd found an antique cookie mold with a sailing ship on it and couldn't resist trying it out.

Edward waved away the cookies, leaned forward, and rested his elbows on his knees. "It was very similar to something I read about in a dream interpretation book." He reached into his pocket and laid a paperback dream guide on the coffee table. "I don't know how reliable these things are," he said, a faint touch of pink coloring his pale face. "I suppose I should have asked you for a recommendation, but the lady at the Corner Bookstore said this was a popular one."

I glanced at the title. I was relieved to see he'd picked one of the classic books in the field.

"Well, there's good and bad out there," Dorien said. "Some dream books are so vague, they're not worth the paper they're printed on. It's like reading your horoscope in the newspaper. You can make anything you want out of it. They keep the details really fuzzy so they apply to everyone."

"Anyway," Edward went on, "I dreamt I was driving alone at night in the country; I think it was the marshlands right outside of town. The night was very dark, with no stars, and I felt confused. Suddenly I didn't know where I was, and I was running low on gas. I felt myself gripping the steering wheel very tightly"—he demonstrated by clenching his fingers into fists—"and I was having trouble controlling the car. It seemed to have a life of its own, and it was swerving all over the road."

"I had a dream just like that last week," Dorien whispered. When Edward glanced up, she quickly apologized. "Please go on. I'm sorry, I didn't mean to interrupt."

Edward nodded, his face tense. "I was going faster and faster. I felt like things were spinning out of control." He stopped and heaved a sigh. "Then suddenly the road changed into a train track." He shook his head, puzzled. "I don't know how that happened, but I was driving down the railway tracks in the pitch dark and the car was bouncing from side to side off the rails. I tried to get ahold of myself, and then I saw that the track was going to end in just a few yards. Somehow I knew there was a cliff ahead and the car was going to go right over it." His voice was low and hushed and he looked around the group.

"Good heavens," Minerva murmured. "What did you do?"

"I tried to slam on the brakes, but they weren't working. Nothing in the car worked; it was out of my control. I was trapped. I knew I was going to die." There was dead silence in the room. All of us were caught up in his story.

"The car kept on speeding down the tracks, and the drop-off was getting closer and closer. I knew I'd be a goner any second because the car was going to plummet over the cliff. It was inevitable. I tried to prepare myself for the end, and then, to my horror, I realized I wasn't alone in the car."

"You weren't alone?" I said, my breath catching in my throat.

"My nephew William was strapped into his car seat right next to me."

"Oh no!" Rose said, her hand flying to her mouth. "That poor little child."

Edward nodded solemnly. "Something terrible was going to happen to him, and there was no way I could save him."

He rested his fingertips on his forehead and hung his head. He had described the dream so vividly, all of us had been affected. I hadn't realized I'd been holding my breath and let out a little puff of air.

"That must have been horrible for you," I said when the silence had gone on for a while. "It sounds absolutely terrifying, Edward."

"Yes, it was," he admitted, looking up at me. "It's gotten so I'm afraid to go to sleep at night."

"Because you wonder if you'll have that dream again," Sybil ventured.

"That's it." He rubbed his hands together as if he needed to restore the circulation. "I don't think I could face it again. I had chest pains when I woke up."

"Chest pains? Edward, that's awful," Persia blurted out. "You need to tell your doctor about this. Please don't delay; it could be something serious."

Edward gave her a wan smile. "I think I was just stressed out from the dream. And from some other things going on in my life," he said cryptically. "I don't hold much stock in doctors," he said. "I try to eat right and I walk five miles every day. And I take my vitamins. I'm a tough old bird, you see."

"That's all well and good," Minerva spoke up, "but you still might need to be evaluated and maybe have some cardiac tests done. Better safe than sorry. Right, Rose?" she said, turning to her sister.

"Right," Rose agreed. "I used to get nightmares all the time, and it turned out that I had an arrhythmia."

"That's an irregular heartbeat," Minerva explained.

"It's like the chicken-and-egg question," Rose went on. "When my heart goes into a crazy rhythm in my sleep, my body knows something is wrong and my mind conjures up a dream to make sense of it. The doctor told me this might be the source of my nightmares. I can wake up with my heart pounding for no reason at all. I'm not stressed out or worried about anything, it just happens." Rose looked around the group and folded her hands in her lap. "I have to turn on the light and read for a little while to distract myself and calm down. Then I can go back to sleep and have a peaceful night."

"I think my situation is different," Edward said doubtfully. "Everyone in my family has good strong hearts. I think these nightmares I'm having are all in my head. I'm letting myself get all upset about something I have no control over." He hesitated and I wondered if he was going to say more, but then he sat back and folded his arms over his chest. He wasn't ready to divulge what was troubling him. We'd just have to be patient and hope he'd decide to share it with us.

"I still think you should go for a complete checkup," Persia said.

"This little nephew who was sitting beside you," Sybil asked, "is this someone who is a big part of your life? You know, Edward, in dreams, one character is sometimes substituted for another. Your dream character might represent a particular quality in someone you know. For example, if you're dreaming of a baby, you might really be thinking of someone who's helpless and vulnerable. Your subconscious translates that person into a baby or a small child in your dream." She smiled. "Another possibility is that you really do have a nephew who's an infant and you're concerned about him."

Edward was listening carefully and nodding. "That's interesting. Well, I can tell you this much: my nephew William is all grown up now, but yes, he's definitely important to me." A smile crossed his weathered face.

"Does he live here in Savannah?" I wanted to keep Edward talking and keep the thread of the conversation going. Edward rarely opens up, and this might be the perfect time to get to know him a little better.

"He went to college here in Savannah," Edward said, "and then he went off to do other things."

He gave an abrupt nod of his head as if punctuating his thought. I had no idea what the "other things" referred to, and I was pretty sure Edward wasn't going to enlighten me.

It seemed this would be a good time to end the meeting, and Edward surprised me by asking if anyone would like to borrow his dream book. Lucinda enthusiastically said she would, and Edward handed it to her. I figured this was a very good sign. Up until that point, I wasn't really sure if Edward was planning on staying with the group.

"Is it all right if I stop by tomorrow morning?" Lucinda asked me as she as she was leaving. "I'm going to be over this way and I'd like to drop off the yearbook."

"Of course," Ali told her. "We're going to be up at the crack of dawn."

"We are?" I said archly.

"Cooking classes," Ali said brightly. "We need to get started on them." When Lucinda gave her a blank look, she added, "It's a new project we're trying out; it's still in the planning stage. Don't worry, we'll tell you all about it when we have the kinks worked out. We'll be featuring cupcakes from Sonia's latest book."

"I can be here at nine tomorrow morning, if that's not too early?" Lucinda said timidly.

"That's perfect," I said. "We're experimenting with the recipe I found online for donut cupcakes, and you can be the first person to try them."

"Donut cupcakes? They sound delicious," Minerva piped up. "Would it be inconvenient if Rose and I stopped by, too? I need some candies and cupcakes for my bridge club."

"The more, the merrier," Ali said gaily. "The coffee will be on and the cupcakes will be fresh out of the oven."

"Sounds heavenly," I heard Rose murmur to Minerva as they headed out the door.

"Do these seem a little heavy to you?" I asked Ali the next morning. It was eight thirty and I'd just slid the first pan of donut cupcakes out of the oven. We'd experimented with two different recipes, trying to get exactly the right texture and topping. I knew our beta tasters would let me know if we'd succeeded.

"They look delicious," Ali said, admiring the streusel-topped creations I'd put on the cooling rack. "They don't seem heavy at all," she said, lifting one up and inspecting it. "They smell delicious and they don't need frosting with that yummy streusel topping. You know, these would be easy to pack and ship to our distance customers." She gave a rueful smile. "That is, if we ever have any. The way things are going with the shop, we may need to set our sights on a national customer base."

Ali and I have been toying with the idea of creating a mail-order business so we could ship our baked goods all over the country. It's an exciting concept, but somehow we've never had the time to go over the logistics. Was it realistic or just a dream? I needed to take a cold, hard look at it from a business point of view before we got too involved. I wasn't really sure how our pastries would hold up in the mail. We use fresh ingredients in our baked goods, with no trace of additives or preservatives. How long would they stay fresh and tasty? This was going to take some serious thought.

"All in good time," I told her. "Besides, once Sonia's murder is solved, this cloud over the shop will disappear."

Lucinda arrived at nine o'clock on the dot, with the Harper sisters right behind her. After we were settled at the kitchen table, Lucinda pulled out the Academy yearbook, her eyes sparkling with excitement. "I found a few photos that you might find interesting. We could start with Trudy's senior picture." She placed the book in the center of the table and we all leaned forward to take a look.

"Trudy Carpenter," Minerva said. "She looks sort of quiet and subdued, doesn't she?" She pointed to a picture of solemn-looking girl with pale skin and long red hair. In this picture, Trudy was about five years older than she'd been in the photo in Clare's locket, but the high cheekbones and the wide, expressive eyes were the same. Once again, the resemblance to Sonia was striking.

"Yes, she was rather quiet," Lucinda agreed. "And she kept to herself. If you look at her activities, you'll see that she wasn't really involved with her classmates. See, nothing is listed under her name. No band, no Spanish club, no volleyball."

"Maybe she wasn't much of a joiner," Ali pointed out. "Some people enjoy spending their free time alone." She glanced at me and I nodded. I remember that Ali hadn't joined any clubs in high school and college, preferring to take long walks in the woods or curl up with a novel in front of the fire.

"She was in AP English," I pointed out.

"Yes, and I almost forgot to show you that poem she wrote." She dug into her bag and pulled out a couple of handwritten pages on lined paper. "She was quite creative. I don't know why I saved it, but something in it just touched me."

I unfolded the pages and began to read. The poem sounded like it was written by an unhappy teen, full of angst and drama, secret sorrow and broken promises. "It seems like she was going through a bad time," I said quietly. "She mentions betrayal. Did something happen in her senior year?"

"Not that I know of," Lucinda said. "Come to think of it, she did seem more withdrawn that year. Maybe it was just the idea of graduating and going on to the next stage of her life. All of her classmates were preparing for college, and it seemed Trudy had no plans at all. She might have lost her way. I was never sure why."

Ali peered over my shoulder. "Blessing, hanging over me like a cloud, swaddling, a dark shroud, a spiderweb of lies." She looked at Lucinda. "What in the world does she mean?"

Lucinda gave a helpless shrug. "I have no idea. She jumps

from idea to idea; I think she was trying to write in a stream-of-consciousness style. She certainly meanders."

"She starts out by saying 'blessing.' An odd choice of word." A frown crossed Ali's face. "'Shroud'? 'Spiderweb'? Such dark images." She paused for a moment. "Why would anyone think these were blessings?"

"Yes, it seemed strange to me, too," Lucinda said. "The images are contradictory, aren't they?" She paused to take a tiny bite of her donut cupcake. "Ali, these are brilliant," she said, brightening. "You've outdone yourself. They really do taste like a cross between a donut and a cupcake."

"Thanks," Ali told her, looking pleased. She blew out a little breath as if to shake off the depressing poem. "I'm so glad you like them. I was aiming for something like a Cronut."

"A Cronut? What in the world is that?" Rose asked.

"A cross between a croissant and a donut. They're new and very trendy. I might try out a recipe and add them to the menu someday."

"I think you've outdone yourself, my dear." Rose sipped her coffee appreciatively. "They are delicious. I'm sure they're going to be a huge hit."

"You know, I just thought of something," Minerva said, tapping her finger on the lined paper filled with Trudy's handwriting. "It could be that we're looking at this in the wrong way. The word 'blessing.' She may not have meant it in a spiritual sense, like a gift. What if she meant an actual place?"

"A place?" Lucinda asked.

"She might be referring to the town. There's a Blessing, Alabama, you know. It's about halfway between here and Tuscaloosa."

"Are you sure? That certainly puts another spin on

things." Rose delicately lifted out another cupcake. She cut it in two halves and placed one half on her sister's plate.

Minerva smiled her thanks. "Rose, dear, don't you remember that Sonia had an aunt living in Alabama? It was her mother's sister Reba, I believe. And I think the town was called Blessing."

"Reba Miller," Rose said. "Yes, I do. As I recall, Sonia was close to her aunt and thought of her as a second mother. It always surprises me that she never mentions her aunt Reba in interviews. Reba was such a big part of her life."

"Is there some reason Sonia might want to forget that part of her life?" I was puzzled at this revelation and intrigued by the mystery aunt.

"I can't imagine what it could be," Minerva said. "I never heard anything about Sonia and Reba having a falling-out or anything like that. I don't think she has any other family there, so maybe she doesn't make many trips home to Alabama."

"It seems like a closed chapter in her life," Lucinda said thoughtfully. She scanned the poem once more. "But it looks like something happened in Blessing that was hurtful. Something dark that led to secrets and betrayal. Or am I reading too much into this? Can anybody think of another interpretation?"

She brushed a loose curl out of her eyes. Lucinda is every inch the Southern lady and was wearing a snazzy navy-and-white blazer with trim white pants and white ceramic earrings. She carried a navy-and-white bag and was coordinated all the way down to her white sandals.

"It might just be that she was copying another poet," Ali said thoughtfully. "When I was that age, I thought poetry was supposed to be very heavy and tragic, so I tried to write that way. I played a lot of sad music, moped around the house, and read Sylvia Plath." She grinned. "It didn't make me more creative; it just made everyone around me depressed."

"I remember that phase," I said with a laugh. "Mom and Dad were happy it only lasted a few weeks."

"I couldn't stand it any longer," Ali admitted. "I guess I'm just a born optimist."

Our guests got up to leave and Minerva stopped downstairs to pick up some red velvet cupcakes and chocolate bridge mix. Minerva leaned over the counter and said, "I have a feeling that poem might be significant, Taylor, and I have no idea why." She hesitated and then said, "Do you think it could be something more than just a teenager being a drama queen?"

"I do," I told her. "I think there's something important here, but I can't put my finger on it. I'm so glad Lucinda brought it over," I said, handing her the package. "Actually, I have an idea I wanted to explore, but I didn't want to say anything just yet."

"Let me know what you find," she said.

"Oh, I will, that's for sure," I told her. As soon as we closed the door behind them, I turned to Ali. "Are you thinking what I'm thinking?"

"We're going to Blessing," she said without missing a beat.

19

"No listing for a Reba Miller in Blessing," Ali said a few minutes later. "There's a Floyd Miller, maybe he's a relative. And it looks like a really small town, practically a whistle-stop." She stared at the computer screen and tried not to jostle Barney, who insisted on curling up on her lap. The friendly tabby kept nudging her to pet him by bumping his head under her hand, forcing her fingers off the keyboard. She scooped him up briefly to kiss the top of his head and then replaced him in her lap. "What do you think we should do?"

I poured the last of the hazelnut coffee into a thermos and grabbed two plastic mugs.

"I think we should drive over there right now and check it out. How far is it, anyway? Didn't Minerva say it was halfway between here and Tuscaloosa?"

"It's not quite that far. I think we can be there in a couple of hours." I heard the shop door open downstairs. Dana was punctual as usual. She'd certainly exceeded our expectations for a college intern and had proven herself to be not only smart and reliable but highly creative. I decided it was time to assign her more challenging projects and give her more responsibility. Maybe even the cooking classes?

"This will be quick trip," I said idly. "We can easily get to Blessing by lunchtime and be back here in the early afternoon."

"Taylor, do you think this is a wild-goose chase? Maybe we should stay home and work on ideas for the cooking classes." *The dreaded cooking classes!* Ali must have read my mind.

I shook my head. "It's not a wild-goose chase. I think something will turn up. I'll drive and we can do some planning on the way. I've got a good feeling about what we'll find in Blessing."

Three hours later, we were trudging up Main Street in Blessing, hot and tired, and I had come to regret my hasty decision. We'd found Floyd Miller, who owned a convenience store out on the highway and lived on the edge of town. He lived practically out in the country and we had to travel down meandering dirt roads to find his white frame farmhouse. He said Reba "wasn't kin" to him, even though they had the same last name. In any case, Reba had moved away a few years earlier. No one seemed to know what had happened to her and she had no family left in Blessing.

We accepted his offer of a "Co-cola," and sat on his front porch, fanning ourselves in the noonday heat. He couldn't help us, but he was certainly chatty, sitting on his rocker spinning yarns with his hound dog, Russ, at his side. Letitia and Cyrus were his grown children, he told us, and proudly pulled out photos of his grandchildren. We dutifully admired them and minutes later, we were on our way.

It felt like a dead end.

Soon we were strolling up the main drag again with no plan in sight. Blessing was a typical Southern town, and Main Street was lined with small shops, two-story brick buildings, friendly people, and a couple of convenience stores. Not a shopping mall in sight. We passed three churches in four blocks, along with the firehouse, the sheriff's office, and a tiny library. I spotted a WELCOME sign advertising that Blessing had a population of five thousand people, was "a good town to be from," and was famous for an annual peach festival.

As we trudged along the dusty sidewalk, my mind had sputtered and stalled. My spur-of-the-moment impulse to track down Reba Miller had led nowhere, and I was at a loss as to what to do next. Maybe Trudy Carpenter's poem had no significance. Maybe Blessing had nothing to do with Trudy and she'd simply liked the sound of the name. I was ready to admit defeat when Ali broke into my thoughts.

"Now what?" she said. There was a tiny hint of exasperation in her voice and her hair was hanging limp on her neck. She pulled a rubber band out of her purse and yanked her thick blond hair back into a makeshift ponytail. The midday sun was beating down on us and my only thought was to get into someplace air-conditioned as soon as possible. The three *R*s. Regroup, review, reassess. My business school training had kicked in. Some frosty air and iced tea might jolt my brain back into action.

"Well, we have two choices. We could try the library," I suggested, "or maybe Shirley's Drop-In Diner."

Ali's eyes lit up at the word "diner" and her lips twitched.

"The diner, please! I'm starving." I should have guessed. Ali is a big fan of diners, with their wide selection of comfort food and oversized portions of homemade pie. "We might get some menu ideas for the shop. And who knows"—she raced on without taking a breath—"we might hear some interesting gossip. People in diners love to talk, don't they? Everybody knows everybody in these small towns. And everyone shows up at the diner. If we strike out, we can always hit the library after lunch."

"I hope you're right. Otherwise today has been a complete wash." I pushed open the double glass doors and was rewarded with a blast of frigid air. Heaven!

"Welcome to Shirley's," a plump waitress greeted us. "Would y'all like a booth instead of a table? We have one left in the back." She was eyeing Ali's laptop, peeking out of her tote bag, with some suspicion.

"That would be fine," I told her, following as she grabbed two enormous menus off the rack. Ali lingered to look at the array of pies in a refrigerated case, but I nudged her forward. "You can have pie later," I promised.

"Now, we do have Wi-Fi, but some days it's uncertain," our server said. So that was why she'd cast a nervous look at the laptop, I thought. I'd figured she was afraid we'd order two iced teas and spend three hours hunched over our electronic devices. Sometimes I have to remind myself not to be so cynical.

"My name's Flo," she added with a wide smile. "Would you like to hear the specials?" Without waiting for us to reply, she reeled off a dizzying selection of typical diner food. Meat loaf and mashed potatoes, mac 'n' cheese, chef's salad, club sandwich, turkey tetrazinni, chicken with dumplings, and four kinds of soups. And, of course, those ginormous pies, which were calling my name with their sugary little voices.

Ali held up her hand, laughing. "They all sound really good, Flo, but tell me, what would you recommend?"

"Well, now, that's hard to say," Flo said, sticking her pencil behind her ear. "Because I like everything on the menu. If I wanted something light, because I knew I was going to have a big dinner later on tonight, I'd have one of our new flatbreads." She opened the menu and flipped it to the back page. "We just added these and they're a big hit. It seems a lot of folks are watching their calories these days and looking for something light and tasty."

"They do sound good," Ali said. "What are your favorites?"

"The flatbread pizza with mushrooms and the spinach artichoke flatbread with feta cheese. You can't go wrong with either one and they come with side salads."

"Let's try them both, "I said. "And two iced teas, please."

When Flo had bustled away, Ali said, "We should add flatbreads to the menu at the shop. They're very trendy and a lot of cafés and restaurants in Savannah are serving them."

Flo was back in a flash with our flatbreads, and just as she predicted, they looked delicious. Business had thinned out in the diner, and I thought this might be a good time to see if we could get any local gossip. After I complimented Flo on our choices, she asked genially, "Where are you folks from? I think I recognize a Northern accent." She raised her eyebrows. "With a touch of Atlanta."

"You have a good ear," Ali told her. "We're originally from Chicago, and my sister lived in Atlanta for a while. But now we call Savannah home."

"Is that so?" Flo said, refilling our iced tea. "How do you like it there?"

"We love it," I told her. "We own a vintage candy shop called Oldies But Goodies, right off the Historic District."

"Oldies But Goodies?" Flo blinked, and I saw her eyes flicker with recognition. "I'll have to check it out the next time I'm in town," she said slowly. "When I have family visiting, we always take them to Savannah for the day. They love the Riverfront." There was dead silence and Flo bit her lip. "Well, I guess I'll just come right out and ask you—is that the place that Sonia Scott was poisoned? The name sure sounds familiar."

I glanced at Ali and saw her face crumple. Even people this far away knew that Sonia was murdered at our shop. "Sonia did die at a book signing at the shop," I said quickly. "But it's not what you think. She wasn't poisoned; she had an allergic reaction. It could have happened anywhere."

"Well, that's mighty sad. I didn't know that." Flo looked toward the front of the diner to make sure no one was waiting to be seated. "I remember her when she was a young 'un, barely out of her teens."

"You knew Sonia Scott?" Ali blurted out. "Do you mean you knew her here in Blessing?"

"Why, yes, that's exactly what I mean. I knew Sonia and I knew her aunt Reba. You couldn't find a nicer lady than Miss Reba. She'd do anything in the world for you. Now, Sonia was something of a handful when she was coming up. She needed a firm hand, and I think Reba did the best she could, but there still were some problems."

Ali and I exchanged a look. Flo was turning out to be a gold mine of information.

"Are you saying Sonia lived here?" I was surprised. I'd read Sonia's press packet, and there was no mention of Blessing. As far as I could tell, she'd grown up in Savannah and Brunswick.

"She was here for a while," Flo said, lowering her voice a notch. "She came to visit Miss Reba in the summers and stay with her. I reckon her parents couldn't handle her, so the minute school was out, she was back here in Blessing, hanging out at the local pool and flirting with all the boys. She was a looker, that's for sure, with that long red hair and slim figure."

Ali raised her eyebrows. This wasn't we'd expected. Sonia had spent her summers in a little one-stoplight town like Blessing? And how come her publicity people kept it a secret?

"Flo," I said softly, "did something happen to Sonia in Blessing?"

She paused to look out the window and ran her hand over her chin. A long beat passed. A shadow crossed her face, and I wasn't sure she was going to continue. "Something happened one summer," she said finally. "It was the last time she came to visit Miss Reba. I'd say Sonia was sixteen or seventeen at the time."

"What happened?" Ali's voice was barely a whisper. Both of us were leaning forward, straining to catch every word.

"My sister was working as a nurse at Blessing Community Hospital," Flo said. "She looked up to see Sonia walking in the front door, holding a baby. A beautiful red-haired baby. A tiny little thing, probably only a few days old." She paused and I felt a catch in my throat. "And when Sonia walked out an hour later, she didn't have the baby."

I felt like the breath had been sucked out of me. Trudy Carpenter. The red-haired baby was Trudy. But why hadn't Sonia ever claimed her as her daughter? And did Trudy ever find out the truth that her "aunt" was really her mother?

Ali looked shaken as I quickly paid the bill and left a hefty tip for Flo. I was happy to get in the car, switch on the AC, and try to make sense of all this as we drove back to Savannah.

I was silent for a moment, mulling over the latest development.

"Do you think Trudy would ever be so furious she would kill Sonia?" Ali asked. "It seems unthinkable, but . . ."

"She might have considered it the ultimate betrayal," I said. "That poem was so full of pain and longing. But Trudy as a killer? No, I don't buy it. Everyone said she was a sweet, sensitive girl back in school. I think if anything, she turned her anger inward, into depression."

"Drugs can change a person, if she really did go down that road," Ali said bluntly. She was right. Ali had known friends in college who'd succumbed to the lure of drugs and had made royal messes of their lives.

"And she's living with Reggie Knox," I said. "Could they have planned this together, or did he force her to be an accomplice?" They had different motives. Trudy may have wanted revenge and Knox probably wanted money, but it still didn't seem to fit.

"I think we need to run this by Sara and Noah," Ali said.

"Definitely. We need to touch base and compare notes. Today was a bombshell, but maybe they have some surprises, too." I glanced at my watch. We could easily be home in time to check things at the shop and then meet for dinner at one of my favorite spots in town.

"Dinner at six?" She pulled out her cell and started punching in numbers.

"It's a date."

20

Sweet Caroline's was doing a brisk business when Ali and I walked in. I spotted Noah and Sara sitting at a table in the back and gave them a little wave before being engulfed in a hug by Caroline LaCroix, the owner. Caroline, chic in that way that only French women can manage, kissed me on both cheeks. "Oh, Taylor," she said, her eyes welling with tears, "what a time you and Ali have had." She looped her arm around Ali's waist and shook her head. "I can't believe the way things turned out. Who knew a visit from Sonia Scott would end in such a disaster! *Quelle horreur!*"

"We certainly didn't," I said ruefully. "No one could have predicted it. It all went downhill at the television taping." I explained that the impromptu book signing had been arranged when Sonia's private jet had developed engine trouble. Sonia, ever the self-promoter, wanted to wring every bit of publicity out of her visit to Savannah, and had asked Olivia to set up a quick photo op. The book signing at our candy shop seemed like the perfect opportunity; who knew it would end with Sonia's death?

"I am so sorry," she said in her French accent. Caroline is an elegant woman in her mid-fifties who moved to Savannah from the south of France.

She ran a much larger restaurant with her husband, but when he passed away, she decided to close it and open the smaller Bay Street bistro. Sweet Caroline's has a friendly, relaxed vibe to it. The chalkboard menu changes daily and all the items are fresh and of high quality. Caroline's chef and sous chef go to the docks and markets each morning at the crack of dawn to secure the most flavorful fish, fruits, and vegetables.

Caroline is an excellent cook and makes the soups herself from scratch; the house specialty is a special *pistou* soup with beans from the south of France. It's so popular with the patrons that Caroline gave it a permanent spot on the menu. Unlike many restaurateurs, Caroline refuses to allow any prepackaged products in her kitchen and never reheats anything in the microwave. All Caroline's food is fresh, and labor intensive, but she wouldn't have it any other way.

"Come, let me show you to your table," she said, her voice warm with sympathy. "Your friends Noah and Sara are waiting for you. I told the sommelier to bring a very nice Pinot Grigio, compliments of the house. I think you'll enjoy it."

"Thank you, Caroline," Ali and I said in unison.

Noah stood up and gave me an appreciative glance as I scooted into my seat. I admit that I took extra care tonight, wearing a classic little black dress I'd picked up at a sample sale in town and wearing my hair loose and tousled, the way he liked it. I could tell from his expression that my efforts had paid off. I kept telling myself not to get emotionally involved with Noah again, but my heart didn't always listen to my head.

Ali is convinced Noah and I will end up together some day, but Ali is a true romantic who believes in happy endings. I'm older and a little more jaded by life. I've learned that wishing for something doesn't make it so, and that relationships can be fraught with danger. Ali falls in love at the drop of a hat, and seems to recover from failed relationships just as easily. I've learned not to give away my heart too quickly. Would I be satisfied having a deep friendship with Noah instead of a passionate love affair? Only time would tell.

"Have you brought Noah up to speed?" Ali asked Sara, as she reached for the bread basket. I opened my mouth to ask the waiter to remove the tempting basket of sliced baguettes and the little plates of seasoned olive oil, but Ali closed her hand over my wrist. "Don't even think of it," she said. "The bread stays." She had a surprisingly strong grip and I smiled to myself. When there's fresh-baked French bread involved, Ali can be surprisingly assertive.

"I wasn't, really," I teased her. "I was going to ask for two more wineglasses." She smiled at my feeble excuse. She wasn't buying a word of it.

As if he'd read my mind, the server appeared and placed two glasses on the table. "Would you like any appetizers?" he asked.

"Thanks, but we're fine for now," Noah said, waving him away. Noah hadn't taken his eyes off me since I'd sat down, and although his attention was flattering, it was also a little disconcerting. The look in his eyes made it hard to believe that he was content with the status quo: for the time being, we were just friends. Not even friends with benefits, as Ali liked to tease me. I reminded myself that this was what I'd wanted, wasn't it?

"So tell us the deets," Sara said eagerly. "You two went to some little backwater town called Blessing, and what did you find?"

"We found a story," Ali said feelingly. "Almost a Lifetime movie." She dipped a small slice of a baguette into seasoned olive oil.

"Really?" Sara looked incredulous. "Well? Are you going to keep us in suspense? What's the big event that happened in the tiny town of Blessing?"

I took up the thread of the story. "We found a chatty waitress at the local diner—"

"Always a good call," Noah said approvingly. "You'd be surprised what you can find out at a diner—who's sleeping with whom, who's running a scam, and sometimes you can even figure out who's buried a body."

"This wasn't quite that dramatic," I told him, "but we did find out that Trudy Carpenter might be Sonia's daughter, not her niece." I quickly told Ali and Noah what we'd learned about Sonia showing up at the local hospital with a baby and walking out empty-handed.

Noah whipped out his tiny notebook and a pen. "What's the name of the hospital? You say it's in a town called Blessing?"

I shook my head. "That's a dead end. The hospital closed years ago. All we have is the word of the waitress, plus the fact that Trudy is the spitting image of Sonia. She doesn't look at all like her mother, Clare Carpenter."

"Wow, you accomplished a lot," Sara said. We stopped the conversation to give our orders. Everyone wanted Caroline's signature dish of caramelized onion quiche with a side salad. And we couldn't resist asking for more of the bread rounds.

"What does this give us?" Noah said thoughtfully. "Besides a motive for Trudy—or maybe her boyfriend—to kill Sonia. They knew they'd inherit a fortune."

"What's the latest on Reggie Knox?" Ali asked. "Did the police pick him up for questioning? As far as I'm concerned, he's at the top of the suspect list."

"Actually, they did bring him in." Noah stared at me over the rim of his wineglass and I felt a little spark of pleasure coil through me. "I talked to my cousin at the Savannah PD and he said Reggie claims he has a rock-solid alibi for the time Sonia was at the book signing."

"Really?" I felt let down. I was fairly sure Reggie was involved in Sonia's murder, at least as an accomplice or a coconspirator. I just had a bad feeling about this guy, and over the years, I've learned to trust my instincts. "What's his alibi?"

Noah snorted. "The crazy thing is, he won't say. He clammed up and insisted on getting a a lawyer. They didn't have anything to hold him on, so they had to release him. If they want to bring him in again, they're going to have the PD's office assign someone to him. They really don't have any evidence he's involved in Sonia's death in any way. He's on their radar screen, but that's about it."

"I still think he's connected with her death somehow. Just a gut feeling," I murmured. "Maybe Reggie knew that Sonia was really Trudy's mother, and he was blackmailing Sonia."

"Then why would he kill her?" Sara asked. "No sense in slaughtering the goose that lays the golden egg."

"I don't know," I admitted. "Maybe she stopped payments, or something like that. Or maybe she was going to do something to land him back in jail. Is the Savannah PD looking into Sonia's financials? If there was a trail of payments going out to Reggie, that would be pretty conclusive, wouldn't it?"

"I think they're on it," Noah said. "Let's run through the suspects again," he suggested, flipping open his notebook once more. "Does anyone like Etta Mae for the crime?"

"That's a tough one," I told him. "My feeling is that she's not capable of murder, but I have to admit, she can be volatile and she had plenty of reason to resent Sonia. She really believes Sonia stole her family recipes and wants her day in court.

"It might be that Sonia was completely innocent in this whole cookbook caper and didn't know anything about it. After all, she was the head of a gigantic empire; she couldn't be responsible for keeping up with every little detail." It would be ironic, I thought, if Etta Mae was furious enough to kill over the cookbook and then ended up killing an innocent person.

We were quiet for a moment, sipping our wine when the server arrived with our dinners. We all tucked into the quiche, and for a moment, all thoughts of murder and mayhem were forgotten.

"Who else are you looking at?" Sara said, breaking the silence.

"There's Jeremy Watts," Ali said. "Sonia's lover."

"What's his motive?" Noah asked.

"I'm not sure," I admitted. "Sonia might have issued an ultimatum: marry her or else."

"But would she really want to go public with the news that she's dating a married man?" Sara said. "She's America's sweetheart. That's not going to help her image, is it?'

"No, I suppose not. And I don't think Jeremy was going to move up in the company if something happened to Sonia. It seems pretty clear to me that Olivia was the power behind the throne. She was probably going to run the company if Sonia was out of the picture."

"I think we should move Olivia up to number one on the suspect list," Sara said. "Especially if this Reggie Knox comes through with an airtight alibi. Olivia had a lot to gain." She stopped to pass a basket of bread the server had just put on the table. Between the French baguettes and dinner rolls, it was carb city.

"What do we know about his wife?" Sara asked.

"Not very much. Her name is Leslie," I volunteered. "She seems to stay out of the picture, although she did come to the taping of Sonia's show. We met her briefly, and I saw her chatting with some of Sonia's staff. Everything looked okay. She seemed friendly and pleasant."

Noah arched an eyebrow. "She was there for the taping? I'd think that would be the last thing in the world she'd want to do. Doesn't she know about the affair? I thought it was common knowledge."

"It is, but some women"—I shrugged—"just decide to look the other way. It doesn't make sense to me, but maybe that's how she's decided to play it. I suppose she had to see Sonia from time to time socially at company events, and she was okay with it. Maybe she just pretended nothing was going on. And, of course, Sonia never said a word, either. Outwardly, everything's fine."

"Sonia was something of a control freak," Ali interjected.

"So they say," I added. "Actually, Lucinda reconnected with Leslie at the taping," I said to Noah. "I think I may have mentioned this earlier, but she seemed happy to run into her. I think Lucinda feels sorry for Leslie. They didn't talk much about Jeremy, but everyone seems to know the gossip. It's no secret that Sonia had her claws in Jeremy and she wasn't going to let go of him."

I stopped talking for a moment, my thoughts buzzing. So Jeremy was cheating on his wife with Sonia. Was he also cheating on both of them with Olivia? Hadn't Jeremy and Olivia looked a little too friendly in the restaurant and outside of the taping? Or was I imagining things? I made a mental note to ask Lucinda for information on Leslie, if she had any from her Academy days. Maybe she could shed a little light on Jeremy and his affairs.

We wrapped things up quickly with promises to touch base in the next few days. Noah looked like he wanted to spend some time alone with me, but he had to meet a new client and reluctantly said good night. I nodded and told him I had to leave, too. After all, I'd promised Ali we'd spend some time on the cooking classes. I knew I'd have trouble focusing on donuts and cupcakes, but a promise is a promise.

21

Sam Stiles called the moment we walked in the door to the apartment. I hadn't heard from her, and I was eager to hear the latest developments in the case, especially the final toxicology report. What Sam said next matched perfectly with the initial findings Noah had dug up when we first started investigating Sonia's death.

"Sonia's stomach contents show no trace of peanuts, but there's evidence of sesame seeds," she said without preamble. "We sent the pastry samples off to the lab for analysis and stomach contents revealed sesame seeds along with flour, sugar, and butter. Do you know what that could be?" Sam asked. "It sounds like cookies, doesn't it?"

Shortbread cookies! That was what Lucinda brought to the book signing. And it was one of Sonia's recipes, straight out of her cookbook. Would Sonia have knowingly included sesame seeds in one of her own recipes? I immediately discounted the idea; it was impossible. She knew she was deathly allergic to peanuts, and peanut allergies and sesame seed allergies go hand in hand. Surely she would have known this. I listened as Sam went on with her description.

"Everything else seems pretty straightforward," she said. "There also was evidence of cream cheese and cherries."

"The cherry cheesecakes! That's what Ali and I made, mini–cherry cheesecakes. It's one of Sonia's favorite recipes, and it's right out of her cookbook." I hesitated, bracing myself for what could be coming. "Was there anything else?"

"It's hard to say. Nothing else was out of the ordinary. Sonia had eaten pancakes for breakfast. She'd ingested a large amount of coffee, and something that looked like lemon pudding. It was only partly digested, so she must have eaten it at the signing."

"Lemon bars," I said quickly. "That was the other recipe Ali and I prepared. And that recipe was also straight out of the cookbook."

"So there were only three types of desserts served at the book signing?"

"Yes, and they were all Sonia Scott classics. Shortbread cookies, mini–cherry cheesecakes, and lemon bars. We followed the recipes exactly."

Sam was silent. "It's really hard to see how she ingested sesame seeds accidentally, if you're sure that's all she ate at the shop."

"I know that's all she ate, because that's all we served." I wondered how this news would affect our customers. The jury was in. It was no longer possible to say that Sonia hadn't died because of what she'd eaten in our shop; in fact, it was conclusive that what she *had* eaten in our shop had killed her. I felt a wave of exhaustion wash over me. Probably mental exhaustion, because it wasn't that late.

"Anything else?" I asked, putting the kettle on to boil. I

use tea as my "calm down" and "rev up" drink. I go through phases, and at the moment I'm hooked on a spicy mix of cinnamon, cardamom, and cloves. Ali had settled herself at the kitchen table, with Barney on her lap, thumbing through a copy of *Southern Living* while I paced back and forth with the phone clasped to my ear.

"We're still keeping tabs on Reggie Knox, but I think he's off the hook for the crime."

"How come?" I stopped pacing, sank into a kitchen chair, and Ali looked up quizzically. "He was one of my top choices. Motive, means, and opportunity."

Sam laughed. "Maybe motive and means, but he didn't have opportunity. He insisted on consulting a lawyer, so we had to get one of the public defenders over to interview him. Reggie finally came clean. He was in a chat room at the time of the book signing. There's no way he could have spiked Sonia's food."

"A chat room? Can you be sure about that? Maybe someone else logged in with his name. You never know."

"We know," Sam said grimly. "He was on Skype. It was Reggie, all right."

"A chat room," I repeated. "You know what I'm thinking," I said finally. "Underage girls, sexual predator . . ."

"You might be right, but we can't nail him on anything this time. He got in and out of the chat room pretty fast, before he incriminated himself. I think he probably has done this plenty of times before; he could be a regular in the chat room. That's why he wanted to consult with a lawyer before telling us what he'd been up to. We'll certainly be on the lookout for him from now on."

"This is really a surprise." I scrawled the word "Reggie" on a pad, scratched a line through his name, and passed it to Ali. Her eyes widened and she shook her head. I'm sure she was hoping it was Reggie as well.

That left us with Olivia, Jeremy, Trudy, Leslie, and Etta Mae. Mentally, I scratched Trudy and Etta Mae off the list. I still didn't want to believe that Etta Mae was capable of murder, and I couldn't bear to think of Trudy killing her own mother. It just didn't seem right.

So we were left with Olivia and Jeremy, weren't we? If Olivia or Jeremy didn't kill Sonia, then everything was up for grabs. The murderer had to be someone who knew Sonia and knew about the nut allergy. My thoughts were going around in circles and my head started to pound.

"So we'll have to see what shakes out," Sam said. "The toxicology is clear, but without more information, the DA isn't going to be able to charge anyone. It's one of those cases that may not go anywhere." I could hear heated voices in the background with a metallic sound like a chair hitting the floor and a muffled curse.

Sam's words were nearly drowned out and I pressed the receiver closer to my ear. "Hey, put him in the holding cell," she called to someone. "He's too disruptive. If he tries anything else, we'll charge him with resisting arrest."

"Sam, are you okay?" I said worriedly. "What's going on there?" Anyone who thinks a cop's life is glamorous hasn't done a drive-along with the Savannah-Chatham Metro PD. Sara and I went along one evening when she was writing a piece on the department, and it was an experience I'll never forget.

"Sorry about the noise," Sam said. "One of our rookie cops just broke up a bar fight and dragged both the contenders back to the station house. One of them is high on something and took a swing at the arresting officer. We'll stick him in the tank to cool off before morning." She gave a harsh laugh. "A night in the drunk tank is enough to make anyone adjust their attitude."

"I hope he's okay," I said, meaning the arresting officer.

"*She*," Sam corrected me. "She's a petite little thing, probably weighs in at a hundred and ten, but she graduated first in her class at the police academy and she has a black belt in karate. I think she'll go far and move right up the ranks." Sam has mentored several female officers and takes pride in their success.

"I better let you go," I said. "It sounds like a madhouse there."

"Yeah, it's a full moon," she said with a laugh. "They're all out tonight."

"Hey, come back to the Dream Club when you can. We miss you."

"I will, just as soon as things settle down a little."

She rang off, and I gave Ali a quick recap of the conversation.

"This feels like one step forward and two steps back," she said. "Did you tell Sam about our trip to Blessing?"

"I texted it to her, earlier today. She didn't have any comment, so maybe she doesn't think it's relevant. Now that Reggie has been ruled out as a suspect, I don't think she's going to look at Trudy too carefully." Unlike on TV crime shows, real police departments are low on funds and have to allocate resources where they'll be the most effective. By spending time on leads that seem iffy, they take time away from investigating the key suspects in the case.

"It doesn't sound like it," Ali agreed.

"Tea?" I offered, deliberately changing the subject. Too much talk about murder and I'd never get to sleep tonight.

Ali shook her head. "I'm going to have hot chocolate."

Ali collects samples from all over the world. We sell a fair amount in the shop, and we've talked about adding it to our holiday menu. It would be a nostalgia thing, since it never gets brutally cold here in Savannah. But Southerners are big on tradition, and a lot of folks think it isn't Christmas unless you serve hot chocolate and a mind-bending selection of Christmas cookies.

Ali and I turned in early, and Scout surprised me by nudging open the door to my bedroom and jumping into bed. She purred like a motorboat, rubbing her head against my face before burrowing down under the covers. I smiled to myself. I guessed I was officially part of the family. Being accepted by a cat is the ultimate seal of approval.

22

Ali and I spent the next morning finalizing the fliers for the cooking classes. Dana had done an excellent job with the design: it was simple yet eye-catching, and it featured a giant, luscious-looking chocolate cupcake right smack in the middle of the page.

After much debate, we decided that the adult classes would feature cupcakes, along with multipurpose tartlets that could be used for both sweet and savory treats. The kiddie classes would rely on no-fail snacks and a fun session learning how to decorate sugar cookies. Dana had come up with some kid-friendly designs that would be easy to duplicate.

I was still concerned about the cost of the free classes—we would have to pay for all the supplies—but I hoped we would reap rewards in terms of community goodwill. We hadn't bounced back after Sonia's death, and this might be a way to lure new customers into the shop.

When the last fliers were packed in cardboard boxes for

Dana to distribute in the district, I asked her if there was anything else we could do. She brushed her glossy black hair off her face and thought for a moment. "I'd still like to do a flier and a coupon we could e-mail to our regular customers. We've collected a pretty decent mailing list from our promotions, and it wouldn't cost anything." Her tone was hopeful; she knew we were almost operating in the red.

"I think that's an excellent idea," I told her. "What will we say in the e-mail?"

"Something along the lines of: *We've missed you! Please come back and see our new menu and have a cookie on the house.* Something like that."

"I love it!" Ali's enthusiasm was infectious. "Taylor, isn't that just the most clever thing you've ever heard of?" She gave Dana a quick hug. "What would we do without you? I don't want you to ever graduate from college," she said feelingly.

"Unless she comes to work for us after graduation," I said. "This time as a paid employee."

"That would be nice," Dana admitted. I knew she was struggling to make ends meet and worked in the university bookstore to help defray her tuition costs. I admired her talent and energy; she showed a lot of initiative and seemed to genuinely love the shop. It was more than just a job for Dana—it was a passion.

Dana left on her rounds, and Ali and I were idly unpacking a new shipment of gummy bears when Lucinda Macavy stopped by. "Glad I caught you," she said, perching on a stool and helping herself to lemonade. "I've got out-of-town relatives arriving tomorrow night and I'm pressed for time. I'm planning a small dinner party for eight people. What would you recommend in the way of snacks and desserts?"

"Well, that depends on what you're planning for dinner," Ali said.

"Oh, what I always have: a nice roast with potatoes and carrots, peas, corn, and some corn bread, or maybe homemade dinner rolls. Men always like meals like that—simple, you know." She blushed a little and I suddenly got the picture.

"Lucinda," I said, "are you inviting Edward Giles to your dinner party?"

Her eyes widened and she blushed. "Why, Taylor, you are positively psychic. How could you possibly know that?"

"Just a lucky guess," I murmured. "I think that's a wonderful idea. He seems to be at loose ends, doesn't he? A bit of a recluse?"

"Well, I'm not so sure about that. I think he's just shy. I hope the Dream Club will bring him out a little, give him a reason to socialize."

"Do you think he's going to stick with the club?" Ali asked. "I had the feeling he was on the fence about it. I'm not sure he even believes in dream interpretation."

"Oh, I think he will. He asked if he could meet me for coffee and loan me another dream interpretation book, and that's when I got the idea of asking him over dinner. He seemed ever so pleased; I don't think he gets too many invitations."

"I think you're right." A customer came into the shop and Ali jumped up to greet her. "What are you serving to drink with your dinner, Lucinda?"

"White wine," she said quickly. "My relatives are bringing it. I know you're supposed to serve red wine with meat, but they prefer white. Do you think that will be all right?" She bit her lip. "I suppose I could ask Edward what he likes to drink, but what if he doesn't drink at all, and disapproves of drinking?"

I tried not to smile. "Lucinda, I don't think there's much danger of that. This is a university town, after all, and Edward must go to some events on campus—faculty parties, things like that. I'm sure he's not going to be shocked by the sight of white wine, if that's what you're worried about."

Lucinda sighed. "I guess I'm making too big a thing of this dinner party, aren't I?"

"I think you should just relax and expect all your guests to have a wonderful time. Now," I said briskly, "how about some cheese straws for an hors d'oeuvre and a nice lemon pie for dessert. The lemon pie is light and tangy, not overly sweet, and it will go well with the rest of your menu. I'll take it right out of the freezer and you can let it defrost at home. Keep it in the refrigerator overnight and it will be perfect for tomorrow."

I reached into the freezer and pulled out a pie and a plastic bag of cheese straws. The cheese straws, along with the homemade potato chips, had become one of our most popular menu items.

"I think it sounds perfect," she said.

I figured this was a good time to broach the subject of Leslie Watts. It was unlikely that Lucinda had any information that would be helpful, but it was worth a try.

"Lucinda, when you invited Leslie Watts home for a cup of tea, did she confide in you about anything?"

"Confide in me?" Lucinda looked puzzled. "I don't know what you mean."

"I mean, did she talk about anything that was troubling her, her marriage, her family life, anything like that?" I knew I was grasping at straws, and Lucinda shook her head.

"Oh, heavens, nothing like that. We just chatted about her days at the Academy and what her former classmates were up to. It was mainly a lot of reminiscing, you know. I love hearing about my students' careers and families. Sometimes I wish I'd never retired," she said sadly. "My life seemed a lot fuller when I was headmistress. It was hectic, but there was never a dull moment."

"I'm sure your students have a lot of fond memories about those days," I said. "By the way, did Leslie happen to say anything about Sonia?"

Lucinda patted her hair. I could tell she'd just been to the beauty shop because her light brown curls made a perfect frame to her face. There was a long pause, and I wondered if she was trying to decide how much to reveal. "Nothing really," she said finally. "She told me that her husband Jeremy travels a lot, but I suppose it goes with the territory. She seemed to accept the fact that his job would take him away from his family from time to time, and I suppose she makes the best of it."

I felt like I'd hit a dead end. Either Leslie hadn't said anything of consequence or Lucinda felt duty bound not to betray a confidence. Still, I wasn't surprised that Leslie wouldn't confide in Lucinda. She hadn't seen the former headmistress in years, and she probably felt it would be inappropriate to lay her personal concerns on her.

I tried one more tack. "When you met with Edward," I began tentatively, "did he tell you anything about his personal life? He doesn't reveal very much about himself at the Dream Club meetings, you know. I have to admit, I'm a bit curious about him. I wonder if he's as much of a loner as I think he is?"

Lucinda smiled. "He's rather reticent, isn't he? But I admire that in a man. You know, in this day and age, people go around telling perfect strangers their business. In my day, you kept your problems to yourself. It seems more dignified somehow."

I sighed. I was getting nowhere with Lucinda, and there was no sense in badgering her for more information.

"I suppose you're right, Lucinda, I hadn't really thought of it that way. Let me ask a little favor of you."

"Of course, anything," she said brightly.

"If you do happen to hear anything more about Sonia from either Leslie or Edward Giles, will you tell me about it? As long as you're not breaking a confidence," I added quickly.

"Why, of course, I will, Taylor." She smiled. "But I don't think Leslie is one to gossip. She's just the sweetest girl, and we had had such a nice chat that evening. She even helped me in the kitchen. We're all trying to solve this case together, aren't we? I'm sure if either Leslie or Edward knew anything that might be helpful, they'd be glad to come forward with it." Her smile was so bright and genuine, I didn't dare tell her that I seriously doubted it.

"That was sweet, wasn't it?" Ali said a few minutes later, when Lucinda had left. "It seems that Lucinda has a 'gentleman caller.'"

"Yes, it was." I hesitated. "I didn't have the heart to tell her about the news from Sam about the cookies."

"But Lucinda won't think she's responsible, will she? No one has any idea where the sesame seeds came from." Ali said, sorting out a giant package of jelly beans. She'd decided to make a display and was arranging swirls of red, orange, and yellow in a sunset pattern. Dana had arranged green and blue Jelly Bellies in an ocean wave pattern and glued them onto a styrofoam board covered with fabric. All we needed was a sunset and a palm tree, and we'd have a homemade mosaic. Very eye-catching and perfect for the front window.

"There were only three kinds of desserts served at the signing," I reminded her. "Lucinda's cookies, the mini–cherry cheesecakes, and the lemon bars. Sonia had pancakes for breakfast at the hotel before coming here, and I'm pretty sure the hotel is off the hook."

"Why's that?"

"Because Sonia's allergy was really severe. The effects would be immediate, according to the coroner. If the sesame seeds had been in the pancakes, she would have collapsed in the hotel dining room; she never would have made it to the book signing."

"A cloud is going to hang over the shop until this is settled, isn't it?" Ali said softly. "It's very hard to change people's perceptions, even when they're wrong. I e-mailed a few of our former customers, and no one has gotten back to me. It's like there's a curse on me," she said wryly. "I feel about as welcome as the Angel of Death."

I understood exactly how she felt. It was impossible to estimate how much of a hit we'd taken because of Sonia's death. We both knew of restaurants that had gone out of business because of health scares—real or imagined—and this was our greatest fear. No matter how often we told people that Sonia had died of a food allergy, we always got the same response: a look of shock and incredulity, quickly followed by a slight shake of the head. They didn't seem to believe a word of it.

We had to turn things around and quickly. When Lucinda called later that day to say she had something to show the Dream Club, I jumped at the chance to schedule an emergency meeting for the following evening.

23

By the next morning, it was clear that Dana's fliers were a huge success. Ali started scheduling guests for the Toddler Chef cooking classes, and twelve members of a local book club signed up for The Magic of Cupcakes. Ali and I had agreed that adult classes should be limited to a dozen participants and the kiddie classes would only have eight.

I still was having visions of little kids in chefs' hats merrily spreading chocolate frosting over everything; I pictured sheer chaos. Ali swore she would keep everything under control, and she enlisted Dana to help her manage the supplies and work with the kiddies. I warned Ali that unless she wanted to completely embarrass me, she would assign me a very easy cooking project.

"The cupcake class!" she said happily. "You know how to make cupcakes, right?"

"From a mix?"

"From scratch!" Dana looked appalled. "Why would we

teach anyone to make cupcakes from a mix? They can figure that out for themselves. All you have to do is read the directions."

"I had the feeling you'd say that." I bit back a sigh. "Okay, what exactly will this entail?"

"Oh, it's easy and it's fun," Ali said with a grin. "We'll do two kinds, vanilla and chocolate, and then use a nice buttercream frosting before we decorate them. Buttercream is so versatile, and it really holds up well."

"Buttercream frosting. I assume that doesn't come in a can?"

"You assume correctly," she said primly. "No canned frostings or cake mixes allowed in this kitchen. Canned frosting would never work; it would collapse. Sometimes people try to thicken it with powdered sugar, but that never works. Besides, if you're going to use powdered sugar, you might as well do it right and make frosting from scratch. That way it's guaranteed to turn out perfectly, every time."

"Got it," I agreed. I remembered that Ali had watched a cooking show with Cheryl Day from Back in the Day Bakery here in Savannah. Cheryl had made some delicious vanilla cupcakes with buttercream frosting and had used a piping bag to create beautiful swirls. How did she do it? It seemed a bit intimidating, but maybe with practice, I'd catch on.

"How are you at rosettes?" Ali asked, thumbing through a copy of Cheryl Day's cookbook.

"Rosettes?" I asked blankly. She pushed a colorful photo of a chocolate cake toward me. It was a masterpiece, a towering delight of dark chocolate, topped with three roses: one lavender, one yellow, and one pink. The cake looked so beautiful, I couldn't imagine anyone actually cutting into it.

"These are rosettes," Ali said, tapping the page with her

fingernail. "See how delicate they are, and how the green leaves really make them look more dramatic against the dark chocolate frosting? You can add just a few rosettes to the top of the cake, or you can cover the entire cake with rosettes. I'm thinking we'll do just one rosette on each cupcake. They're pretty, aren't they?" She turned the page, revealing a dozen perfect cupcakes in rainbow colors, each topped with a perfect rose.

I was so out of my element, I could only nod appreciatively. "Yes, they're gorgeous"—I swallowed hard—"but you have to understand, this stuff is way above my level." *Rosettes with pretty petals and delicate green leaves—is she kidding?*

"But you have to start someplace," Ali protested. "And look at all these cupcakes with the beautiful swirls. Cheryl Day is a genius."

"How do you usually frost your cupcakes?" Dana asked, as if this was something I did every day. I squinted and tried to remember the last time I'd made cupcakes. I think I was ten years old, back in Indiana. And naturally, I'd used a mix. A box of cake mix, a can of frosting, and I made enough Halloween cupcakes for everyone in my class. Nothing fancy. Just basic chocolate cupcakes with vanilla frosting that was tinted orange with food coloring. Except I used too much food coloring and the resulting color looked like Cheetos.

"Well, first, I would spread frosting on them with the back of a spoon," I began. I didn't confess that sometimes I licked the spoon as I worked. Some secrets should remain buried.

"I remember you doing that. The cupcakes weren't too pretty, but we had fun, didn't we?" Ali smiled at me. "You can't get good coverage with the back of a spoon, though," she added, on a more serious note.

"And you certainly can't get a nice swirl design," Dana chimed in. I was outvoted; it was two against one.

"And then sometimes I would just dunk the top of the cupcake into the bowl of frosting," I admitted as the memory of my mother's kitchen came into focus. "If I was in a hurry."

Ali and Dana nodded their heads sadly. I think they realized they had their work cut out for them. "I can see we have some catching up to do," Ali said soberly. "That's okay, we have a couple of days before the cooking classes start. Dana and I can walk you through it."

"Don't worry, you'll pick it up really fast," Dana said. I don't think she believed a word of it, but it was nice of her to be encouraging.

"Did you say Lucinda was coming over early tonight?" I was making a fresh pitcher of iced tea and vacuuming the living room in preparation for the Dream Club meeting that was starting in twenty minutes.

"Yes, she has something she wants to show us. She didn't want to talk about it over the phone. She said it was something of a surprise and it may—or may not—be significant."

"How mysterious. Did she seem worried or upset?" I found myself wishing Lucinda had given us a hint and wondered if her surprise had something to do with the case.

"No, not at all." Ali shrugged and lifted Barney off the sofa. "But you never know with Lucinda. It could be nothing; she might want to show us some new drapery fabric. Or it could be something important." She moved Scout from the armchair to the rug in front of the fireplace. The cats seem to sense when we're having company and immediately snare the comfiest spots in the room. I always have to go over the furniture with a roll of tape before guests arrive.

I left a quick message for Noah and arranged some raspberry thumbprint cookies on a plate along with tiny squares of German chocolate brownies. If the brownies were a hit, I planned on adding them to the menu downstairs.

Noah was something of a puzzle. I hadn't heard from him in the past few days, and he hadn't answered my last couple of texts. Was he busy working a case, or was there something going on in his life?

I was debating what the next step with Noah should be when I heard Lucinda coming up the stairs. I always leave the downstairs door unlocked for our Dream Club guests, and Lucinda called out a cheery hello when she reached the landing.

"I have something to show you," she said, her eyes shining with excitement. She pulled a yearbook out of a paper bag. "This was quite a surprise. You never know what you're going to find when you go poking around in the attic."

"What is it?" Ali said, hurrying over. She motioned for Lucinda to take a seat on the sofa and poured her a glass of iced tea.

"One of my friends taught at Centreville High School, and we retired at the same time last year. She wanted me to see some photos of her retirement party, and she also brought along an old school yearbook. I took a few minutes to leaf through it, and who do I see but William Giles!"

"William Giles?"

"Edward Giles's nephew," she said, the words tumbling out in a rush. "Remember when Edward talked about that weird nightmare he had about his nephew? This is William, the nephew. He even looks a lot like Edward, doesn't he? A young version of Edward."

"Are we sure this is the same William Giles?" Ali asked.

"Yes, of course I am." Lucinda raised her eyebrows and

there was a slight edge to her voice. "Look. William wrote about the most influential person in his life, and it's none other than his uncle Edward Giles." She paused and locked eyes with me. "*Our* Edward Giles," she said. "William was the class valedictorian and they printed his graduation address in the yearbook."

"It sounds like Edward was instrumental in him getting into college," I said, my eyes scanning the speech. "He's been involved with him every step of the way and guided him into a career."

"Keep reading," Lucinda said with a cat-that-swallowed-the-canary smile. "Look where William did his college internship."

I read the next paragraph and my mind did a cartwheel. "'Next year, William Giles plans to be an intern at Sonia Scott, Inc. He's looking forward to working in her broadcast division and will be a crew member on her TV show.'"

"Edward's nephew worked for Sonia and he never said a word? How is that possible?"

Lucinda shot me a puzzled glance. "Well, you know we agreed that he's reticent," she said mildly. "I suppose he doesn't want anyone to know his business."

"But this is important," I sputtered. "I can't believe he sat here listening to us talk about Sonia's murder and he never volunteered this information."

"Why should he?" Lucinda countered. "It couldn't possibly be relevant to the case." She hesitated. "Besides, his nephew isn't working for Sonia's company anymore. He was only there for a very brief time."

"How do you happen to know that?" Ali asked.

"I spoke to his former teacher, of course. She read all about it on TMZ. Apparently they wrote a rather unflattering story about Sonia and described her as a diva. They mentioned

William Giles as an example of what happens when Sonia blackballs someone." *TMZ? Lucinda never fails to amaze me.* She sipped her iced tea. "I was hesitant to mention this, because one should never speak ill of the dead. At least that's the way I was brought up—"

"Yes, yes." I cut her off. The rest of the Dream Club would be here shortly, and I wanted Lucinda to cut to the chase. "Lucinda, I don't mean to be rude, but please go on with your story." I tapped my watch. "The rest of the group will be here any second and I'd like to hear why he left Sonia."

"Well, that's the part that's a bit unsavory," she began.

"Unsavory?" Ali exchanged a look with me.

"I mean, it makes Sonia sound rather unkind. Not a very nice person," she said, shaking her head. "It seems that William was working on a technical crew and hoped to become a lighting designer. I think that's what they're called. Of course, the competition is fierce in television; there are very few jobs open."

"Yes, I know," Ali said, sneaking a peek at the kitchen clock. "But what happened?"

"Poor William made a mistake in rehearsal. Somehow he pressed the wrong buttons and the whole set went dark. It wasn't a live show; it was just a rehearsal, you understand. So it wasn't a complete disaster, but Sonia went absolutely ballistic and fired him on the spot. She said that the episode would have to be reshot and since it was nearing the end of the day, the cast and crew would be paid overtime. What a mess for William. He was so apologetic. He begged her to reconsider, but she went storming off to her dressing room to cool down. That was the last he ever saw of her."

"It sounds dreadful," Ali said sympathetically. She pumped up the pillows and sat on the sofa. "It must have been a terrible blow to an ambitious young man. Of course, everyone has some setbacks in their career. I suppose he went on to find another job in television?'

"Oh no, my dear, that's the whole point of the story. He never could get another job. Sonia was very powerful, you see. She told him he would never work in broadcasting again, and she was right. She blackballed him. Very vindictive of her. She made sure that no one hired him. It must have been devastating for him."

"That's awful," I burst out. "Anyone can make a mistake."

"Not if they want to keep working for Sonia's company," Lucinda said, raising her eyebrows. "There's no forgiveness, no going back."

24

A few minutes later, everyone gathered in our apartment, and the meeting began. All the members, including Detective Sam Stiles, showed up tonight. She arrived a few minutes late, gave an apologetic wave, and squeezed in next to Persia.

I half expected Edward Giles not to make an appearance, but he was right on time and snared a seat next to Lucinda. He cast shy glances at her from time to time, and it was obvious that he was attracted to her. I was wondering how I would broach the subject of his nephew and his association with Sonia's company when Lucinda beat me to it.

Without preamble, she opened the yearbook and showed it to Edward. "Edward," she said quietly, "I was surprised to learn that your nephew William worked for Sonia Scott." She smiled at him. "It must have been an exciting experience for him. I was surprised you didn't tell us about it."

Edward looked at the yearbook photo, turned beet red, and

began to sputter. "How did you—" He broke off and rubbed his chin with his hand. "Yes, he did," he said, his tone angry, defensive. "It wasn't for very long, though. I didn't think it was worth mentioning." He quickly grabbed a glass of iced tea and chugged half of it.

Everyone stopped chattering and stared at him. Usually we have a few minutes of socializing before getting down to business, but the group members seemed to sense that something important was happening. Etta Mae licked her lips and leaned forward in her chair, straining to hear every word. The Harper sisters exchanged a puzzled look, and Persia sat back with a self-satisfied expression on her face as if she'd known what was coming. I was surprised at her reaction and decided to ask her about it after the meeting. Sybil lifted her shoulders in a shrug and reached for a cookie, her expression serene. Maybe she'd seen the whole thing in a dream? As a dream-hopper, she certainly was capable of dropping in on one of Edward's dreams.

Lucinda didn't let him off the hook, and I decided to sit back and enjoy the show. "But, Edward, it's so exciting. Not many people have the opportunity to work in show business. You must be so proud of him. Where is he working now? Did he leave Sonia's and start work on another television show?"

Edward let out a long slow breath and clenched and unclenched his fingers. "He's working in a bank," he said shortly. "And no, there's nothing exciting about it, except the pay is good and he has a real chance of advancement." He set his iced tea back on the coffee table and looked directly at Lucinda. "Yes, I'm very proud of him. That young man has suffered some serious setbacks and could have let himself spiral down into depression, but he pulled himself together and made a different life for himself."

"Well, that's good to hear," Lucinda said brightly. "All's well that ends well, isn't it?"

"I suppose so," Edward said grumpily. It was clear Edward wasn't going to say another word about his nephew, despite Lucinda's prodding, so Ali called the meeting to order and asked if anyone had anything to report.

"Tell us about the cooking classes," Etta Mae said. "I saw a flier on a bench in Forsyth Park. Can anyone come?"

"Yes, of course," Ali told her. "And there's no charge, not for the classes or the supplies. I think it will be fun!" she added in a burst of enthusiasm. "Be sure to pick up a sign-up card as you leave tonight, if you're interested. The classes are filling up so quickly, and we're keeping them small, because we want to give a lot of personal attention to each student."

"Well, I think it's a fine idea," Etta Mae said. "Your baked goods are excellent," she said, biting into a lemon tart. "And as you know, I come from a long line of Southern cooks, so that's high praise indeed."

"Etta Mae," Minerva said suddenly, with a keen expression on her face, "what's the latest with your case? Or do you have one? I remember you said Persia was going to arrange a meeting for you."

"Yes, she did," Etta Mae said, smiling her thanks at Persia. "Persia really came through for me. I met with one of the attorneys at her firm yesterday morning and he was very encouraging. He wants to look into the case a little more before giving me his opinion, but he said I have every reason to feel positive. And he's not charging me; that's the best part."

"Adam Lloyd is taking the case on a contingency basis," Persia explained. "If he wins the case for Persia, he takes a percentage of the settlement, but if he loses, then she doesn't owe him a penny."

"That seems like a smart way to operate," Edward interjected. "When William left Sonia's company, I thought of sending him to a lawyer specializing in employment issues, but he wouldn't hear of it. I suppose he just wanted to get out and put the whole nasty business behind him."

His tone was so bitter that Rose Harper looked up in surprise. "Good heavens, did something go wrong when he worked for Sonia? I thought he left to take another opportunity."

There was a long, uncomfortable silence. "Well, I probably shouldn't discuss it," Edward said, his mouth turned down in a scowl. "But since the cat's out of the bag, he didn't leave under ideal circumstances. Let's just leave it at that." He lifted up his glass and then set it down with a thump. "That woman—that woman," he said, his voice shaking with anger. "She changed the whole course of William's life and destroyed everything he'd worked for."

"I'm so sorry to hear that," Rose said softly.

"I'll never forgive her, never," Edward added, his voice heavy with emotion. "William is a fine young man and he believes in letting bygones be bygones, but I don't share that view."

"An eye for an eye," Persia said knowingly.

"That's right!" Edward looked at her in surprise. "That's exactly how I feel. William worked so hard to achieve what he wanted, and he chose a very competitive field. When he left Sonia's show, he left under a cloud."

"What happened?" Dorien asked bluntly. Tact has never been her strong suit, and she made no effort to soften her tone.

"I'd prefer not to get into all that," Edward said. "Let's just say William made a small mistake, the kind of thing anyone could do, and Sonia was furious. She fired him on the spot."

I glanced at Lucinda. The story certainly jibed with what she'd told me earlier.

"Sonia was a very powerful woman," Sybil said thoughtfully. "I suppose she wouldn't give him a reference for another job?"

"Right you are!" Edward burst out. "Not only did she refuse to give him a reference, she made sure he never worked in television again. All those people know each other, you see, and connections are everything. A word from Sonia could make or break someone's career." He snapped his fingers with such a loud cracking sound that Barney woke up from his nap with a frightened squeal. "His career went right down the drain, just like that," Edward said, staring morosely into his glass.

There was an awkward pause and I was at a loss for words. Finally, Ali broke the tension by saying, "That's horribly sad, Edward. I wish we could help you and especially William. Is there anything we could do?"

"No, no, that's quite all right." He waved his hand dismissively. "I just have to learn to accept it the way William does. Please forgive me," he said earnestly, looking at Lucinda. "These are just the grumblings of an old man. Let's go on with the Dream Club. I could use a change of subject and I'm sure everyone else could, too."

We immediately moved on to dream reports, but I found myself staring at Edward, remembering the strange, disconnected expression on his face when Sonia collapsed in the shop. His expression was so blank, it was almost as though he was willing himself not to react.

Could he possibly be someone we should consider as a suspect? Until Lucinda found that yearbook, I never thought Edward had any connection with Sonia, and even now, I still found it hard to believe that he would be capable of murder. And how would killing Sonia help his nephew? It wouldn't change a thing. It sounded as though Sonia had done as much damage to William's career as she could and her blackballing him had a permanent effect. There was no way to undo it.

Etta Mae also had a strange look on her face that day, I remembered. A small, gloating smile that twisted her features in a way that made me shudder. I couldn't tell if she was surprised, or if she was just happy that something had happened to a woman she considered her archenemy. I still wasn't certain Etta Mae would have a strong enough motive for murder. Did it really help her case that Sonia was dead? It seemed that Etta Mae was going forward with her lawsuit against the company, and thanks to Persia, she even had a good lawyer on her side. So any anger or resentment she felt at the time should have dissipated by now.

The dreams tonight were nothing out of the ordinary. Sybil did one of her dream-hopping experiences and talked about a troubled young girl who was torn between two boys in her high school class. "High drama," Sybil said with a self-deprecatory laugh. "You'd think I'd find a way to drop in on something important. This poor girl was completely obsessed over whether she'd make cheerleader and which boy would ask her to the prom."

"You really have no way to control it, do you?" Etta Mae asked. "Because this is a skill I sure would like to learn. If I knew what people were dreaming about, I'd know what they were thinking. I'd have a huge advantage over them," she said with a cackle.

"I don't think you can learn it," Dorien cut in. "It seems like it's some sort of gift, like being psychic or clairvoyant. You either have it or you don't."

"I don't know what I'd do if I had that gift," Lucinda said.

"I think I'd feel overwhelmed with the responsibility. Sybil, do you ever know the people whose dreams you visit?"

"Sometimes." Sybil shifted uncomfortably and I immediately thought that maybe she had dreamt about someone in the room.

"Wow, I didn't know that," Dorien said. "Do you ever tell them?"

"Oh, heavens, no," Sybil said, flushing. "That would be too embarrassing. What if they thought I did it deliberately? I don't do it on purpose," she added quickly, "but I wouldn't want people to get the wrong idea. They might think I'm stalking them."

"Oh, well, I didn't think of that," Dorien countered. "I suppose it could be awkward."

"Very," Sybil said tartly and folded her hands neatly in her lap to signal that the conversation was over and she wanted to move on.

The other dreams were fairly mundane and Sam Stiles had nothing to share. "When I'm under a lot of stress, I tend not to dream," she said wearily. "It's like my brain wants to shut down completely and give me a few hours of oblivion. Does anyone else feel that way?"

"Oh, heavens, yes," Lucinda said. "It can go either way. When I'm upset, I have these awful 'rescue' dreams. There are always cats or puppies in trouble, and it's up to me to save them."

"Probably from your days at the Academy," Persia noted. "The kitties and puppies probably represent your former students."

"That could well be," Lucinda said. "And sometimes it goes the other way. When I'm really troubled by something, my head hits the pillow and I go out like a light for eight hours straight. I always feel so much better when I wake up."

"I have the same experience," Sam piped up. "It's almost like my brain reboots itself, like a computer. I wake up energized, ready to take on the day."

"I don't suppose you can tell us any news about the investigation?" Dorien asked. Her tone was polite and conciliatory. I think she's a little afraid of Sam. Sam can be just as blunt and direct as Dorien, and she's not afraid to tell Dorien off if she feels she's stepped over the line.

"Afraid not." She threw me a quick look, and I wondered if she planned on staying after the meeting and giving us an update.

"Oh, speaking of poor Sonia," Minerva said, "I completely forgot that I have some photos of the book signing to show everyone."

"The shop looks so nice," her sister Rose added. "I thought you might like to have them, Ali. We can make copies."

While Minerva dug into her purse for the photos, I asked, "Who took the photos? I didn't think anyone on Sonia's staff came equipped with a camera that day."

"Oh, they didn't," Minerva said. "This is from Mrs. Martha Whittaker. She's a longtime friend of ours and she snapped them with her camera. Her grandson gave her one of these point-and-click cameras for her birthday, and you'll be surprised at how clear the photos are." She finally dug out a manila envelope and spread the photos on the coffee table.

"Wow, these are lovely," Ali said. "Look Taylor, here's a shot of the window display and here's a nice one of Sonia smiling at the guests."

"Look, here's Bernice Tuckerman," Persia said. "She used to work at the law firm with me. I'd love to have a copy of one of these, if I may."

"Of course, we'll have copies made for anyone who wants them. Someone start a list. I've numbered the photos on the back."

As we passed the photos around, Lucinda said suddenly, "Oh, this is my favorite. Sonia is answering a question. Look how happy she is and the people in the front row are smiling at her."

The photo made the rounds and when it reached Sam, she gasped. "How did we miss this?" she said in a strangled voice.

"Miss what, my dear?" Minerva asked calmly.

"The drink! Sonia's holding a cardboard coffee cup."

"I don't think so," Rose said, "I remember she was drinking iced tea at the signing. At least, that's what Ali and Taylor served that day."

"We did," I said slowly, leaning forward to see the photo. "But I don't know that Sonia actually drank any of it. Where did this cup come from?"

Minerva dug into her giant purse again and pulled out a magnifying glass. "Here, your eyes are better than mine," she said, handing it to Ali.

"Java Joe's," Ali said, squinting at the photo. "That's the little coffee shop right next to the hotel. Sonia had breakfast at the hotel, but she must have stopped by Java Joe's and grabbed a cup of coffee to go."

"I can't believe we overlooked this," Sam said. She looked pale and exhausted and I knew she'd been working overtime at the precinct. "I'm positive this paper cup wasn't in any of the crime scene photos."

"Is it important?" Rose asked.

Sam ran her fingers through her short, curly hair. "I have no idea." She gave a short laugh. "But it adds another element to the mix, doesn't it? We need to find that coffee cup."

"What can you do?" Ali asked.

"Can I borrow this photo?" Sam asked Minerva. When Minerva nodded, she said, "I'm going to see if the CSIs remember seeing this paper cup at the scene. They certainly would have bagged it, unless somehow it got overlooked. Maybe someone dumped it, but we took all the trash with us. I gave very clear orders on bagging all the trash. I have no idea why it's in the picture, but it didn't show up in the evidence."

I thought guiltily of us inviting the Dream Club upstairs to the apartment for an impromptu meeting right after Sonia was taken away. Should I have thought to shoo everyone out the door to preserve the crime scene? In hindsight, it would have been the wise thing to do. But at that time, we didn't know the downstairs was a crime scene. As far as we knew, Sonia had died of natural causes. It had seemed perfectly normal to want to join together after such a traumatic event.

"I think we may be overlooking something. Are there any photos of her actually *drinking* the coffee?" Sybil asked. "It looks like it's just sitting there in front of her." *A good question. Maybe Sonia bought the coffee and brought it to the shop, but never drank it during the book signing.*

"I don't think so." Ali swept up all the photos and riffled through them as if she were shuffling a deck of cards. "In fact, I think this is the only photo that even shows the coffee cup."

We went back to our dream discussion then, but Ali looked worried and preoccupied. I think she was feeling the same emotion I was: guilt. Had we made Sam Stiles's job a lot harder by not preserving the evidence?

But how could we have known? Sonia's collapse was so sudden and shocking, we weren't thinking clearly. Our focus was on getting Sonia to the hospital as quickly as possible.

Somehow I couldn't shake the gray cloud hanging over me, and I was happy when the meeting was over and the members filed out. Sam received an urgent phone call on the landing, so she left immediately. If she really had some inside knowledge she wanted to share with us, it would have to wait until the following day.

25

The next morning, I debated whether or not to call Noah. Again. I'd already left two messages and the idea of leaving another one seemed, well, *needy* somehow. The shop was going to open in ten minutes and I was restocking a rainbow assortment of Necco Wafers. I love their Easter-egg colors and was trying to figure out something creative to do with them when Ali spoke up.

"You really should call him, you know." Sometimes she can read my mind. It's uncanny, and it usually happens when I feel troubled or indecisive about something. Ali seems to have a sixth sense, and her protective instincts kick in, even though I'm the older sister. I gave a slow, deliberate shrug as if I had no idea what she was talking about. "Him," she added pointedly. "Call him. Noah." A long beat. "You know you want to. Don't be so stubborn."

"Ah, Noah," I said innocently, as if the thought had never crossed my mind. "Yes, I suppose I could." I gave up on the

Necco Wafers. Dana would be here any minute, and she was a genius at display. I'd let her tackle them.

I watched as Ali wrote today's specials on a blackboard with colored chalk. Flatbread pizzas; Mediterranean panini with black olives, artichokes, and Feta cheese; and a light version of Ali's favorite potato soup that was catching on fast. And, of course, cheese soup served in a bread bowl. Ever since we'd added soups and sandwiches to our menu, we'd attracted some street traffic. "You're letting your pride get in your way," Ali said softly. She let out a little breath as if she was tempted to say more but was holding her peace for the moment.

"I don't think so," I said, pretending I really didn't care either way. The trouble is, I did care, and when I didn't hear from Noah for a while, my mind zipped down dark paths. What did I really want from him? One day, in a fit of exasperation, he'd asked me that. I'd replied that I wanted us to be friends, but deep down, I wondered if I really wanted something more.

Did I want to go back to the hot romance we'd once shared? It was a crazy-making, exciting time, being in love with Noah. Like walking on a tightrope with no net. Every step was fraught with danger, with the potential of plunging to the earth. So why did I want to go back to that? I couldn't even answer my own question. Every time I thought about Noah, my thoughts were more confused than ever. Maybe the best thing to do would be to just dive into my work at the shop and put all romantic notions aside for the time being. *Que cera, cera*, as Ali is fond of saying.

"He's not ignoring you, you know. He always gets involved when he's working on a case. He develops tunnel vision, and everything else flies out of his head."

"Is he working on a new case? Besides Sonia's death, I mean?"

"I'm sure he is. I spoke to Sara briefly a couple of days ago and she said he's right in the middle of a big harassment case. She didn't know too many details, but it sounded like it was very high profile."

"What sort of harassment?"

"One of those he-said-she-said cases. He's doing a lot of collateral interviews, trying to figure out the background of both the parties involved. He's convinced it's not an isolated incident."

Dana arrived a few minutes later and immediately took charge of stocking the shelves, putting her own stamp on things. "Shall I make a pot of tea?" she asked. I'd been so absorbed thinking about Noah, I'd forgotten to put out tea and cookies for the customers.

"Yes. Let's make it iced tea; we could try some of that spiced ginger tea Ali ordered."

"Sounds good."

When Lucinda dropped by a few minutes later, we were debating the merits of adding more salads to the café menu. Dana was opting for smoked turkey salad with candied pecans and cranberries and Ali had her heart set on a marinated fennel and red onion salad she'd sampled at a party. I told her I wasn't sure about the fennel and wanted to do a taste test.

"Good morning, ladies," Lucinda called out cheerfully. "I can tell you're all busy, so I'm just going to pick up one of those cookie stamps you advertised in your flier." Offering upscale baking supplies had been Dana's idea. The cookie stamps were an imported item, and rather pricey, but nothing deters die-hard bakers.

"We have a new selection," Dana said, pulling out a box of cookie presses. "They're gorgeous; take a look and see what strikes your fancy."

"Oh, I do love these," Lucinda said. "I'm putting together a gift basket for a raffle, and I want to add a few cooking tools. Something very Southern. The cookie presses are adorable. I didn't realize they came in so many different designs."

"They're a very popular item," Dana told her. She spread an array of presses on the counter. "I think the pineapple and the sailing ship are my favorites."

Lucinda leaned over to inspect them. "I'll take the pineapple, the acorn, and the sunburst," she said finally. "And I have to have this little rabbit." She turned to me. "I already have the sailing ship. You know, you'll think it's silly but I haven't been able to use the sailing ship press since poor Sonia died. That was the one I used on the shortbread cookies I brought to the shop that day. What a dreadful morning that was." Lucinda's voice wobbled and Ali quickly rushed to her side.

"Oh, you shouldn't think about that sad day, Lucinda." Ali locked eyes with me over the top of Lucinda's head, probably hoping I would say something comforting. I had barely noticed the ship imprint on the cookies that day, and I took a closer look at the mold. It looked exactly like a nineteenth-century ship, with its full sails and broad hull. An amazing coincidence.

"That's odd," I said softly.

"What is?" Lucinda raised her head.

"Well, this sailing ship," I began, "is just like the one Edward told us about in his dream. Remember, he described the Savannah Harbor and the sailing ships with their cargoes of spices for the New World?"

"I'd forgotten all about that," Lucinda said, perching on a stool by the counter. "But now that you mention it, yes, I think this is the kind of ship he described. He said he was lecturing on trade routes in the nineteenth century in his history classes at the university. He's such a fascinating man. His description of the wharf was very vivid, wasn't it?"

"It was," I agreed. "Do you remember Sybil had a similar dream?"

"The one about the woman with the basket of benne chips," Ali said. "I remember that. I thought it was striking that two people in the group had dreams about the past and the same location, the Savannah Harbor."

"It's a pretty press, isn't it?" Lucinda said, turning it over in her hand. "Except I'll probably never be able to use it again without thinking of that dreadful day."

"I need to figure out how to arrange these," Dana said, picking up a rose cookie press. "I wonder if we could use them in a window display? They're small, but maybe if they were grouped in a dramatic way, they would make a statement."

"It would be nice if you could sell boxes for them," Lucinda added. "You know how I can't stand clutter. I had to look all over for a plastic box that was the right size." She gave me an apologetic smile and I nodded. Lucinda's passion for order is practically pathological. Ali and I have visited her home, and her kitchen looked like it was ready for a photo shoot. It was so spotless, I had been hesitant to sit down.

"I think I could order some boxes like that," Dana said, snapping her fingers. "I saw one the other day in a catalog. A rectangular plastic box, and it had slots inside. Would that work?"

"That would be perfect," Lucinda said, sipping her iced tea. "My, this is delicious. What is it?"

"Ginger spice," Dana said promptly, pushing the box toward her. "We have a new shipment, but I haven't marked them yet." She pulled a few tea bags out of the box and handed them to Lucinda. "Here, try them at home and see what you think." I had to smile. Dana has shrewd retailing instincts and never misses a chance to make a sale or promote a product. "Going back to the boxes, how many cookie stamps do you own, Lucinda?"

"Oh, more than a dozen, probably fifteen. I keep them in alphabetical order."

Dana smiled. "You are the most organized person I've ever met."

"She alphabetizes her spices, too," Ali piped up.

"Well, of course I do," Lucinda, raising her eyebrows. "Doesn't everybody?"

"Not everyone," Ali said, grinning. "But I suppose it makes things easier when you're in a hurry."

"Yes, it does." Lucinda's expression was placid. "I'm afraid I'm getting careless as I get older, though. Just the other day, I reached for thyme and grabbed the turmeric by mistake."

"Wow, how did that happen? It would have been a disaster," I said, remembering that turmeric was a potent spice used in Indian cooking.

"It was very strange. I still can't fathom how I mixed them up. I know the lineup because they're alphabetical. *R*, *S*, *T*. Rosemary, sesame seeds, thyme. Some nights when I can't sleep, I visualize my spice cabinet and go through each shelf, listing all my spices." She gave a self-deprecatory smile. "Some people count sheep or list the states, but I always turn to my spices. It focuses my mind, although I suppose it's not for everyone."

I nodded as if this made perfect sense, wondering where in the world she was going with her story. "The turmeric, of course, should be to the right of the thyme," she continued. "But the sesame seeds weren't in their usual place between the rosemary and thyme; they were two bottles away. So the turmeric was sitting where the thyme used to be."

"Did you stop yourself from adding turmeric just in time?" Dana asked. I could tell she was asking out of politeness.

"Oh, heavens, yes, I did. It's a good thing I happened to glance at the bottle." She reached into her purse and handed Dana a credit card. "I think I'd like to add one more cookie press: the sailing ship," she said. She pushed the press with the schooner across the counter.

"Well, sure, but I thought you said you already had one of these?" Dana asked, puzzled.

"I do, but I'm going to send this as a gift to someone. Do you remember Leslie Watts? She really admired it the night she visited me. I bet she'd like to have one, and she'll probably never get around to buying one for herself. She has those little children and she doesn't get out much, poor thing."

Dana started to wrap up Lucinda's purchases when my brain did a cartwheel. "Lucinda," I said breathlessly, "did you just say Leslie admired your cookie press—"

"Why, yes, dear, she did—"

"Were you in the kitchen—I mean, were the two of you in the kitchen when you made those shortbread cookies?" I could hear the tension in my voice and a look of concern flitted over Lucinda's face.

"Of course we were," she said in her gentle voice. "We were having tea and just enjoying a wonderful conversation about friends we hadn't seen in years. It's amazing how time flies and life gets in the way of our keeping in touch with old friends. Friendship is a precious thing, you know, and I have to remind myself never to take it for granted." She signed her name to the receipt and looked up at me. "It's a shame that census taker came to the front door when he did. You know I try to be polite to everyone, but he just talked and talked." Lucinda threw up her hands. "I finally had to shoo him off the porch by telling him I had cookies ready to pop into the oven."

"What happened then?" I asked, willing myself to slow down. My heart was pounding, and I could feel the hairs standing up on the back of my neck.

Lucinda shot me a puzzled look. "Why, I went back into the kitchen and Leslie was admiring my cookie press. Is that what you mean, dear?"

"I—I don't know what I mean," I said, shaking my head. "Was Leslie still sitting at the counter? Where were the cookies?"

"You certainly are in an inquisitive mood today," Lucinda said playfully. "I feel like we're playing Twenty Questions." Her expression turned sober. "Is something wrong, Taylor?"

"I'm not sure," I said truthfully. "You walked back in the kitchen and Leslie was still sitting there and the cookies were on the counter in front of her. I just want to make sure I understand. I want to picture the scene."

Lucinda blew out a little sigh. "Yes, it's just as I described. Leslie was still sitting there, and the cookies were on the cookie sheet, all set to pop in the oven. She must have finished rolling out the dough and used the cookie press. Such a sweet girl. She did a good job, too. They looked lovely, all lined up in rows. Wasn't that thoughtful of her?"

26

Dana looked puzzled at the discussion, but Ali knew exactly what was going on.

"Lucinda," she said innocently, "was there any dough left over from the shortbread cookies?"

"Well, there were scraps, if that's what you mean. You always have some cookie dough left over when you use a cookie press. It's inevitable. I like to save it and use it in another recipe."

"You saved it?" This was even better than I'd hoped. I could hardly restrain myself. I felt like jumping off the stool and rushing over to Lucinda's. The picture was finally coming into focus. Leslie had been alone in the kitchen with the cookie dough. Lucinda had been distracted and had spent a long time talking to the young man taking the census. The sesame seeds weren't in their usual place in Lucinda's spice rack. How tempting it would have been for Leslie to just reach into the spice cabinet and give a good sprinkle of sesame seeds to the shortbread cookies. No one would be the wiser. At least, that's what she was counting on.

"Well, Leslie tried to throw out the scraps"—my spirits plummeted—"but I told her I always save them for a cookie-crumb crust. You know how thrifty I am. Waste not, want not. They're perfect for a pie crust, you know. They're excellent with key lime pie; it's one of my favorite recipes. It's ever so easy to make, especially if you already have leftover dough. You just press it into a pie pan and bake it at 350 degrees before adding the key lime filling. Anyway, I gathered up all the shortbread scraps and froze them."

"They're still in your freezer?"

Lucinda blinked. I knew she was baffled by my questions, but I didn't want to let her know my suspicions. At least, not yet.

"No, I used them up for the key lime pie I just told you about—"

"You've already made a pie with them?" My voice was spiraling downward in dismay. I thought we were on to something, and now my hopes were dashed.

"Yes, the hospital guild was running a bake sale and asked me to contribute something. My key lime pie is always popular, so I made one right away. Cheryl Simmons stopped by and picked it up last night." She paused and laid a hand on my arm. "Taylor, my dear, is something wrong? I can tell you're troubled, and I have no idea why. Please let me help you."

"No, it's nothing, Lucinda, really." I forced a lame smile. "I'm just a bit out of sorts today; don't give it another thought."

By the time we ushered a very puzzled Lucinda out the door, I was exhausted. Ali and I retreated upstairs, leaving Dana to manage the shop. Ali made iced coffee and wordlessly passed me a frosty glass. It's one of my favorite pick-me-ups. I started sorting through my thoughts out loud. Sometimes it helps me focus and get clarity on a situation.

Ali beat me to it. She flopped on the couch, put her feet up on the coffee table, and said, "It might not be anything, you know. The whole thing could have been perfectly innocent. Leslie stopped by for a visit, and she just wanted to be helpful. And Lucinda could have mixed up the spices herself."

"But now we'll never know, will we?" I said, letting out a deep breath. "What are the odds we could track down that pie?"

"Taylor," Ali said, "I think you're getting carried away. You're obsessing over Leslie."

"She had every reason to dislike Sonia," I pointed out. "She was breaking up her family, urging Jeremy to leave her and the kids. Sonia was the ultimate home-wrecker. It's only natural for Jeremy's wife to despise her."

"A lot of people had reason to dislike Sonia," Ali reminded me. "We have other suspects, you know."

I nodded. She was right, of course. Maybe I was clutching at straws. My mind was doing somersaults, trying to integrate what I'd just learned about Leslie and the shortbread cookies into my theory of the case. Now that I had new information, should I shuffle the list of suspects? Where did Leslie fit into the new lineup? I could see that Ali didn't share my suspicions about Leslie, and I wasn't sure why.

"What do you think about Edward?" Ali said suddenly. "I know he doesn't look like a murderer—"

"They never do." I interrupted her with a little snort. "That whole story about his nephew doing an internship for Sonia's company was certainly a surprise. It makes me feel a little uncomfortable that he didn't mention it before. How could he just sit there and not say anything? We were all talking about Sonia and her personality and how she rubbed some people the wrong way, and he just sat there like a bump on a log! You have to admit, that's pretty strange."

"It does seem a little odd," Ali conceded. "But would that be a motive for murder? Or is there something else you're not telling me?"

I shook my head. Ali was right; I was leaving something out. I hadn't told her that Edward had seemed completely unmoved when Sonia collapsed in our shop. His expression had never changed. His features could have been chiseled in stone. Could it be that Edward was just a reserved sort of person who didn't show his emotions? Or could it be that he wasn't surprised by Sonia's collapse because he had something to do with her death? I wasn't completely sure if I'd accurately read Edward's expression that day, so I didn't want to use that to bolster my case against him.

"It doesn't seem like much to go on. The only way Edward could have killed her is if he slipped something into that coffee cup from Java Joe's," Ali said. "He'd have to know about her allergy, of course, and he'd have to know something about anaphylactic shock. He would have had to come prepared."

"Which wouldn't be hard," I countered. "After all, his nephew used to work for Sonia. He could easily have gotten the information from him. And who knows, maybe it was written up in a magazine article someplace. Sonia liked to give interviews. Maybe she mentioned it to a reporter and Edward read about it."

"And what happened to that cardboard coffee cup?" Ali pondered. "Sam Stiles said it's not part of the evidence they collected at the scene. It couldn't have just walked away."

"Someone could have crumpled it up and stuck it in their

pocket. They could have walked right out the door with it if they really wanted to. No one would suspect anything or try to stop them."

"And if someone did spirit it away, what happened next?" Barney entered the room with a soft meow and jumped into Ali's lap. Scout was trailing behind and decided to make a quick detour to her food dish.

"I imagine they'd want to get rid of it right away. They probably tossed it in the nearest trash can, or maybe a Dumpster."

"Taylor, what if they couldn't get rid of it right away? What if they were forced to stick around with the incriminating evidence right in their pocket?"

I allowed myself a little smile. "I'd say they were probably a nervous wreck, hoping they could leave before the police arrived and interviewed them, or worse, found the evidence on them." I paused as the picture began to take shape in my mind. "Ali, what are you suggesting?"

"Think about it, Taylor. We called an impromptu meeting of the Dream Club because everyone was already in the shop. Didn't a couple of the members seem reluctant to stick around? I have a vague memory about that."

I had a memory, too, but it wasn't vague, it was crystal clear. "Etta Mae and Edward Giles," I said promptly. "I practically had to twist their arms to get them to come upstairs. They were all set to leave when the crowd poured out."

"That could be it," Ali said, her eyes bright with excitement. "What if one of them was holding the paper coffee cup? Or they'd hidden it somewhere in their clothing? Of course they wouldn't want to come upstairs; they'd want to make their getaway as soon as possible!"

"Or," I said, playing devil's advocate, "wouldn't it be perfectly normal to want to leave after such an upsetting sight? A famous celebrity collapses during a book signing, the paramedics arrive and whisk her away to the hospital? That would be enough to turn anyone off. If you remember, you and I were pretty shattered by what happened." She nodded solemnly, her eyes widening. "And Etta Mae and Edward are the newest members of the group, so they don't know everyone like we do. They could have been so upset by what happened to Sonia, they just wanted to go home."

Ali cocked her head to one side, considering. "It's possible," she said finally. "Why do I feel like we're back to square one?"

"I don't know. I keep trying to put the pieces together, but something just doesn't fit. I think we need to talk to Sam Stiles. I'd like to hear her take on this. She doesn't know about the scene in the kitchen with Lucinda and Leslie. She's probably focusing all her energies on that Java Joe's coffee cup." I paused. Maybe Sam was headed in the right direction with the investigation and I was off base? Still, we had to tell her about Lucinda and the shortbread cookies, just in case.

"And I think you need to talk to Noah," Ali said. She's always had a soft spot for Noah, and I know she'd be thrilled if we got back together, not as friends but as a couple.

"Ali . . ." I said warningly.

"I know, I know," she said in a singsong voice. "You want me to play little sister and mind my own business."

I laughed. "Something like that." I could never stay annoyed with Ali; she has my back, as she loves to tell me. There is no one more loyal than my kid sister, and she's been there for me in some very tough times.

I was just about to call Noah when Dana's voice, low and hushed, came over the intercom.

"Ali and Taylor, are you there?" she said hesitantly. I could hear the tension in her voice. "You need to come downstairs right away; you have a visitor."

I shot Ali a puzzled look. "We'll be right down," I said, lifting Barney off my lap and depositing him gently on the floor. He didn't even wake up and began purring in his sleep as he curled up on the rug. "Is it Noah?" I said, hazarding a guess.

"No," Dana said quickly. "I'm afraid not, but it's someone I know you'll want to see." She lowered her voice to a breathy whisper. "She says she's Trudy Carpenter."

I clicked the OFF button and turned to Ali. "You're not going to believe this, but the elusive Trudy Carpenter is downstairs in the shop. And she wants to see us."

"You're kidding!" Ali darted toward the stairs, stopping at the landing to make sure I was following her. "This should be interesting," she said, her expression somber.

27

"I should have come to see you ages ago," Trudy said a few minutes later. I could hardly take my eyes off her. She was the spitting image of Sonia, with flaming red hair and enormous blue eyes. She looked nothing like Clare Carpenter, the woman Ali and I had visited.

"Have a seat," Ali said, pulling out one of the counter stools. "Let me get you something to drink." She quickly poured a glass of iced tea and put it in front of Trudy, who was looking around the shop.

"I just wanted to see where it happened." There was a hitch in her voice, and her eyes suddenly welled with tears. "It was right here, wasn't it?"

Ali looked helplessly at me. "Yes, it was," I said gently. "Right here in the shop. She was surrounded by people who loved her and loved her books," I added. I wanted to say something comforting but was coming up short. The truth was, except for her paid employees, Sonia was surrounded by strangers when she died. And as far as we knew, her killer's face might have been one of the last things she saw. I remember how distraught Olivia had seemed when Sonia had been wheeled out by the paramedics. Had it all been an act? I remember thinking at the time how devoted Olivia was to her boss; her shock and worry had seemed genuine. But maybe Olivia was a skilled actress and none of us knew?

"Her fans, you mean." There was a sardonic twist to her mouth. "She could never get away from them."

"Do you think she wanted to?" Ali asked in surprise. "I remember how she seemed so energized that day. She hadn't planned on staying overnight in Savannah, but there was a problem with the plane, and her flight was delayed till the next day." She pushed a plate of cookies toward Trudy and continued. "But you probably already know all this, don't you? Sonia wanted to take every moment to promote her books, so we set up a last-minute book signing for her that morning." Ali smiled. "Sonia seemed like someone who didn't want any downtime in her schedule."

"It was probably Olivia who suggested it," Trudy said, sniffling. "Olivia was always pushing Aunt Sonia to do more book signings, more TV appearances, more cooking shows. She could never do enough to please Olivia." She looked up, with her lower lip quivering a little. "I don't understand it, do you? This endless desire to make her business bigger and bigger? I remember when Aunt Sonia baked cakes and cookies for her neighbors. And then she branched out and a lot of clubs hired her. Why couldn't she have just kept things the way they were? I think the TV show and the books changed everything," she said sadly. "She never really had time for anyone after that. I always felt like someone snatched her away."

I pulled out a stool and sat down next to her. "When someone reaches that level of success, their life really doesn't belong to them anymore. Sonia had an empire. So many people relied on her; she had hundreds of employees. I think she took that responsibility very seriously."

Trudy nodded. She was wearing a T-shirt with jeans and sandals and her coppery hair was pulled back in a ponytail. Without a trace of makeup, she looked very young and vulnerable.

"I know what you're saying. Still, I keep wondering what would have happened if she hadn't stayed overnight here in town. She'd be safely on the next stop on the tour and none of this would have happened." Her voice broke a little and Ali moved swiftly to put her arm around her.

"Trudy, you mustn't let yourself think that," Ali told her. "Sometimes, things just happen and they're out of our control."

Trudy glanced at me, her eyes tearing up. "Do *you* believe that, too?"

"Ali's right," I said with as much confidence as I could muster. I wondered how much Trudy knew about her mother's death. Did she think it was an accident? Did she have any idea that someone had been plotting to kill her and managed to pull it off? Of course, if Leslie really had slipped sesame seeds into the shortbread cookies, it was a crime of opportunity. Leslie saw her chance and took it. The deadly sesame seeds were sitting on the spice rack, just waiting for Leslie to grab them and sprinkle them on the cookies.

But there was another theory of the crime. If someone really had slipped sesame powder into Sonia's coffee from

Java Joe's, the killer must have carefully planned it in advance and waited for the opportunity to slip it into Sonia's food or drink. Something about the last scenario seemed a bit off to me, but I couldn't put my finger on it. I resolved to ask Ali once Trudy left.

I was trying to think of a delicate way to ask Trudy how much she knew about Sonia and her medical condition when she answered the question herself. I wasn't sure if allergies could be inherited and if Trudy also suffered from nut allergies.

"Allergies can be so dangerous, can't they?" Trudy said. "My mom had me tested for allergies when I was a little kid, since they run in the family. Aunt Sonia had them ever since she was a little girl."

Aunt Sonia. I realized Trudy probably had no idea that Sonia was probably her mother and that Sonia and Clare had been living a lie all these years. Even if it was true, there was no reason to divulge any family secrets now. And it still wasn't certain. Sonia had been seen carrying a baby into a hospital and coming out empty-handed, but nothing was written in stone. Maybe there was another explanation. And I still couldn't think of any way it affected the case. Trudy's dreadful boyfriend had a rock-solid alibi, so he was off the suspect list. And when I looked at this sweet, shy girl, I realized there was no way she could be a killer. Her grief was genuine, and I had no doubt she had loved Sonia.

"Have you already had the funeral service?" Ali asked.

Trudy nodded. "Yes, my mom thought it was better to do it quietly. She didn't want any media there. I went with my boyfriend and it was very sad. We only stayed a short while." She stood up, giving a rueful smile. "My boyfriend isn't exactly popular with my family," she said sadly. "He's really a good guy, but he's had some problems with drugs and alcohol."

"I'm so sorry to hear that. Your family should be there for you. You need a lot of support right now." Ali gave her a quick hug.

"I'll be okay," Trudy said, shrugging into her jeans jacket. "We don't see too much of my family. I can only deal with them in small doses. Reggie is all I need right now. Thanks so much for talking with me." She smiled and hugged me. "I feel much better now."

As soon as we closed the shop door, Ali sank onto a stool at the counter. "Wow," she said softly. "That was one visitor I wasn't expecting."

"Me, either," I admitted, "but now that we've met her, I feel pretty certain about ruling her out as a suspect, don't you?"

"Absolutely." Dana emerged from the storeroom as Ali added, "That girl couldn't hurt a fly, I'm certain of it."

"So where does that leave things?" Dana asked. She poured herself a glass of ginger tea and took a tiny sip. "Are you any closer to solving the murder?"

"Not really," I admitted. I suddenly remembered what was troubling me about the coffee from Java Joe's. "Ali, if someone really spiked the Java Joe's coffee with sesame seed powder, how could they be sure Sonia wouldn't drink it right away? If she drank it in the limo, it would be obvious that it was the coffee that sent her into anaphylactic shock. Whoever was close to her at the time would surely be a suspect. Anyone who had access to the coffee cup would be a suspect. They'd be taking a huge chance of getting caught, and I don't see why they'd risk it."

"That's a good point—" Ali began when Dana cut in.

"I think I know the answer to that," she said excitedly. "Sonia always drank her coffee lukewarm, and Java Joe's serves it steaming hot."

"Are you sure?" Ali asked, puzzled.

"I'm positive," Dana replied. "I offered to heat it up for her at the book signing and Olivia told me not to bother. She told me Sonia always waited until it was lukewarm to drink it. Apparently, Sonia would wander around holding a cup of cold coffee all day long and it drove her staff crazy."

"But how does this affect the case?" Ali continued.

Dana put her glass down and stood up as some tourists wandered into the shop. "Don't you see? Anyone who knew Sonia realized there was no way she would drink the coffee right away. Sonia would hold the cup in the limo—or maybe someone held it for her—but it was pretty certain she wouldn't take a sip until she got to the book signing."

"And once they arrived at the book signing, there were dozens of fans milling around," I said slowly. "The pool of potential suspects widens. And there was food there, the cookie trays, just to add to the confusion."

"The possibilities are endless," Ali said softly. "And the coffee from Java Joe's is a new element."

That's what had been troubling me: the coffee. But I see now that it could have worked exactly the way Dana had just described. My mind raced on, ticking off the possibilities. Sonia was carrying a cup of coffee from Java Joe's and any one of her staff members would have had time to spike it with sesame powder. They would have been safe, as long as she didn't drink it in the limo.

If this scenario was true, Lucinda's cookies had nothing to do with anything. And Leslie's visit to Lucinda's kitchen had been completely innocent. Was I really back to square one? And without the coffee cup, how could we ever prove anything? It was all speculation.

"Are we back to Olivia?" Ali asked as Dana checked in with the tourists to see if they needed help.

"I think so. We really don't know much about Sonia's

other staffers, but I'm sure the police ran a background check on them."Ali picked up her sunglasses and purse.

"Are you heading out?"

"Yes, and you're coming with me," she said firmly. "We're going to see Noah. But first we're making a stop at Java Joe's."

28

"Of course I remember Sonia Scott and her visit to Java Joe's. What a charming lady she was." Erica Morrison, the manager at Java Joe's, glanced at her watch before ringing up a sale. Ali and I were sitting at the counter with steaming lattes in front of us.

"Can you talk for a minute?" Ali asked. "We don't want to interrupt you. I know what it's like trying to take care of customers while someone's chattering away at you. My sister and I own Oldies But Goodies, the candy shop right off the square." She pulled out a business card that Dana had designed and handed it to Erica.

"Oldies But Goodies. I've been meaning to stop by. I've heard great things about you." Erica slipped the card into her apron pocket. "This is actually a good time for me to talk; I can take a quick break," she said. "I just hired a new assistant, and from the looks of things, she's going to be wonderful.

This will change my life," she added. She motioned to a young girl wearing a black Java Joe's apron to take over the cash register for her and then walked around the counter to sit with us.

"Thank you so much. We won't take up too much of your time," Ali promised.

"I'm happy to talk about Sonia. What a surprise it was when she walked in that day! And so sad what happened afterward." She paused. "What would you like to know about Sonia's visit? Was there something in particular? She was only here for a few minutes. Probably ten or fifteen minutes, all in all."

"We'd love to hear your impressions of her," I said quickly. "What you remember about the visit, anything at all. One of our friends is a journalist and she's thinking of doing a piece on Sonia's visit to Savannah. Maybe there are some anecdotes you could share."

"Well, her visit was a complete surprise. We knew she was staying at the hotel right next door because the bellman had told us that morning. He stops in at seven thirty every morning like clockwork. He said everyone at the hotel was excited to have Sonia staying with them."

"Do you have any idea why she stopped in here that morning?" Ali asked. "Hadn't they already checked out of the hotel?"

"Oh yes, they'd checked out, all right. I know that because we were watching the valet parking attendant pile their luggage into the back of the limo. We were all standing at the window, hoping to catch a glimpse of Sonia."

"What happened next?" Ali asked.

Erica laughed. "Well, she spotted us and came right over to the front window and yelled, 'Hi, y'all!' Some of the baristas were waving for her to come inside and she did. That caused quite a stir, I can tell you. All the customers were applauding."

"I suppose everyone wanted to meet her and say hello," Ali offered.

"Oh, they did. And they wanted to take pictures, too. She was so charming and gracious to everyone. We knew she was in a mad rush to get to the book signing, but she still took some time to pose for a few photos. I have one, myself, if you'd like to see it."

She went back behind the counter and opened a drawer. "I haven't had time to get it framed yet, but it's going to have a place of honor, right up on the wall near the cash register. And I'll have it enlarged, of course." She pulled out a small photo of Sonia with her arm around her. They were standing in front of the coffee machine flanked by Olivia and a couple of smiling baristas. "I'm having copies made for everyone. This is probably the closest they've ever been to a real celebrity; it will mean a lot to them."

"I'm sure it will," I said, passing the photo to Ali. "Everyone looks so happy," I commented. It was sad and ironic to think that Sonia would meet her death just a couple of hours later.

"A lovely picture," Ali murmured, and then she gave a little gasp. "Taylor," she said breathlessly, "look at that man in the background. Isn't it—"

"Jeremy Watts," I blurted out. "Yes, that's definitely him." He was in profile, staring out the coffee-shop window toward the limo parked outside. He must have been unaware he was caught in the photo; he looked moody and tense, not involved with the happy crowd gathered around Sonia.

"Is something wrong?" Erica asked as I slid the photo across the counter to her. "That man you're looking at"—she tapped her fingernail on the photo—"I think he was part of the group, because they all came in together. He must have worked for Sonia."

"Yes, he did. He was one of her employees. Nothing's wrong," I reassured her. "We were just surprised to see him here, that's all." I exchanged a glance with Ali. Jeremy had told us at the hotel that he'd returned home that night and wasn't able to attend the book signing the next morning. Yet here he was, still in town, just minutes before the book signing. So he had spent the night in town? What was going on? A simple change in plans or something more sinister?

In any case, I figured we'd learned as much as we could at Java Joe's, and after thanking Erica for her time, we stepped outside into the bright Savannah sunshine.

My cell was chirping and I glanced at the readout. Noah! As I mouthed his name to Ali, she scrambled for her own phone, which was playing "Material Girl." Both of us ran under an awning to escape the heat, with our phones clasped to our ears.

"It's Sara," Ali said, just as I answered my cell.

"You must be a mind reader," I said to Noah, "because I was just going to call you."

Noah's warm, sexy chuckle raced over the line. "Really? I'm glad to hear it. I was going to suggest lunch at Caroline's if you can slip away. I want to give you some updates on the case." I heard phones ringing in the background and the whir of a fax machine. It seemed like business had picked up at the detective agency, and I wondered if Noah had finally settled on an assistant. "Lunch sounds perfect," I began as Ali tapped my arm.

"Sara wants to meet us at Sweet Caroline's," Ali said. "Is noon okay?"

"Wow," I murmured, "we all got the same idea at the

same time. Tell her yes. Noah will be there, too." I turned back to my cell. "Synchronicity," I told Noah.

"Is that a code word for something?"

"No," I laughed. "It just means there will be four of us at Sweet Caroline's, that's all. Sara's going to join us."

"I *told* you he'd call," Ali said archly as we continued our walk. The sun was high in the sky, the air soft and balmy as we headed for a stroll by the Riverfront.

"Yes, you did," I told her. "But it's all business. He said he wants to give me an update on the case."

"It can't *all* be business," Ali said, determined to have the last word. "He could have gone over the details by phone, if that's all he wanted." My sister, the eternal optimist.

Business was brisk at Sweet Caroline's, but the hostess had saved us my favorite booth in the back. Sara and Noah were deep in conversation when Ali and I arrived. Remy, Sara's adorable dog, was lying quietly under the table. Caroline LaCroix, the owner, says that well-behaved dogs are usually welcome in cafés in her native France, and she decided to continue this tradition in Savannah.

As always, Sara had her notebook spread out on the table with an assortment of pens and highlighters. She has her own system of organizing her notes; quotes are highlighted in yellow, unless they're off the record, and then she colors them bright red.

"Noah's bringing me up to speed," Sara said as we slipped into the booth. I saw that Noah had already ordered white wine all around. Ali looked at the label and grinned at me. I knew what she was thinking. She was impressed that Noah had remembered my favorite wine and had decided that our relationship was in its "on-again" phase. I didn't have the heart to tell her the choice of wine wasn't as significant as she thought. It happens to be Noah's favorite as well.

The server appeared and everything on the menu looked tempting to me. The panini special sounded delicious, and we all decided to try it. Creamy goat cheese with roasted red peppers. Noah was already sampling Caroline's famous handmade potato chips while we waited for lunch to arrive. Caroline served them in a little basket lined with a red-and-white checkered napkin, and they were a huge favorite.

I idly thought of serving them at the shop and didn't know if Caroline could bear to part with the recipe. I know they're made out of russet potatoes, sliced paper-thin, because the server told me. And they're sprinkled with olive oil and baked in a very hot oven. But Caroline adds some sort of herb that gives them an extra kick. Maybe rosemary? I wasn't sure.

"So where do things stand with the case?" I asked as soon as we'd ordered.

"Have you talked to Sam Stiles?" Noah asked. He was eyeing the potato chips as if he was tempted to reach for a handful and was trying to restrain himself. Caroline's potato chips are seriously addictive, and I knew we'd have to order another basket at some point. The first basket is always on the house, and after that, they are considered a menu item and Caroline charges for them.

I shook my head. "I haven't had a chance to talk to her. What's up?"

"The police found the Java Joe's coffee cup." He sat back with a smug smile.

"You're kidding!" Ali blurted out. "Taylor, did you hear that?"

"Yes," I said, "I'm still trying to get my mind around it."

"I can't believe you found out before we did," Sara told him.

"I have my sources," Noah said, smiling as the server poured the wine.

"But where was it? That day when Sam and the CSIs came over, they went through the whole shop with a fine-tooth comb."

"They did find it, but somehow it got misplaced at the station house and never got logged into evidence." Noah gave in to the urge and helped himself to a handful of potato chips. "But they have it now, and they can still run tests on it."

"So that means the chain of evidence was broken," I said. Noah nodded and I went on, "And that means it might not stand up in court. Tell me about the paper cup. Did they analyze it? Was there any evidence of sesame seeds in the cup?"

"It's possible but they're keeping this quiet for the moment," he said, lowering his voice. "Don't go public with this, not even to the Dream Club."

"I won't breathe a word," Ali said solemnly. "So this is a dead end?"

"Maybe not," I said, sitting up straight. "Ali, remember when Olivia turned up at the shop, looking for her day planner?"

"Yes, she seemed really upset that she didn't find it."

"What if"—I leaned in across the table and lowered my voice—"what if she was really looking for the coffee cup? The day planner was just an excuse, something she made up on the spot."

"It's certainly possible," Noah offered.

For a moment no one spoke, and then Sara said, "But I don't still understand why she left the coffee cup in the shop. She could have shoved it in her bag and just taken it with her. "Maybe it wasn't possible," I said, trying to re-create the scene in my mind. "Or maybe she forgot all about it in the heat of the moment. Everything was so chaotic, she might have dropped it somewhere under the table where Sonia did the book signing. And then Sonia collapsed, and in all the commotion, she couldn't retrieve it." Another thought bugged me. *If the chain of evidence was broken, how important was the coffee cup, anyway? Maybe we're going down a blind alley.* I really needed to talk to Sam Stiles myself and see what her take was on the coffee cup. Was it significant to the case or not?

"That's certainly a possible scenario," Ali said. "If she really did slip something into Sonia's coffee, she knew she had to get that cup back right away. There was no way she could let the police find it. Her only hope was that the police missed it in their initial search. So that meant she had to come back to the shop with a phony excuse."

"So maybe she came up with that story about losing her day planner," I said. I took a sip of white wine. It was just as delicious as I remembered. "It really seemed suspicious. I remember thinking that she wasn't very convincing."

"It could have happened that way," Sara said in her breathy voice. "Olivia was holding the coffee cup and could have slipped in the sesame powder whenever she had the opportunity. If that's what happened, Olivia must be in a panic right now, wondering what happened to the cup. She's probably terrified that it will turn up."

"But the chain of evidence was broken," I piped up. "So the cup probably isn't even admissible."

"But Olivia doesn't know that," Sara retorted, raising her eyebrows. "Ali is right; Olivia doesn't dare take a chance. If there is any way she thinks she can retrieve that cup, she will."

"How are the police going to handle this information?" I asked Noah.

"They're going to pretend that they're launching a

massive search for the coffee cup," he told me, "along with some plastic plates and platters from the signing. They figure if they rattle a few cages, they might get some interesting results."

"This puts another whole spin on things," I said. I tried to imagine Olivia holding the Java Joe's coffee cup and slipping in sesame seed powder. I rolled the idea around in my mind. It wasn't definite, but it was a possibility. Something nagged me about this theory, and I couldn't quite identify it.

Before I could figure out what was bothering me, Sara asked, "Did you mean the police actually ruled out any trace of sesame seed powder, or were the results inconclusive?"

"Inconclusive," Noah said. "The sample was too degraded, and there's no way to know for sure if that's the way the sesame seeds were ingested." He turned to me while the server placed our lunches in front of us. "Is business still slow at the shop?"

"I'm afraid so," I told him. "No matter how many times we try to reassure people, they still seem to think we 'poisoned' Sonia somehow." Noah nodded. We both knew that perception was everything, and how hard it was to regain the public's trust once something like this happened.

"What about the news closer to home?" Sara asked. "Where do things stand with Etta Mae and Edward Giles?" she added, referring to the two new Dream Club members whom we originally had considered as suspects.

"Persia has been helping Etta Mae investigate whether Sonia's company really did steal recipes from her family cookbook," Ali said. "I talked to Persia this morning," she said to me. "I didn't get a chance to tell you."

"How are things going with the lawyer?" I asked, remembering how Etta Mae's face was contorted with rage when she talked about the "theft" of her beloved family recipes.

"Etta Mae is much calmer, it seems," Ali continued. "She feels relieved that she's gotten legal representation, and she seems more rational about the whole thing." She turned to me. "Remember how emotional she was at the Dream Club?"

"I certainly do. She looked positively murderous." I didn't add that I'd spotted a gloating expression on Etta Mae's face as Sonia was whisked away by the paramedics. It could have represented a vindictive pleasure in her enemy's fall, or it could have meant something more sinister.

"Are we taking Etta Mae off the suspect list?" Sara asked, highlighter in hand.

"Maybe not quite yet," Noah said. "But she's not at the top anymore."

"That leaves us with Edward," Sara said. "Is he still paying visits to Lucinda?"

"I'm not sure," I told her. "I never got a chance to follow up on that. I think Lucinda was tickled to have some male attention, and I believe that Edward is lonely and socially awkward. I think he's flattered that Lucinda is taking an interest in him."

"Do you still consider him a suspect?" Noah grabbed the last of the homemade potato chips, and Ali signaled the server for another basket.

I shook my head. "I don't think so. He might have been upset over his nephew being treated so badly by Sonia, but murdering her certainly wouldn't change anything. Plus, he seems like such a gentle, quiet soul, I can't imagine him deliberately hurting anyone."

"I agree," Ali said quickly.

"What else has happened since we talked?" Noah asked.

His tone was innocent, and he didn't explain why he'd been out of touch the last few days. Ali insisted that it was because he was busy with his new detective agency, but I wasn't so sure. There's something mercurial about Noah. He can appear and disappear at will—both physically and emotionally—and I've never really understood it.

I told Noah and Sara about Trudy's visit and how both Ali and I were convinced that she had nothing to do with Sonia's death. And Noah repeated his story about Trudy's ex-con boyfriend and his rock-solid alibi. When we seemed to have exhausted all the news on the case, Ali gave a quick update on the baking classes we were offering.

"Baking classes? I want to sign up!" Sara said impulsively. I tried not to smile. Sara can barely boil water for tea.

"You're certainly welcome to come," Ali told her. She whipped out a flier and passed it across the table. "I think you'd enjoy the cupcake class. I'll add you to the list right away, because the class is filling up very fast."

"Thanks. I'll write it up and submit it to the style section of the paper; they love articles on food and cooking classes."

"Do you think they'll publish it?" Ali asked excitedly.

"I'll do my best," Sara assured her. "They're always looking for local features."

29

The moment we left Sweet Caroline's, I realized what had been bothering me about the coffee cup. "Ali, do you mind if we make a quick stop at Java Joe's again on the way home?"

"Of course not," she said, putting on her sunglasses. The bright sun was beating down through the leaves of the banyan trees and making interesting patterns on the sidewalk. "What's up?"

"Just an idea," I told her. "Did you take a good look at that photo of Sonia from Java Joe's?"

"Well, I think I did," Ali said tentatively. "It just looked like a typical fan snapshot. Sonia and Erica and the baristas, all looking happy and smiling at the camera." She turned to me, her brow furrowed in concentration. "What are you getting at?"

"Did you notice anything special about Jeremy Watts standing in the background?"

She hesitated. "I noticed he didn't look too thrilled to be there, and I'm sure he didn't realize anyone was snapping his picture." She took off her sunglasses as we stopped at a crosswalk and gave me a searching look. "Did I miss something?"

"Not necessarily," I told her. "Or if you did, then I missed it, too. Something about that photo has been bugging me, and I need to go back and check out it."

"You certainly are being mysterious," she said. "I could tell something was bothering you during lunch."

"You could? How did you know that?"

"You never asked Noah a word about his new receptionist," she said archly. "And you didn't ask him why he's been out of town or what cases he's been working on."

"I didn't think it was the time or place," I said, hearing a touch of defensiveness creep into my voice. "If he wanted me to know, I guess he'd tell me."

Ali smiled. "I think he was waiting for you to ask him. You know, Taylor, in some ways, I think I understand Noah better than you do."

"Well, I'm glad you stopped in," Erica said a few minutes later, "I was just leaving to take it to the framer." She pulled the photo out and passed it across the counter to us. She looked puzzled, and I knew she was wondering why in the world we'd returned to Java Joe's for another look at the snapshot.

"I just had to see it again," I said guilelessly. "Ali, take another peek. Neither one of us really took a good look at Jeremy Watts before."

"What am I looking for?" Ali said under her breath as Erica turned to ring up a sale. She stared hard at the photo and even held it up to the light.

"You'll know it when you see it."

"Okay," she said finally. "I give up. There's nothing wrong with the picture. At least nothing I can see. It's Jeremy Watts, all right, and he's standing over by the wall, at the station with the creamer and sugar packets and the flavored syrups for the coffee."

"And . . . what else do you see?" I prompted.

"And he's holding a coffee cup!" she said and immediately clasped her hand over her mouth. "Olivia is nowhere in sight. It's Jeremy holding the cup. Could this be the cup Sonia had at the book signing? She turned and looked at me, her eyes wide with shock. "This isn't what I expected."

"Yes, I know—"

"And this means he would have had the perfect opportunity to tinker with Sonia's coffee and add some sesame seed powder. He had access to the coffee, and he had the perfect excuse. He could just pretend he was adding cream and sugar or whatever she liked in her coffee. It would have been so easy for him. I can't believe we missed this."

"He couldn't have planned it better," I said softly. *If indeed that's what happened*, I thought. We still had no proof that anyone had tampered with Sonia's coffee; all this was circumstantial and more in the realm of guesswork. Just speculation. We had no real proof of anything yet.

"All this time we thought it was Olivia, but now I'm beginning to think it could have been Jeremy," Ali said in a hushed tone. Erica was finishing up with her customer and turned back to us expectantly. "Was there anything else you needed?" she asked, taking off her apron. She was clearly going off duty and eager to be on her way.

"No, we're fine," I said. "Thanks so much." I pulled some fliers out of my purse. "Would you mind if we left a few of these with you? We're offering free baking classes at the shop. Some of your customers might be interested."

She quickly scanned the flier and broke into a broad smile. "Cupcake classes! What a great idea! I'll keep them right here by the cashier and make sure we drum up some business for you. Local businesses need to support each other."

"Yes, we do!" Ali said enthusiastically. "What next?" she said to me as we left the shop.

It was midafternoon, and I had an idea I wanted to run by Sam Stiles. We could visit her at the precinct house, but it might just be easier to head for home and call her. I was embarrassed that Noah had found out about the coffee cup before we had, but I blamed myself. I'd been so busy tracking down dead-end leads and setting up promotions for the shop, I'd neglected to contact Sam.

"How much is left to do on the cupcake classes?" I asked her.

"Nothing," she told me. "Dana has ordered all the supplies, and as soon as we have twelve people who've signed up, we can start immediately."

"I'm sure we have a dozen people right now," I told her. "If necessary, we can pull in members of the Dream Club. You know they'd be happy to help."

"Why are you so eager to do this?" Ali asked me.

"Because I want to lure Olivia back to the shop," I told her. "I've got to have some excuse, and I'm going to tell her that we have a window display of Sonia's books."

Ali frowned. "Will she fall for that?"

"Why not? If she really did tamper with the coffee cup, she'd be glad to have the opportunity for a second look around for it."

"So we lure her back to the shop and . . ." Ali's voice trailed off uncertainly.

"And we sit back and see what happens."

As soon as we got back to the shop, Ali consulted with Dana about the supplies and asked her for a rough estimate of how long it would take to set everything up. My plan was to get Olivia to the shop early enough that she could poke around on her own, and we could catch her looking for the cup. But we needed to take things a step further, and that's where Detective Sam Stiles would come in. I curled up on the living room sofa and called her.

She answered on the first ring, and I told her I knew about the coffee cup from Java Joe's.

"Yeah, the coffee cup," she said, a note of weariness creeping into her voice. "I can't believe the way it went down. I guess you heard the CSIs actually found it, but someone at the station house screwed up and it was never entered into evidence. What a mess." She sounded tired and dejected.

"Well, it didn't contain any evidence of sesame seed powder, did it? And the chain of evidence is broken, so you couldn't really use it to nail Olivia, right?" *Or Jeremy*, I thought, remembering that photo at Java Joe's.

"No, you're right, we couldn't," she said, her voice flat. She gave a bitter little laugh. "But you know how I hate sloppy police work. There was no excuse for what happened."

"I know what you mean," I said. Sam is the ultimate perfectionist. The so-called eighty-percent rule doesn't work with Sam. She believes in giving any effort a hundred and ten percent, and she has very high standards for her detectives and her CSIs. I knew that she was probably angry and embarrassed that such an important piece of evidence would slip through the cracks.

"I'm still hoping someone will slip up or some new information will come to light. At the moment, we don't have much to go on."

"Who's at the top of your suspect list?"

"Olivia," she said slowly. I quickly told her about spotting Jeremy holding the coffee cup in that photo taken at Java Joe's. I was glad that Sam was willing to exchange information with me; technically, she shouldn't be talking about an ongoing investigation. "Well, I still like Olivia for the crime. I don't see Jeremy having a motive. At least, not a strong motive." She paused for a beat, and I said, "It might help his career if Sonia was out of the way, wouldn't it? Maybe he was tired of being a midlevel executive and wanted a shot at the top spot." Barney jumped on my lap, and I gently shifted him onto the sofa cushion next to me.

"Not necessarily," Sam said. "I'm not sure he'd move up in the company if Sonia died. From what I hear, he's not a very valued employee, and who knows, he might get fired in the shake-up." There was a long beat while I considered this.

"What about Leslie Watts?" Ali mentioned she'd called Sam a couple of days ago and told her about the strange incident with Leslie in Lucinda's kitchen.

"Taylor, I know what you're thinking. That Leslie grabbed some sesame seeds from Lucinda's spice rack and dumped them in with the cookies." There was a short pause while someone was talking in the background. "I just don't buy it. What are the odds of Leslie even knowing that Lucinda had sesame seeds? And how could she be sure that Lucinda wouldn't come back and catch her in the act? It sounds really risky to me."

"Risky or improbable?" I was a little disappointed because I still thought Leslie was a strong suspect.

"I'd say risky *and* improbable. I think the whole thing was perfectly innocent. Here's the way I see it. Leslie was just trying to help out by putting the dough on the cookie sheets for Lucinda. You know how flustered Lucinda gets sometimes. She might have been standing at the front door for sixty seconds and she thought it was ten minutes. Plus, let's face it, at times Lucinda gets a little ditzy. She probably mixed up the position of the spice bottles herself." Sam gave a short laugh. "Who alphabetizes their spices anyway? I barely have time to feed the dogs and cats and open up a can of soup when I get off duty." It was true; Sam worked harder than anyone I knew.

"Do you have a plan? Is there any way to flush out Olivia?"

"Funny you should say that," she said, lowering her voice. "Can you get Olivia to come back to the store for a chat?"

"I think so. Dana's window display is drawing a lot of attention and I was going to ask her to stop by to take a look at it."

"That would really help," Sam said, relief evident in her tone.

"Do you want me to just watch her? I could give her the opportunity to look around for the coffee cup and report back to you."

"I thought of something better. What if you told her that the police are still looking for the coffee cup and that we're going to try the dump at the edge of town in a couple of days. I'm going to leak a piece to the newspaper that we're looking for paper and plastic products from the signing that day."

"I can try. I could tell her that all the trash cans in the district were emptied and the dump is your last hope of finding it."

"Let me know what happens," Sam said. "I'm counting on you." She started to click off and added, "Oh, and Taylor, thanks for this."

"I'll do my best," I promised. I flipped the phone shut and felt a little buzz of excitement. Were we finally close to finding the murderer? Would Olivia fall for the ruse? She'd have to be pretty desperate, but if Sam thought it would work, I'd be happy to give it a try. And the perfect time to do it was before the cupcake baking class.

30

"Was it hard to get twelve people to show up?" I asked Dana the following morning. It was nine thirty, and The Magic of Cupcakes class was going to start in half an hour.

"Not at all," she said, checking the supplies she'd laid out for the students. She'd brought in two folding tables she'd found in the shed behind our building and had covered them with bright blue-and-white gingham cloths. Each student would have a workstation, complete with mixing bowls, cupcake tins (both mini and full-sized), and a nice selection of colored frostings.

"It looks very nice," I told her. Dana has a creative flair. "Will this be enough frosting for everyone?" I asked, pointing to the little dishes filled with frosting in Easter-egg colors—mint green, buttercup yellow, and soft pink.

"Oh yes; those are just for adding color for the flowers," she explained. "We use buttercream frosting for the base, and I made a big batch of it this morning." She pulled a giant mixing bowl out of the refrigerator and showed it to me "We're going to teach them to create flowers and rosettes to top the cupcakes."

"Flowers and rosettes?"

Dana opened a cookbook and pointed to a beautiful cupcake topped with pale blue hydrangea petals. There was a row of snowy cupcakes with pink rosettes on the next page. It was hard to believe it was all made from tinted frosting.

"It looks impossible," I told her.

"It's easy with the right tip on a piping bag," Dana said. "Why don't you try your hand at it?"

"I don't think so," I said quickly, but Ali laughed and pushed a piping bag into my hand. "Taylor, you can make a rose. Watch, I'll do one and then you do one."

Dana handed her a cupcake already topped with buttercream frosting, and Ali expertly used a piping bag to form soft pink petals on the top. She leaned over, biting her lower lip with concentration, and then stood back to admire the results. It was perfect. A lovely pink rose topping off a snowy white cupcake. *How did she do it? It only took a couple of minutes. And a very steady hand.*

"See, it's easy," she said. "I can teach you how to make a couple of tiny green leaves to go with it, but we'll save that for another time. Go ahead and try it, Taylor. Dana, give her a cupcake."

At first I was all thumbs, but somehow I followed Ali's guidance and produced not a perfect rose, but something resembling one. She coached me on how to make the petals by starting on the inside and going clockwise, making tiny petals by dabbing pink frosting from the piping bag. I could see that this was going to take some practice, but it didn't seem as impossible as it had a few minutes earlier.

"Perfect," she said approvingly. "Taylor, you're a natural.

You can help the students while Dana and I fill the piping bags for them."

"I thought each student was going to do her own," Dana said.

"Well, it's a lot quicker if we do it for them. If they don't have the bags tightly secured, the frosting oozes out the wrong end. They'll be discouraged before they even get started."

"I appreciate your faith in me, Ali, but I don't think I'll be able to offer much help."

"Nonsense, Tayor. It's the effort that counts," Ali said. "Just keep encouraging them. That's all they need: a bit of self-confidence."

Sara arrived a few minutes later, and I knew something was up. I glanced at the clock. Twenty minutes before the students would arrive. I was grateful that Dana seemed to have everything under control.

"What's up?" I asked Sara, pulling out a stool for her.

"I just heard something interesting about Jeremy Watts," she said, her face flushed with excitement. She sank onto the stool, her eyes dazzling. "Do you remember that purse snatching at the grocery store? An elderly woman left her purse in the cart and someone followed her around and then snatched it when they had the chance?"

"I think I read about it," I said slowly. "And Rose told me about it. The woman used to live on this street. She was a friend of the Harper sisters."

"It seems that the police pulled the store security tapes, hoping they could identify the guy."

"And what happened? Did they get him?" Ali asked, joining us.

"Yes, he has a long history of thefts. But here's the interesting part. Jeremy Watts was shopping in the same store.

At least, there's a guy on the tape who looks just like him. And"—she paused dramatically—"it was the night before the book signing." She raised her eyebrows, and I wondered what was coming next.

"Why would he be shopping at a grocery store here in Savannah?" Ali asked. "He said he was going straight home."

"He lied," Sara said flatly. "Sam's going to send one of her detectives over to the store this morning to see if anyone recognizes him from a photo. It certainly looks like him on the tape, but it would be better to have an eyewitness."

But an eyewitness to what? I didn't have more time to ponder the issue because the students started streaming in, all smiles and enthusiasm. Within minutes, Dana had them settled at their stations and launched into her welcome speech, telling everyone to "have fun" with the decorating and not to worry if their first attempts weren't perfect.

"After all," she said, "it doesn't matter what they look like; they'll still taste good." And she was right. Dana had made dozens of vanilla cupcakes from scratch yesterday, and the enticing aroma had filled the shop. "Now let's get started," she began. Sara joined the students, with her notebook at the ready. I hoped the local paper would feature the event; it would be good for business.

I drifted away to talk to Ali, who was making another pitcher of iced tea. "You can never have enough sweet tea for these ladies," she said.

"Very true. What did you think about what Sara told us about the security tapes?" I asked.

"It's interesting, but I don't know what to make of it." She shook her head. "Maybe nothing. We'll have to wait and see what the detectives come up with when they visit the grocery."

Olivia arrived a few minutes later. She looked tired and

stressed out, and I wondered if running Sonia Scott, Inc., was taking a toll on her, or if it was something else.

"Olivia, it's so nice you could stop by." I gestured to the cupcake class in progress. "All our customers are making cupcakes from Sonia's book. And we're hoping the local paper will cover the event. It will be good publicity for the store, and for her book, of course."

"That's nice," she said idly. "You made a lovely window display with Sonia's books. I looked at it when I came in. Very colorful." She glanced around the shop. "I see you've moved things around a bit."

"Not too much, just a little. We had to fit two card tables in the center aisle so Dana and Ali could hold the class."

Once again, Olivia was looking at the floor. Was she looking for her missing day planner, or for the coffee cup from Java Joe's?

"I have some bookmarks I found," I said, reaching into a drawer. "I thought you might like to have them. I see that Sonia autographed some of them, so they could be valuable."

"Thanks," she said dispiritedly and shoved them into her blazer pocket. "It's weird it didn't turn up," she said. "The day planner," she added when she caught my puzzled look.

"Oh yes, the day planner. We looked everywhere," I said glibly. "Who knows what could have happened to it. I hope it wasn't thrown out. A few things went missing from the shop that day."

"Really?"

I nodded. "A coffee cup and a plastic cookie tray. Who knows what happened to them?"

"A coffee cup and a cookie tray. Does it really matter at this point?" Olivia asked in a world-weary tone.

"The police seem to think it does. They've searched all the trash bins around here, and they're going to check the city dump tomorrow. All our trash from the shop is stashed in bright red plastic bags with our logo, so maybe they'll come up with something."

"Maybe they will," she said in a tired voice. *Interesting.* She hadn't taken the bait. "Thanks for saving these," she said, patting her pocket. "I guess I'd better get going, I've got a million errands to do," she added, moving toward the door.

"I suppose it must be pretty nerve-wracking, trying to take over the reins of a conglomerate."

"It is," she said with a wistful sigh, "and it's not at all like I pictured. Sonia was a workaholic, you know. I always admired that quality in her. She was my mentor, and I've never met anyone with such drive and enthusiasm. The company was her baby, her whole family." Her mouth twisted in a sardonic smile. "No time for anything else, no need for anything but success." There was a little catch in her voice, and she blinked rapidly.

"She must have sacrificed a lot to achieve what she did," I said slowly. I was surprised at Olivia's mood; I'd never seen her so vulnerable and tentative. And I'd never expected her to be emotional. She had been so self-contained on previous visits. Was I seeing another side of Olivia? Or was this the "real" Olivia and she had kept her true self hidden up until now?

"Well, it's only for a little while longer," she said. "Surely I can hold myself together for another month or two."

"What will happen then?" I asked, puzzled.

"I'm leaving the company," she said, and for the first time, I saw a genuine smile cross her face. "It's something I should have done years ago. I suppose I was just so much in awe of Sonia, I stayed with her. She was my idol. I wanted to be just like her. And now that I've seen what her life was like, I don't want any part of it."

We heard a round of applause go up from the students, and I glanced over at Dana. She gave me a thumbs-up. Someone had probably produced the perfect cupcake.

"But what will you do? You've devoted so much of your life to the company."

"Too much," she said ruefully. "I feel free for the first time in my life. I'm going back to Chattanooga and opening up a little bed-and-breakfast with my sister. It will be low stress, and I can't wait to connect with my family again."

"Wow, I'm stunned."

"Everyone is." She smiled. "Good luck to you, Taylor. You've been very kind, and I know your shop will be a success."

"Good luck to you, too," I said warmly.

"And the day planner I was looking for—" she added.

"I can keep on looking . . ."

She laughed and shook her head. "Don't bother; I don't need it anymore. I don't know why I worried about it in the first place. In the scheme of things, it doesn't even matter."

And with that she was gone. I went back to the cupcake class and Ali shot me a puzzled look. Olivia had totally surprised me. My whole theory of the case was turned upside down. If Olivia had no desire to run Sonia's company, then what would have been the point of killing her? Unless Olivia had murdered her because she'd *thought* she wanted to take over the company. And then once the deed was done, Olivia realized she'd made a terrible mistake? I was more confused than ever.

31

"She didn't seem the least bit worried?" Sara asked. The Dream Club meeting was about to start, and I'd just told Sara about Olivia's visit to the shop.

"Not the tiniest bit."

"And you told her the police were looking for the coffee cup?" Sara reached out to grab a raspberry thumbprint cookie off a tray I was carrying into the living room.

"I told her. And it had no effect whatsoever. She seemed completely disinterested. I told her they'd already checked all the trash bins in the area and they were going to check the dump tomorrow morning. No reaction at all."

Sara bit into the cookie and grinned. "Delicious." I bit back a smile. She'd already sampled something off each tray. "Well, killers can be really cold-blooded. They don't experience emotions the way we do, so that could explain how she kept her cool."

"But Olivia also told Taylor that she wasn't going to take over Sonia's company," Ali pointed out. She poured iced tea and coffee and took a quick look around the living room. "Why bother killing Sonia if she was going to leave the company and move to Chattanooga for a quieter lifestyle?"

"It doesn't make sense," Sara admitted, "if Olivia really was telling Taylor the truth. Maybe the whole Chattanooga story was a ruse to get her off the suspect list."

"She seemed pretty convincing to me." I picked Barney up off the sofa and put him in his cat bed on the floor. He prefers the sofa, but some of the club members have complained about cat fur on their clothes. I quickly went over the sofa cushions with a roll of sticky tape. Barney watched me carefully as I set about the task, and the moment I finished, he bolted out of his cat bed and jumped back up on the sofa.

"Cats!" Sara said with a laugh. Her golden retriever, Remy, was curled up asleep in my bedroom. Remy is one of the quietest, gentlest dogs I've ever met, and that is why Sara can take her everywhere.

"Where does that leave us?" Sara asked.

"In a state of confusion," Ali said ruefully. "Sam Stiles still likes Olivia for the murder, but after hearing about her plans to go to Chattanooga, I'm not so sure. That could change everything. It seems to take away her motive, doesn't it?"

"What about Jeremy Watts? There's the security tape I told you about earlier," Sara pointed out. "Sam's going to call later and tell me if that really was Jeremy in the grocery store. Maybe they can find someone who remembers what he bought."

"That could be interesting. Especially if it was sesame seeds."

I tried to connect the dots in my mind. Jeremy had been

caught on tape the night before the book signing. Instead of leaving Savannah as originally planned, he'd stuck around and gone to a grocery store near the hotel. Why? And we know he was holding a Java Joe's coffee cup the next morning, because we saw the photo at the coffee shop.

Could Jeremy really have bought sesame seeds at the grocery store? Was the idea completely far-fetched? Maybe he figured out a way to grind them up and saw his opportunity at Java Joe's the next morning. He could have slipped the sesame seed powder in Sonia's coffee and then taken off. As far as he knew, he was in the clear and no one would be able to connect him to the murder. Sonia liked her coffee lukewarm, so there was no way she would drink it in the limo. She would drink it at the book signing, collapse and die, and no one would be the wiser. Jeremy would be driving home, beyond suspicion.

I could see this as a possible scenario. But what was his motive? If Olivia was really leaving the company, she wouldn't be there to protect him and further his career. One possibility is that Sonia was going to tell Jeremy's wife about their affair, but since the affair seemed to be an open secret, that was no motive after all. I was stymied.

"I don't see how we can connect Jeremy or Olivia to the crime without some hard evidence," Sara said. "Everything is circumstantial, right?"

"That's true," Ali said, "but a lot of cases are solved with circumstantial evidence. The killer is confronted and then he caves and confesses. I've seen it happen again and again. On television, I mean."

I had to chime in. "But Jeremy doesn't look like the type who would break down and confess to anything." I thought of the day I'd spotted him having breakfast with Olivia at the hotel. He'd been uncomfortable when he'd spoken with us a few minutes earlier, but he'd kept control of the conversation and hadn't revealed a thing. A cool customer, indeed.

"I suppose you're right," Ali agreed. "He plays his cards close to his vest, but I still think he's weaker than Olivia. She's a pretty tough cookie and definitely the stronger of the two."

The Dream Club members started arriving then, and it looked like everyone but Sam Stiles had made it. Ali took a quick phone call in the kitchen while I welcomed everyone. The Harper sisters settled down on the sofa, Sybil and Persia claimed armchairs, and Lucinda perched on an ottoman.

Sara hunkered down on the floor, by the coffee table, where she could pet Barney and Scout. And where she had access to the desserts, I thought with a smile. We always tease Sara about her sweet tooth, but maybe we're just jealous. She manages to eat copious amounts of sugar and never gain an ounce. I envy her.

"Who's missing?" I said, counting heads.

"Sorry I'm late," Dorien said, bustling in. "I had a reading to do." Since Dorien's catering business took a nosedive earlier this year, she's gone back to reading tarot cards. She's managed to pick up some business by advertising in local papers and passing out fliers, but she's barely scraping by. I've often thought of hiring her at the shop, but her abrasive manner would be off-putting for customers. She must turn on the charm for her tarot readings, I decided, since she seems to be fairly successful.

"That was Sam Stiles," Ali whispered, pulling over a kitchen chair. "She sent a couple of detectives out to watch the garbage dump tonight. Just in case." She raised her eyebrows. "She expects to find Olivia there, looking for the coffee cup."

I shook my head and let out a breath. Obviously Sam was

a detective and had more experience than I did, but I just couldn't see Olivia as the prime suspect anymore. *But maybe I've been conned by Olivia,* I thought. *That whole story about Chattanooga might be bogus. Maybe the woman is a born actress and I've fallen for her spiel.*

"We're still missing two more people," Ali said, scanning the group.

"Etta Mae is out of town," Rose Harper told us. "She had to visit a relative and asked me to give everyone her apologies. She'll be here next week."

"And that leaves—"

"Edward Giles," Lucinda piped up. "I'm afraid he's decided not to continue with us." She looked troubled and twisted her hands in her lap. "I swear, I don't know what's going on with that man. I thought he enjoyed our little group."

"Hah, I'm not surprised," Dorien said caustically. "I never had a good feeling about him. And he was reluctant to share his dreams; remember how we had to prod him each time?"

"I think he was just shy," Lucinda said, shooting Dorien a look. "Not everyone is as outspoken as you are, Dorien. I think in time, he would have come around."

I think Lucinda had been hoping for a personal relationship with Edward that never materialized. I'd figured the two lonely people would get together, but maybe they just hadn't connected. The former headmistress and the university professor had seemed like a perfect match to me, but relationships are tricky, and who can predict the outcome?

My thoughts drifted back to Noah, and I quickly reined them in. There was no use speculating on what was going on with him: either we'd resume our relationship and remain friends or we wouldn't. I was trying to take a very Zen approach to it, but I wasn't all that successful. I still caught myself thinking of Noah at odd hours of the night and day. Did he think about me? Only time would tell.

"Well, it's sad, but it's not completely unexpected," Sybil said. "I never thought he was really into dream interpretation."

"He was certainly pleasant enough," Lucinda said. "A real gentleman." I could tell that she was disappointed that Edward wouldn't be joining us anymore. She turned to me. "He's going to write to you and Ali with his apologies. He wishes everyone well, but he just doesn't feel this is the right direction for him at this time."

I shrugged. "It's not for everyone," I admitted. Sometimes dreams reveal secrets that we'd prefer to leave buried in our subconscious. A couple of people have dropped out when they felt a little uncomfortable at the feedback Sybil and Persia gave them. Ali always does her best to moderate the discussion, but some members are lacking in tact. Dorien, in particular, has a way of always putting her foot in her mouth, and a couple of people have taken offense at her blunt remarks. It's hard to juggle different personalities in a group like this, especially when the discussion turns personal and some "interpretations" hit too close to home.

"Who wants to start?" Ali passed a plate of meringues. She'd added chocolate chips and chopped nuts and tinted them with food coloring. Rose and Minerva Harper admired them while scooping some into a napkin.

"Such pretty pastels," Rose said. "Were they difficult to make?"

"They're a breeze," Ali told her. "You leave them in the oven overnight. I'll text you the recipe."

"Well, I had an interesting dream for tonight," Lucinda said, "but the strangest thing happened. It flew right out of my head. I can't remember a single thing about it. How embarrassing."

"That happens to all of us," Ali said soothingly. "Don't worry yourself trying to recall it. You'll see something or you'll hear something and the whole dream will come back to you in a flash."

"Ali's right; that happens to me all the time," Dorien offered. "Don't waste your time trying to chase it down. It will come back when you least expect it."

"But it's not just the dream that's troubling me. I've been forgetting other things as well." Lucinda looked genuinely distressed, her lips drawn downward in a frown. "I don't know if it's old age or if it could be something more sinister."

Everyone was silent for a moment. Minerva Harper said, "Nonsense, my dear. We all forget things from time to time. You shouldn't worry about it."

"I suppose you're right," Lucinda said in a downcast voice.

"As long as you're not forgetting things that could be really important," Rose said. "You're not leaving things cooking on the stove, are you?"

Lucinda looked relieved and gave a faint smile. "Oh, nothing like that. That would be quite dangerous. No, these are just little things. Maybe it's just carelessness; that could be it. The sesame seeds are a perfect example."

Sesame seeds? Ali and I exchanged a look. "Do you mean finding the sesame seeds in the wrong spot on your spice rack?" Ali asked.

"Well, yes, that was the first thing I noticed. But then something else came up. I noticed the seal was broken, and I'm positive it was a brand-new bottle."

"Then don't use it, my dear," Minerva urged. "It could

be contaminated. Take it right back to the store and demand another one."

"Normally, I would, but when I looked inside, I saw that half the sesame seeds were gone. You know how pricey they are. How could I have used up half a bottle and not remember doing it?" She looked around the group, but no one spoke up. Finally she waved her hand in the air like she was swatting a fly. "Let's move on," she said briskly. "Enough of my memory problems. We're here to talk about dreams."

I sat there, stunned at what Lucinda had just revealed. Should I follow up on it or wait until the meeting was over? I was trying to decide what to do when Dorien's voice cut into my thoughts.

"I'd like to go first," she said, taking the floor. Dorien started to describe what's known as the classic "House Dream," but my thoughts were elsewhere. I was so shocked by Lucinda's story about the bottle of sesame seeds, I could hardly concentrate on the discussion.

I tried to picture the scene in Lucinda's kitchen that night. Not only was the bottle stashed in the wrong place after Leslie Watts's visit, but now Lucinda had admitted that half the contents were gone. Lucinda seemed clueless about what may have happened. And all I could think was, *Leslie Watts. Leslie Watts.* Her name echoed like a gong, over and over in my brain.

I forced myself to tune back into the group. Dorien was describing how she explored the stately mansion in her dream: to her delight, each room was more beautiful than the next. A typical wish-fulfillment dream, and very easy to analyze, I decided. The "house" represents our hopes and aspirations, and it wasn't surprising that Dorien would dream of a glamorous mansion. Her own financial situation was grim, and her dreamworld let her fantasize about living in a beautiful house, even it was only for a few blissful moments.

The group is skilled at dream interpretation, and as soon as Sybil said, "It sounds like the House Dream to me, Dorien," everyone chimed in and agreed with her. "Did you feel comforted by it?" Persia asked, and Dorien reported that she had. People usually enjoy experiencing the House Dream and hope to have it again.

"Who wants to go next?" Ali asked, and Lucinda timidly raised her hand.

"I'm still dreaming about roosters," she said. "Bright red roosters on a blue-and-white background. I don't know why I'm so fixated on roosters."

I looked at Ali. Lucinda had brought that plate to the book signing and it had been piled with shortbread cookies, imprinted with the sailing ship. *The cookies that might have been deadly.*

"It was a weird dream," Lucinda said. "I guess I'm still thinking about the signing and what happened to poor Sonia."

"We all are," Sara said. She gave me a steady look. She had been listening intently while Lucinda related the story about the bottle of sesame seeds, and I think our thoughts were running along the same track. Lucinda, on the other hand, still didn't seem to make the connection.

The rest of the dreams were fairly mundane and could be analyzed quickly. Minerva had an anxiety dream, and she thought it was probably related to an upcoming visit to the eye doctor. Rose dreamt that she was driving an out-of-control car—even though she doesn't drive—and Sybil reported dreaming about a fellow from the early nineteenth century who resembled Mr. Darcy in *Pride and Prejudice.* We all drew a blank on Sybil's dream and agreed to discuss it again at the next meeting.

I glanced at my watch. The meeting was winding to a close, and still no word from Sam Stiles. Maybe the detectives on garbage-dump detail had been wasting their time after all.

And then my cell rang.

Ali looked at me questioningly and whispered, "Go get it. I bet it's Sam."

I hurried to the kitchen, my pulse racing. It wasn't Sam after all; it was Noah. His voice was low and pressured. "I just heard from my source with the PD," he said without preamble. "You know that Sam sent a couple of detectives out to a stakeout at the city dump, right?"

"Yes, she told me—" I began before he quickly cut me off.

"Well, they've been there for three hours and nothing's happened. But now that it's getting dark, they think they've spotted some action."

"Action?"

"A dark blue sedan has circled the dump twice. The cops aren't in the right position to see the plates, but someone is definitely interested." My thoughts winged through the possibilities: Jeremy, Olivia, Leslie. Maybe Etta Mae. Was it just a coincidence that she'd missed the Dream Club meeting tonight?

"But why would the car be circling the dump?"

"Who knows? Maybe the driver's waiting for it to get completely dark before making a move." A loud burst of laughter from the living room made me jump. Sybil was telling a story about one of her dream-hopping adventures, and Ali had dashed out to the kitchen for another pastry platter.

"It's Noah," I said quietly to her. "He's on his way to the city dump. The police think they've spotted someone lurking around. This could be it."

"Go with him," Ali hissed. "I'll take care of everything here."

"Noah," I said into the phone. "Shall I come with you?"

"I'll see you in five," he said. "I'm calling from my car."

32

Minutes later, Noah and I were heading east out of town, the buildings and houses falling away, acres of marshland lining both sides of the road. Dusk was falling and there was a special softness in the air that I've learned to associate with Savannah. I could hardly believe that the killer might be revealed in the next few minutes and there would be justice for Sonia. The idyllic scenery was at odds with the adrenaline spiking through my veins.

"So this could be it?" I said when a few moments had passed.

"I think so. The end of the chase," Noah said. This was the first time he'd spoken since I'd slipped inside the car; his features were tense and his mouth was set in a grim line. I noticed his hands were clamped hard on the steering wheel and he was driving over the limit. He didn't seem inclined to talk, but there were a dozen questions I wanted to ask him.

"I was surprised when you called," I said finally.

"You were in on the beginning of the investigation," he said shortly. "You need to be here at the end." I nodded, unsure what to say next. "The detective agency," he went on in a weary tone, "is taking longer to set up than I thought. That's why I haven't been in touch with you." He took his eyes off the road for a split second and let his gaze sweep appreciatively over my lemon-yellow shift. His features relaxed, and he grinned. I'd worn that dress before with him, and it was one of his favorites. "Do you remember that day you dropped by the office and I was interviewing assistants?"

"I do. I wondered who you finally settled on. How did it go?" I pictured someone who was a top-notch assistant and just happened to look like a Victoria's Secret model.

"I should have let you interview them for me. I made the wrong choice every time. I hired and fired three assistants during the first two weeks, and I finally settled on Mrs. Englethorpe."

"Mrs. Englethorpe? I'm picturing an English nanny."

"No, she's American. But she was born in London and has very strict ideas on how to run an office. We were like oil and water at first, but now we've settled down to a comfortable arrangement."

"Why do you call her Mrs. Englethorpe? Isn't that a bit formal?"

"Well, for one thing, she's old enough to be my mother. She's very prim and proper. She wears sensible shoes and has a blue tint in her hair. Her first name is Edith, but I don't know if I'll ever get comfortable calling her that. You'll have to meet her; you'd like her."

"I like her already." I chuckled, thinking of how I'd let my imagination get the better of me. Here I'd pictured Noah having dinner and drinks with a gorgeous blonde, and the truth was far different. It shows what happens when I let my imagination go into overdrive.

"Here they are," he said softly, hitting the brakes. He pulled up behind a police cruiser, parked on the shoulder, lights off. "It's Riggs and Morton. I know both these guys." We were on the outskirts of town, but I couldn't see the city dump. Night was creeping up on us and the road was dark, not another car in sight.

Noah got out of the car and motioned for me to stay put. "We may have to move the car. Let me see what's going on." I watched as he greeted the officers, talked for a few minutes, and then returned to the car. "They're waiting for the signal to move," he said quietly. "There's another black-and-white at the entrance to the dump, and they're just about ready to apprehend someone."

My heart thumped in my throat. "They already have someone in their sights? Is it a man or a woman?"

"No idea. They're watching someone in a dark gray hoodie approaching the front gate, and they're getting ready to move in." Just as he spoke, the police car zoomed off and Noah sprang into action. "That's our cue. We can drive up to the edge of the perimeter, and then we have to stop." I nodded, knowing Noah was eager to get as close to the action as possible.

A minute later, he pulled up behind the empty police cruiser and I saw two officers—presumably Riggs and Morton—taking someone into custody at the front entrance to the dump. The slim figure suggested it was a woman, but her face was shrouded by the hoodie, and I squinted hard, trying to identify her. It looked like she never made it inside the dump, because I could see the heavy chain locking the doors was still in place. A tool was lying on the ground next to her, possibly a bolt cutter—I wasn't sure.

"Noah, can you see who it is?" I said, my voice tight with excitement.

"It looks like a female," he said, and that moment, the hoodie fell off as the suspect was hustled into the police cruiser and I recognized a familiar face. *Leslie Watts!*

"It's Leslie," I said to Noah.

"Who?"

I suddenly realized Noah had never met Leslie. "Leslie Watts. She's married to Jeremy Watts, Sonia's director of communications."

Noah's cell phone chirped and he flipped it open. "It's Riggs," he said. He listened for a couple of minutes. "You're kidding," he said, shaking his head. "When it rains, it pours."

"What is it?" I grabbed his sleeve the moment he flipped the phone shut. I could hear the wail of police cars in the background and decided it must be the CSIs. I glanced over to my right. Leslie looked small and vulnerable, huddled in the back of the police cruiser. Her hands were probably locked into cuffs, and her head was bowed as if she wanted to hide her face and burrow into her sweatshirt. I pulled my thoughts away from Leslie and turned to Noah, puzzled. If the police already had Leslie in custody, what else could be happening? "What's going on?" I repeated.

"They stationed an officer at the back entrance of the dump, and he just took someone else into custody. Do you believe it? Two suspects showing up in one night." He let out a low whistle. "What are the odds of that happening?"

"Two suspects?" I said, feeling like events were spinning out of control. "It can't be anyone connected with the case; they already have Leslie in custody. So who else did they arrest?" *And why is anyone else prowling around the dump in the dead of night?* I wondered.

"Olivia Hudson. She was holding a pair of wire cutters and was trying to cut through the back fence of the dump."

"Leslie Watts and Olivia Hudson? They can't *both* be guilty," I said, my mind reeling. "That's impossible."

Noah quirked an eyebrow at me. "Are you sure about that?"

His question stopped me dead in my tracks, my mind buzzing with possibilities. "At the moment, I'm not sure of anything." Could Leslie and Olivia have been working together to kill Sonia? It didn't seem possible. And why were they at opposite ends of the dump?

"I'm going to head down to the station house," he said. "There's nothing left to see here. Do you want to come with me?"

I shook my head. "No, it will take hours while they interview Leslie and Olivia. Just drop me off back at the shop, if you don't mind. I have Sara and Ali waiting for me. I know they're going to have a million questions."

"Everyone's left," Ali said when I raced up the stairs to our apartment. She was collecting the empty cups and saucers and piling them in the sink.

"Sara?" I said, looking around. The door to the bedroom was open, so I guessed she'd taken Remy with her.

"She left, too. She heard what was happening and headed down to the precinct house. It's going to be a long night for her."

Ali pushed a cup of steaming ginger spice at me. "This is the last of the tea," she said. "Shall I make another pot?"

"No, this is fine." I accepted it gratefully. "You're not going to believe what happened," I said, still dazed by the course of events.

"From what Sara heard on the police scanner, the police made an arrest down at the dump."

I sipped the tea, feeling a wave of exhaustion wash over me. "Not one arrest, but two." I quickly filled her in on what had happened. "I have no idea what Leslie and Olivia told the cops. They'll interview them separately, of course. They were both trying to break into the city dump." *But at different entrances*, I reminded myself. I was still trying to wrap my mind around it. *Could it be that neither one knew the other was there, and they were working independently?* Anything was possible at this point.

"But what does it mean? Surely Leslie and Olivia weren't working together to kill Sonia, were they? I figured they were mortal enemies, both in love with the same man."

"I don't think they were working together," I said, "but I can't come up with an explanation. None of this makes any sense." I stood up, feeling slightly unsteady. "We won't know anything till morning," I told her. "Can we schedule a breakfast meeting of the Dream Club? We might have some news by then."

Ali grinned. "I've already scheduled it for nine sharp. Right here. I bet we'll have a full house; everyone is on pins and needles." She gave me a sympathetic look, her features softening. "You look shattered," she said.

"I am," I confessed. "Let's call it a night. I have the feeling tomorrow will bring a lot of surprises."

"Do you mean they both were looking for something in the dump?" Etta Mae asked.

"Yes, that's the amazing part about all this," I answered. It was just after nine the following morning and Noah had called me with the details a few minutes earlier. "Leslie was looking for the plastic cookie tray, the blue one with the rooster—"

"The one I brought to the book signing!" Lucinda exclaimed.

I nodded. "Yes, she was afraid there might be traces of sesame seeds left from cookie crumbs. The shortbread cookies."

"Oh no," Lucinda wailed. "So she did add sesame seeds to them? She *admitted* it? How could I have been so silly? I let her sit right there in my kitchen. I had no idea she'd tamper with the cookies. She was such a sweet girl." She raised a handkerchief and dabbed her eyes. "I must be a very bad judge of character," she said sadly.

"You couldn't have possibly known," Ali told her. "None of us did. I never thought she really had a strong enough motive to kill Sonia."

"She was protecting her family," Dorien said, "like a lioness with her cubs. She wanted to keep her family together, and I suppose she thought Jeremy was going to ditch her and marry Sonia."

"I don't think he ever would have," Sybil said. "It was one of those workplace affairs, I believe. I don't think it would ever have gone any further."

"You may be right, but Leslie couldn't take the chance. At least that's what she told the police."

"I still can't believe it," Lucinda said, her face pale. "To think I sat in my own kitchen with someone who was capable of murder. I must have missed a lot of clues along the way." She paused. "But I still don't understand how Olivia figures in all this. If she wasn't working with Leslie to kill Sonia, what was she doing at the dump last night?"

"Love drew her there," Ali said.

"Love?" Minerva and Rose chorused.

"Love for Jeremy," Ali continued. "She was convinced

that Jeremy had slipped some sesame powder into Sonia's coffee at Java Joe's, and she was afraid the police might do a sweep of the dump and find the coffee cup. If there was even a trace of sesame seed powder, that would be the end of Jeremy. Remember that picture of him holding the coffee cup at Java Joe's? He had access to it, and she figured that's when he made his move."

"So she was willing to risk breaking into the dump to save someone she thought was a murderer?" Minerva asked.

"Love is blind," Rose said with a knowing smile.

"I thought their affair was over and Olivia was going to move back to Chattanooga," Persia pointed out.

I shrugged. "That's what I assumed. But maybe she still had feelings for him. Or maybe she hoped he would move with her."

A long beat passed while we all tried to absorb what had happened.

"If Leslie confessed, then there won't be a trial," Lucinda said.

"That's right. She confessed to acting alone," Ali said. "And she admitted everything. I think she feels badly that she got you involved, Lucinda."

Lucinda rolled her eyes. "I should say so. It's going to take me a long time to get over this," she said. "If I hadn't invited her to my house that evening, none of this would have happened. I'll always blame myself."

"Lucinda, you can't look at it that way," Ali told her. "Leslie was determined to kill Sonia, and she would have found another opportunity. It was just a matter of time."

"But what about Jeremy popping up on the security tape at the grocery store?" Dorien asked. "Didn't that mean anything? I thought he must have slipped into the store to buy sesame seeds."

"We all thought that, but we were wrong," I piped up. "Nothing sinister about his trip to the grocery store; he needed some aspirin."

"What will happen to the company, with Olivia gone?" Rose asked. "I always thought she was poised to take over Sonia's position."

"Apparently not." I thought of the wistful expression on her face when she talked about Chattanooga. "I think she'll be more eager than ever to get away. Her affair with Jeremy will end, and I think she'll want to move back to her hometown and start over."

"And that sweet little girl Trudy Carpenter?" Minerva asked. "Do you suppose she'll ever be told the truth about Sonia?"

"There's probably no need to drop that bombshell on her," I said quickly. "And we really don't have proof. Just a conversation with a waitress in Blessing."

"Sometimes you should just let sleeping dogs lie," Etta Mae offered. I had the feeling she was referring not only to Trudy but her own dispute over the family cookbook. With Sonia gone, who knew if the company would even continue? Without Sonia at the helm, the whole empire could collapse.

"And where does that leave us?" Rose asked. "It's ten in the morning, and I suppose we should all get started with our day. Unless," she said hesitantly, "we want to have a quick meeting of the Dream Club?"

"I'll make a fresh pot of coffee," I offered.

"And I have some chocolate croissants in the freezer," Ali offered. "I'm trying to decide if we should add them to the menu downstairs."

"Well, let's do a taste test," Lucinda said, perking up. "I love chocolate croissants. I haven't had them in years."

"Who wants to start with the dream reports?" Ali called from the kitchen.

Etta Mae raised her hand. "I had a really weird dream last night," she said, "and I don't know what to make of it. I found myself in an Irish castle surrounded by acres and acres of wildflowers. Everything was light and airy and beautiful. I heard music coming from downstairs—I think they were having a ball—and I tiptoed down a carved oak staircase to see what was going on. Suddenly the scene shifted, a dark cloud crossed the sun, and . . ."

Ali joined me in the kitchen, and I scooted aside to give her room to defrost the tray of croissants. Just a few seconds in the microwave and they'd be perfect. The hazelnut coffee was already brewing, and the Savannah sunlight was slanting in the windows and making interesting patterns on the pine floors. Barney and Scout were curled up nose to tail for their morning naps on the windowsill.

I could hear Etta Mae's voice rise in excitement as she relayed the events in her dream. Sybil and Rose were already talking over each other, chiming in with interpretations. Dorien came up with a different take on the dream and was forcefully making her case, while Lucinda was trying to be diplomatic.

I was half listening to Etta Mae's dream and wondering what direction it would take. Would her dream hint at romance, happiness, and bliss? Or would it be a dark tale of death, destruction, and murder? I had no idea. Dreams are ephemeral, full of light and shadows, hinting at a reality that we can't fully grasp. They're elusive, mercurial, just outside our understanding. We can guess, but never know, their true meaning.

I glanced around the living room at the happy group deep in discussion and analysis. As long as we had the Dream

Club, there would be more dreams, more interpretations, more mysteries to solve. Some stories would end well; some would end in sadness and loss. I couldn't begin to predict what the future would hold for any of us. But for now, in my sunny Savannah kitchen, all was right with the world.

Dream Symbol Guide

What are your dreams trying to tell you? Do you ever dream of being stranded in a strange city in the dead of night, alone and afraid? Do you dream of wandering through a beautiful house, discovering hidden rooms filled with treasures? Dreams are our passport to the unconscious and understanding dream symbols can help you unlock their secrets.

* Being lost and alone is a frequent theme in dreams and suggests that you feel powerless and vulnerable in some area of your waking life. You literally don't know where to turn, and there is usually a strong element of danger in these dreams.
* Finding yourself in a beautiful house, filled with hidden rooms, is another common theme. The hidden rooms represent your potential, parts of yourself that you have never explored, skills and talents you have never developed.
* Standing on the edge of a cliff is another well-known dream feature. You might be facing a turning point in your life, facing a momentous decision. Sometimes in

the "cliff" dream, you see a canyon across the way. The distance is insurmountable; there is no way you can bridge the gap. This usually means that there is an obstacle to an important goal in your waking life; the gap represents the barrier you must overcome.

* Driving a car—or riding in a car—features prominently in dreams. Are you driving or is someone else driving? If the car is careening down the road, it could mean that some element of your life is spinning out of control and needs to be addressed. If you are in the backseat, or unable to reach the pedals, it could mean that you seriously doubt your ability to control your own life and destiny. You may be overly dependent on others to make decisions for you.
* Cellars in dreams represent the deepest level of your unconscious. There is usually an element of darkness and danger in these dreams. Dreaming of being in a cellar can signify there is something in your conscious life that is hidden, something that you are afraid to face.
* Drowning in dreams usually means you are having trouble "keeping your head above water," and water is a very powerful symbol of the unconscious. A flood represents the notion that you are about to be overwhelmed by a force more powerful than you are.

Symbols in dreams embody our greatest hopes and fears; understanding their significance can help uncover material that is useful in our waking lives. There is no single way to interpret your dreams because you are the architect of your life. Sharing your dreams in a dream club can offer valuable insights into dreams and the power of the unconscious.